VISIONS

VISIONS

A Science Fiction Western

by

JAMES C. GLASS

The Borgo Press
An Imprint of Wildside Press

MMVII

CONTENTS

CHAPTER ONE

THE ENCOUNTER

In the light of dusk a splash of blood looked black against the straw covered ground. Jake Price froze when he saw it, and then closed one hand tightly around his rifle. The cattle moved nervously around him, eyes rolling, still fearful of whatever had happened only moments before. *Must have been quick*, he thought. Otherwise every cow would have stampeded down the canyon. Jake cradled the rifle in one arm and pushed his way forward until the puddle was at his feet and he could smell salty musk. A part of his mind was screaming for a drink. The thing had killed before, and only in this canyon. He had seen it and heard its cry, but when he'd warned the men they'd only laughed. Poor old Jake, drinkin' his own stuff again. Well, this time he'd make sure it wouldn't be so funny.

He worked the lever of the Winchester, and put the hammer on half-cock. The grass was bent and crushed where the bleeding animal had been dragged, and he followed it up a steep hill. There was less than an hour until sunset, and he had no lantern. *I'll follow until sunset*, he thought, *then pick it up in the morning, but no way will I spend the night up here, rifle or no rifle.*

The trail led straight up the canyon towards cliffs of grey slate towering three hundred feet above his head in a series of shelves. Jake's heart was pounding when he reached the field of boulders and rubble separating grass from cliffs, for the trail had suddenly become a scramble climb. *How the hell could it drag a cow up here? Maybe a calf, but that's still two hundred pounds of dead weight! Jesus, I can't catch my breath!* He breathed deeply, then reached into his back pocket and pulled out a flask. He took a long pull from it, and closed his eyes as the whiskey burned a path into his stomach. He took another pull, then studied the rocks ahead of him. The trail had disappeared, but the canyon was getting narrow, and he had

7

seen nothing moving up the cliffs. Plenty of places to hide in the boulder field.

Ahead of him there was a crashing sound.

A cascade of pebbles bounced down the steep slope, narrowly missing his left foot.

Jake raised the rifle, aiming at shadows, swinging the barrel back and forth.

Silence. Nothing moved. Even the birds were still. So many shadows, so many places in which to hide. It could be waiting for him anywhere, eager for the chance to tear out his throat. He remembered his dog Bustard, a hundred pounds of mongrel, throat gaping, belly slashed open from neck to testicles, and the shadowy form loping up the hill behind his barn after slaughtering everything in the hen house.

The lip of a prospector's test hole loomed ahead, a miniature moraine. Jake stepped up to it, holding the rifle across his body, peering into the darkness. Something was there, a form, on its back, legs splayed out and very still. He took a deep breath, then climbed down the shallow moraine side of the hole in soft dirt.

It was the carcass of an adult cow, gutted and partially eaten, the head nearly torn away and dangling limply. The stench of blood and decaying organs engulfed him in a wave of nausea that undoubtedly saved his life, for as he scrambled out of the hole *they* were coming for him, relying on surprise against an armed man.

Jake Price scrambled gasping from the hole, a cocked rifle clutched in one hand, gasping for air, looking up to see three nightmarish figures descending on him from the surrounding boulders. Two beings crouched, ready to spring, the third standing tall, arm drawn back, startled by Jake's sudden appearance. A whirring sound as Jake ducked beneath the edge of the hole, and a fist-sized pebble smashed into the shale at his back. He sat up and fired without aiming, a deafening explosion in the narrow canyon and then a gratifying shriek of fright. Rising up on his knees as he aimed the rifle, Jake saw low sloping foreheads and bared, yellow teeth in grimaces as two figures rolled out of sight over boulder tops. The third bounded lightly from one boulder to the next, then turned and looked at Jake defiantly, daring him to shoot.

It was a kind of man: brute face painted with streaks of red and yellow, amber eyes close-set, small, flat nose and narrow forehead above a tiny chin. A sling dangled from his hand, and when he smiled a malevolent smile there were fine white teeth, and the level, intense stare of a hunting wolf. A quick pirouette on the rock, and the creature-man was gone from view as Jake tugged in vain on the rifle trigger. He'd forgotten to lever a new round into the weapon. Now he remembered, levering and firing in every direction until the firing pin was poking air. Ears ringing, he waited a moment, then scrambled out of the hole and stumbled down the steep gorge, rocks slashing at his knees and thighs until he reached the grass and was running, not looking back, past startled cattle bellowing protests and banging into each other to clear the way for him. An instant later he was clawing at the cabin door, barring it behind him and stumbling to the big oak gun cabinet where he kept cartridges for the rifle. He tore open a drawer, and found only two cartridges in a box.

Jake's face felt flushed, and the room was spinning fast. He sat down hard on the floor, and fell over on his side, eyes open, a little line of spittle running from his mouth. When he slipped into his blackout, devoid of sight and sound, everything was peaceful again, and there were no dreams.

* * * * * * *

By late morning, Jake had split half a cord of wood, and he was reasonably sober when the sheriff arrived. Tom Henley, the one-man police force and county sheriff based in Crosley, heaved his two hundred sixty pound bulk off of a tired looking mare and strolled smiling over to where Jake was leaning on his axe, eyeing him coolly.

"Mornin', Jake."

"Nearly noon, Tom. How ya doin'?" Jake said it amiably enough because he liked the man, but he knew right away it was a business call.

"Pretty good: full stomach, and a nice sunny day to visit folks. How're *you* doin', Jake? Feelin' okay today?"

Jake sighed. "Get on with it, Tom."

Tom looked down at his size thirteen boots, and shuffled from one foot to the other. "Oh, it's nothin' to get over-concerned with, I guess. Lot of shootin' up here yesterday. Scared some folks, so I thought I'd check it out."

"People complain and say a lot of things about me, Tom. What else is new?"

"Oh, this is different, Jake. I hear about when you get drunk and puke in the Athens, and Pete ends up finding you a room for the night. And the whole town has heard your stories about the critters a hundred times. But there was a lot of shootin' here yesterday, and folks is nervous. What happened?"

Jake looked at the round, friendly face: clear blue eyes, a pea-sized brown wart clinging to a jaw line. How many nights had this man put him up in an empty cell, door open, then fed him breakfast the next morning? How many times had they talked about Ester, and what she'd done to him? Here was a man he'd cried in front of. He was a friend.

I was drunk and scared, Tom."

"Okay. But what happened?"

Jake looked hard at the big man. He felt his mouth moving, and knew he was going to sound crazy again, but with Tom it was somehow safe. "They—they came back—yesterday. I heard 'em screaming up by the cliffs all afternoon—darin' me to come out."

"The critters," said Tom.

Jake swallowed hard. "Yes."

"The same ones you say hit your place before, even though nobody else has had any trouble?"

"They killed five of my hens, and—"

"We didn't find anything, Jake. Not a single feather, not a drop of blood. Nothing."

"I saw them this time. Close up. Three of them. Big. They had weapons. A sling. Nearly brained me with a rock. Not injuns, Tom. Half-men, sort of. They killed one of my cows, Tom, and dragged it up to the cliffs. I found it there. A whole cow they dragged up a steep hill, and I followed the blood and—"

"Easy, Jake, you're shakin' all over." Tom put a huge hand on Jake's shoulder.

"I took my rifle and went up to the cliffs, and the dead cow was there in a hole, and then they ambushed me. I drove 'em off, emptied the rifle and scattered them good, but then I panicked and my head was spinning. When I came back to the cabin I guess I passed out for a while, but they was screamin' up there most of the night, and I sat by the window with the rifle in my lap."

Tom looked sadly at him. "Oh, Jake, what am I gonna do with you?"

Jake looked straight into the friendly, blue eyes. "I'm cold sober, Tom, and this is no bull shit, no hallucination. I know what I saw, and they're killing my animals. I want it stopped."

Tom's faint smile suddenly evaporated, and he stood up straight. "All right, let's go up and look at that dead cow of yours, and I'll file a report."

Jake could hear the disbelief, and felt foolish again. "I'll get my rifle."

"No need for that. This here is all we need." Tom patted the Colt forty-four holstered at one hip. "Let's go."

Jake led the way up the hill, feeling scared and guilty, and wondering why he'd said anything at all. *You're the town crazy because you talk too much, stupid. Let 'em find out when their animals are torn apart. Or their kids.*

As they approached the cliffs, Jake felt colder and colder. A welcome morning rain had been hard, sending rivulets of mud running down the hill. "I found a big splash of blood about here," he said, "but looks like it's been washed away."

"Well even that rain wasn't hard enough to wash away a whole cow. Shit, my boots is covered with mud all ready. Let's get on with it."

Somehow Jake knew what they would find before they got to the hole. It made sense, all the screaming last night. Covering their tracks. Tom went ahead, a hand on the Colt's grip, peered over the edge of the hole and sighed. "There's nothin' in here, Jake."

Jake felt his face flush. "They moved it, then. Dragged it away last night. I *heard* them, I told you."

"Oh come *on*, Jake. There's nothin' here but mud and a foot of water in the bottom of a hole, and my clothes are a mess. God damn it, there's nothing *here*! Believe your eyes, for Christ's sake!"

Jake looked down at mud and water, shaking his head. All feeling seemed to drain from him as his jaw set stubbornly. He walked over to a boulder, pointing to a jagged chip at the top. "That's where a bullet hit. They couldn't rub that out or drag it away, but a dead cow they could move, and the rain would obliterate everything else."

For just an instant Jake saw a hint of belief in Tom's face, but then the eyes clouded again. Tom stumbled and slid down the moraine of the diggings, and put an arm around Jake's shoulders. "Come on, let's talk, but not in this mud." They hung onto each other on the way down while Jake babbled about man-like critters who screamed like banshees and threw rocks with slings and dragged his animals away. Tom listened quietly, but seemed to be thinking about something else. When they reached the cabin he suddenly turned Jake to face him, taking a deep, slow breath before he spoke.

"We've been friends a long time, Jake, and I really believe you think you saw something, so I'll look into it. I don't know what I'll do, maybe set up some kind of watch, but I'll do *something*. Okay?"

Jake nodded.

"Now, whether I find anything or not, there's something I want you to do for me and—well—for yourself. Ever since Ester left you've sort of fallin' apart, and it's worrying me. You're drinkin' too much, Jake, and I think you've got a problem with it. I want you to do something about it, put the cork in the bottle for a while, maybe get Doc Ellis to check you out. Do some good for yourself, Jake."

"You're right," said Jake. "I've been hittin' it too hard, and I don't need to. Guess I've been feelin' sorry for myself, Tom. Losin' Ester hit me harder'n I expected, is all. First woman I ever fell for."

"You need help, you yell," said Tom

"Thanks, Tom, you're a friend. You've always been a good friend."

The two men hugged like two standing grizzlies, embracing awkwardly, then Tom walked back to his horse and climbed on. Jake stood forlornly by the woodpile, looking like a reprimanded forty-year-old child.

"Check back with you in a couple of days. Take care of yourself," said Tom, and Jake watched until the horse disappeared in thick stands of trees. He went back to the cabin and ate some jerky and bread, then found a bottle in a cupboard and poured a tumbler full of whiskey for himself. He sipped whiskey all afternoon and into the evening, so that it didn't bother him so much when the screaming began again later that night, continuing until dawn of the next day.

He returned from oblivion at noon, and discovered that another cow was missing.

CHAPTER TWO

THE CAVES

The high Sierra valley cupping the town of Crosley was untouched by the recent gold rush, but was gouged deep, having been scoured out to bedrock by an ancient relative of the crystal clear river now flowing there. Tributaries had emptied into the ancient one, and now there were hanging canyons lined with slate and quartzite cliffs dropping down into the town from both sides, making the mountains seem larger than they really were, and providing a spectacular view for the townspeople.

It had been exceptionally hot in the summer of 1880, and this day was no exception, dry and without wind, and now after the sun had set and a full moon risen the air was suddenly cool so that people went out on their porches to sip drinks and watch the night. In one canyon well east of town there were no porches, only a tangle of rattlesnake infested underbrush, and nettles beneath fir trees clinging tenaciously to steep rocky slopes glowing in moonlight. On the north wall of the canyon, barely within view of the scattered kerosene light of Crosley, a broad, pegmatite seam ran vertically between slate platelets on both sides, filled with crystals formed by mineral saturated waters of a distant past. Water and wind had carved the rock, gouging shelves, depressions and holes into cliff faces as if searching for an artistic theme. Halfway up the seam, a bear-sized hole disappeared into darkness, surrounded by rock gleaming yellow.

Suddenly, the hole seemed to move, growing larger, then drifting to one side.

A dark figure emerged from the hole, moving carefully like a shadow along shelves only inches wide until it reached broad, horizontal slabs of grey slate, blending into the background and effectively disappearing from ground view.

The figure settled itself on smooth rock, back against the wall, and sighed deeply, for it had come to watch a beautiful night. Peaceful. A second sigh of contentment followed the first.

Genetic wisdom of countless generations radiated from amber eyes gazing serenely upon the scene. Long, brown hair, with a reddish tint covered a massive head, flowing down to the nape of a muscled neck and covering the sloped forehead above heavy brow ridges. A full beard had been recently trimmed and decorated with streaks of blue and red mud which clotted in otherwise smooth hair. Thick lips, painted with ochre, were visible within the beard-forest, nostrils flaring in a broad, arched nose sucking in lungfuls of cool night air. The hands were thick, massive palms and stout fingers capable of the finest articulation and now folded together limply on drawn up knees. A man, yet different, so different that the slant-eyed black-haired nomads had never settled the valley, had fled the terrible visions given to their shaman by the strange inhabitants who had arrived long before them. But now the Others had come, and they did not see The Visions.

The big head turned slowly towards the hole going deep into the rock. A shadow within a shadow was there at the entrance, then moving cautiously across the narrow ledge. He had felt her presence long before she reached the top of the tunnel, and now, sensing her fatigue and fear of losing balance in such a high place, he projected to her a feeling of confidence, exhilaration and awaiting love at the end of the short journey. She was smaller than he, with tiny feet making the traverse easier, and in a moment she was with him. They embraced when she had seated herself, and he touched her again with a love feeling, marveling as usual how she retained so delicate a beauty at such an advanced age. She smiled at The Vision, noting the way he always enhanced her good features and eliminated the poor ones. His mind was the perfect mirror, reflecting only the best.

"Anka, I hesitated to disturb you, but the children were restless before sleep and wanted to have a story about the days in the valley. You hide yourself well; this was the last place I thought of." Her tongue clicked against the roof of her mouth in precise articulation of the old language, for she was also an Elder, and Keeper of The Memories.

"You worry too much as usual, Tel. I come here only to watch the night and smell the trees, and obtain relief from the noise below. I'm getting too old for it."

"The children?"

"Not so. I enjoy watching their faces when I take them to the places of our youth, but it is impossible for them to sit still, and they insist on chattering away in the new tongue, asking questions, wanting to put a name on everything, making jokes. Can't they take anything seriously? I show them the way things used to be, the way things can be again for them. How will it be if they walk about marveling at common trees and animals? They'll be discovered, and then what? Weapons and torches? A trek across the mountains to avoid those with fears so easily aroused? The Hinchai spread everywhere, infecting the world, living apart from it. They do not have The Memories."

"They are our cousins, dear heart."

"Yes, but it is difficult to accept. They have come another way."

"Yet you have made the decision to be one with them. Oh Anka, how can you be so grumpy on such a night? And don't you think that down there, near the lights, right now, there are others watching the sky and feeling the cool breeze? Perhaps cuddling?" She snuggled up to him, draping an arm across his broad chest.

"No use trying to arouse me. I'm getting too old for that, too," he said, giving her a toothy grin.

"Teasing again!" She slapped his shoulder hard, then snuggled close again. "All I want is to keep you warm out here. You've been sick."

"I'm fine, now; you don't have to be my mother." He didn't tell her about the horrible, bloody mass he'd spat up earlier in the evening, and how when he breathed it felt like something was loose inside of him.

"What else can I do? Our children are grown, and you're the only baby I have left."

Anka glared at her in mock anger, but before he could touch her she reached out with her own love feeling that made his heart quiver and loins stir, and then her hands touched him there as well. "Ah, the wind and the sky lights make you young again tonight," she said, eyes bright with anticipation.

He seized her, but gently, pulling her around so she was straddling him, and he was instantly inside of her, thrusting hard as she wrapped strong arms around his neck, pulling his face to her withered breasts. He wanted her so much, feeling her passion and her need and wishing to satisfy her, but again he could not. As quickly as it had become hard and proudly erect, his organ was limp and he could do nothing more to revive it. He ceased his thrusting, feeling old and ashamed, burying his face against her shoulder as she caressed his neck and back. His breathing was now a wheeze, and there was a dull ache low in his back. Face against his chest, Tel could hear a rattling sound from deep inside him.

"My love," she said, squeezing him tightly, "you keep me young, but I'm getting cold out here. Can we go in now? I told the children I'd find you for them, and now it's my sworn duty to bring you back."

"If you insist," wheezed Anka.

"I do." Tel stood up, then inched her way back along the ledge, fearful as always of the long fall to the rocks below. Anka followed closely behind, his breath escaping in gasps, head spinning by the time he knelt to squeeze through the narrow entrance to the tunnel leading below.

"The trail grows narrower each year," she said.

"The trail is the same. Perhaps your feet are growing larger."

"From chasing you," she said, holding out a hand to guide him through the entrance.

The tunnel sloped severely for several yards so that they crouched in a duck-walk position until the rock was reasonably level and the ceiling high enough for standing. The walls and ceiling were lined with crusts of tiny quartz crystals, clear and white, but streaked with the yellow of citrine and purple of amethyst. The floor was worn smooth by countless footsteps of those who climbed upwards to see the sun or the moon, smell the sweet scent of pine, hear a bird, or stick a tongue out in falling rain, for except for the great vent carrying hot air, smoke and body odors directly to the top of the cliffs, this was one of only two entrances to the caverns.

They spiraled downwards on a gentle slope, squinting ahead in dim light of torches placed in the walls several meters apart, acrid fumes of burning sap stinging their eyes and nostrils. The noise was faint, at first, growing steadily louder until they could hear individual voices, especially those of the children playing some kind of hiding game. Odors of cooked food and sweaty bodies wafted through the tunnel, along with faint, sweet smoke of hard wood fires. Anka scowled as senses once again saturated, and then ahead of them a shadow raced along the walls, squealing. A pubescent girl, naked and long-legged with blonde hair tumbling in a tangled mass down her shoulders, came around a corner and nearly ran into them. She stopped short, seeing Anka and Tel, her generous mouth spreading into a smile that showed delicate, even white teeth.

"They're back!" she shrieked, startling both Anka and Tel, and then she raced back down the tunnel.

"They're back! They're back! She found him!"

Anka put a hand over his pounding heart. "Spirit of the world, my heart might explode. Catch me."

Tel laughed. "Dear Baela, always running. Her spirit is our youth, my heart."

"She looks like a water lizard, and runs like one."

Tel frowned. "She, and the children like her are the true immortality of the Tenanken, my heart. Not us."

"I know, I know, but appearances must count for something. She should cover herself, Tel. She is not a child anymore."

The tunnel ended at last, and they stepped out onto a flat shelf overlooking the great bowl of the main cavern thirty meters below them, a vaulted ceiling rising sixty meters above their heads to a single fumarole going up hundreds more to the outside world. The cavern was round, over a hundred meters across, a series of concentric shelves dropping down into the bowl until at the bottom there was a large, flat area worn smooth by community meetings and ceremonies. The spiral of shelves began where they stood, and ahead of them raced Baela, spreading the word that Anka had returned.

Children of all ages cascaded down from rocky shelves, spilling into the bottom of the great cavern where the eldest Keeper of The Memories would take them once again into the past. Most were clothed in shirts and pants brought to them by Pegre, but all had cast aside the heavy footwear for the moment, and were bare-footed before him. The only connection to the past was visible in the elderly, sitting high above the babbling throng, wrapped in heavy robes and dozing after a satisfying meal.

"Already we are as the Cousins," said Anka. "I do not see Tenanken here, but something foreign."

"You see their clothing, and ignore their hearts and minds," said Tel. "All are Tenanken, even the Cousins, but we have The Memories, dear heart. You give us that."

"And after you and I are gone, who will be Keeper of The Memories? Where are the Tahehto faces among the young? Where are the heavy features promising remembrance of the ice days, and the great sea, and the long trek south? I see only Hanken features, and a future for the mind touch, but without memories what will there be to tell? We have lost all examples of ancestral purity, Tel. We have become Hinchai."

"Dear heart, the gifts come and go, and the bloods of Tahehto and Hanken are in all of us. You rely too much on appearances. It is a curse of The Memories you bear. Now go to the children who await their favorite teacher."

"Very well," said Anka wearily, "but it is an effort tonight."

"The strength you need will come to you as it always does," said Tel. "Besides, they will not go to sleep without some kind of story, and it is you who have given them the habit. Go, now, so we can *all* sleep!"

"Enough!" grumbled Anka, and he shuffled off along the spiral shelf with an expression of painful resignation on his face while Tel grinned after him. In retaliation he took his time getting there, stopping to share a greeting with each family unit perched on the shelf, for even the adults were gathering to share The Memories, and he loved being the center of so much attention.

Tel settled herself at a tunnel exit near the top of the great room to cool in the gentle breeze from outside, watching her mate of two generations move ponderously downwards while the children scrambled aside to make a path for him to the center of the gathering place. He held himself with great dignity, though she knew his knees ached when slowing the descent of his bulk, and it had become so bad he occasionally allowed himself to complain about it.

Tiny hands reached out to touch him as he followed a winding path into the center of the gathering place. Anka enjoyed cuddling with Tel and close relatives, but was ordinarily not a toucher, preferring to express himself most intimately with the Mind Touch, and finding the grabbing and pulling by the children an irritating distraction to his thoughts. But he was careful to hide such feelings, for this would hurt the children terribly, and he knew he could not bear to do that.

He allowed them to grab at his beard, but their hands were gentle. They withdrew a little when he reached the center of the gathering and carefully lowered himself into a sitting position, and then they were rustling and bustling about, jostling each other to try to get as close to him as possible. As movement subsided, he found himself facing Baela at such close range he could see his face reflected in her amazingly blue eyes. He made the sign for quiet, and all movement ceased in the cavern, even to the high shelves where the elders sat dozing in the flickering light of exhausted cooking fires, stomachs full of meat and vegetables taken in during the bountiful summer.

Anka looked up at Tel, and she smiled, and then he closed his eyes, reaching out to slow the heartbeats of all around him, drawing from them all anxieties that might interfere with their vision experience. He held this posture for several moments, sneaking a look once to find the children relaxed, hands folded peacefully in their laps, eyes closed and chins up to look inward where he would meet

18

them. Far above him, a faint snore was interrupted rudely by a sharp jab from an elbow, and then it was quiet again.

Shadows danced on yellow walls. There was the smell of wood smoke from dying fires, and a moaning sound as the great cave breathed out through a tunnel to outside night air. These sensations were the first to disappear as Anka drew them deep within themselves for a moment of rest and inward focus. When at last he felt them together he gave them a vision of the sun rising over mountains and in the foreground was a forest of pine. Birds with long beaks, colored in reds, blue and yellow were flying to and fro, calling to each other. Small animals with long, furry tails raced up and down the trees and along the branches. He heard a collective sigh from the cavern, then took them beneath the trees where they looked up through a forest canopy towards blue sky, and felt the ferns and grasses beneath their feet. A large, blue bird with a hooked beak shrieked at their presence, and followed them from above as Anka recalled in complete detail another day of his youth when the Tenanken lived beneath the blue sky and the sun.

Before the caves.

A rushing sound filled their ears, and mist hung before them like fog. They came out of the forest at a cliff's edge where a river cascaded down a steep slope into a green pool surrounded my meadows filled with flowers saturating the mind with color and scent. There were fish swimming in the pool. With effort, Anka suppressed his memories of catching the fish with his bare hands, eating them raw after playing with the slithering animals. Living in caves, the new generations of Tenanken had little contact with forest creatures, and feared them. The Visions were like a dream, and when there is fear the dream can be a nightmare to be escaped by awakening, and so Anka avoided anything that might cause fear. Instead, they only watched the fish swimming, and felt hot sun on their faces. It was an unusual vision, for they did not see each other in it. It was as if each was suddenly alone in the outside world, exploring it for the first time. It was, in fact, the world as seen by a young Tenanken child over a hundred years in the past.

They stayed in the meadow until the grass turned golden, and shadows stretched around them, and then they climbed a steep slope to the base of slate cliffs where they watched the sun turn red and disappear behind a ridge. Birds settled for the night, and antlered creatures with large eyes emerged from stands of trees to browse before them on the hillside. High up on the cliff was the yawning maw of a cave, which they reached by climbing wide, ascending slabs of green rock, and when they had entered it an unseen hand pushed a large tangle of leaves and vines over the entrance so that it was very dark, and then—

They opened their eyes to flickering torchlight and yellow rock walls, and the smell of wood smoke. For some, back in their world-cavern, it was a welcome return, for they felt secure here surrounded by rock on four sides. But for others Anka could feel sadness, could read it in their faces when they opened their eyes. The world of the caves was surely not for them. They needed to be free in open air and sunlight, or they would wither away. And suddenly the plan to infiltrate them into the outside world was good, and newly justified in Anka's mind. He wondered why he had ever doubted Pegre's wisdom. Now he was tired, and yawned mightily.

The gathering broke up quietly, everyone going to his or her place on a shelf somewhere in the cavern, and always in view of the others. Baela remained behind for just a moment, smiling at Anka, then lowering her gaze to the floor and rushing away from him. He suspected she had been about to say something to him before suddenly deciding to remain silent. A welcome change from the noise of talk barely understood. Now it was time to sleep, and he struggled to stand, looking up as Maki, his oldest and only living son, made a loud entrance to the cavern, carrying a huge piece of meat over his shoulder.

"Ho, everyone, see what I bring! While all of you are dreaming, some are hunting so that all can eat!" There was a murmur of approval as Maki paraded around the top shelf of the cavern with his burden until reaching Tel, who regarded him coldly. He walked up to her with a wide grin and dropped the huge, bloody mass of flesh at her feet with a grunt. "See, Mother? Not only is it enough here for a feast, but Han and Dorald soon arrive with more like it. Eh?"

"You've done well, son of a proud mother. I'm surprised to see you've completely butchered the animal. It was an antlered creature, or a boar?"

"A large boar, Mother, fat and choice. They are difficult to find, and fierce to bring down, but my sling found the mark again. We butchered it on the spot because it was so large, and there were only three of us to carry the meat."

Tel looked closely at her well-muscled son, the square, brooding face and amber eyes, strong shoulders and long arms lightly covered with reddish-brown hair. A beautiful child, as the others had been before dying in a landslide that had nearly broken her heart as well as Anka's. Maki himself had narrowly escaped death in the accident, and so his life she regarded as a miracle of The World Spirit. Maki's success in the hunt was far beyond anyone's, and she had

20

every reason to be proud, but she despised his good-for-nothing friends, and worried about their influence on him.

Tel prodded the chunk of meat with one foot. "There is more, you say? Most boars I've seen have been the size of this one piece, and were much leaner."

"Much more, Mother, a large herd running together. Enough meat for many months, but they move fast, and we will chase them again tomorrow."

"Be careful, Maki, and don't allow yourself to be seen by our Cousins. It could be dangerous for all of us."

Maki's mouth curled into a snarl. "The cousins, as you call them, are deaf and blind. Why do you make relatives of our enemies?"

"Because we are related, my son. The Plan has said so. We must avoid all contact until the proper time. Please honor this."

Maki's face softened. "We disagree about The Plan, Mother, but I will honor what you say. I want only to please you, and my father."

Tel smiled. "And you do please us, Maki, very much. Here comes you father now. Anka, see what our son has returned with!"

Maki turned, and embraced his father, who was puffing hard from the climb back to the high shelf. Anka clung to his son, patting him on the back, his breath a wheeze again. "Maybe some strength will flow into me if I hold my strong son long enough. It is not so nice to become old."

They parted, and Anka looked down at the meat. "A choice morsel, but I am also too fat. Someone please take this temptation away from me. I'm going to sleep, now, and as a privilege of my age I will leave the hunting chores to those most capable of performing them."

It was a strong compliment, and Maki beamed proudly, his mother quietly gratified and soothed by the obvious strong bond between father and son. It neutralized to some extent her worry over his activities with his friends.

Anka shuffled away towards their sleeping cove above the shelves as Maki jerked the meat to his shoulder again. "I'll leave this in the grotto to cool, Mother. We leave again early in the morning, and I promise you much more of this." He stalked away with his burden, his mother smiling after him, but her smile faded when she saw Han and Dorald, unkempt and dirty as usual, enter the cavern bending over from the weight of meat slabs on their backs.

Tel's heart sank as she watched them greet Maki noisily then follow him towards the grotto. She had seen many boar in her advanced age, and no two of the largest had yielded such a quantity of meat. Sadly, she knew with near certainty what kind of animal her son and his undesirable friends had slaughtered.

It was not a forest creature.

CHAPTER THREE

NIGHT RAIDERS

Maki awoke at the first sign of fire in the eastern sky. He had slept by the cave entrance the entire night, lulling himself to sleep by watching the sky-lights, and straining to hear sounds rising from the distant town. Twice he had heard laughter, loud and boisterous, had felt a growl of vain anger at the existence of those who lived beneath the sun.

The impotent leaders of the Tenanken, old, wobbly and locked in The Memories, had fled to the caves instead of claiming their heritage under the trees by killing the newcomers when they had first arrived. Now there were too many Hinchai for them to wage war against. Even individually they were dangerous when carrying the pointing weapons that hurled tiny, penetrating missiles at blinding speed. He had first seen such a weapon dropping an antlered one at a distance of hundreds of paces; hiding in a nearby tree, he had stifled a cry, watching the great, bloody hole gush open on one side of the animal. And the sound! His heart had beaten erratically for several minutes after that.

But the ones his father and mother called The Cousins *could* be taken individually, for they were physically weak, and slow afoot. Someday he would surprise one carrying a weapon, and in one violent moment that weapon would be his. Then he would determine who ruled the Tenanken.

The fantasy had kept him awake for several minutes, but then he'd succumbed to the rigors of an exciting day and slipped into a deep and dreamless sleep from which he now awoke alert and refreshed. Han and Dorald were still asleep nearby, two bulky chest-mounds rising and falling in near darkness. They were with him wherever he went, would do whatever he told them to do, he using their strength and easily manipulating the feeble minds of orphans born to inferior parents unable to survive. Both were throwbacks to

23

the days before The Plan when births of the slope-heads were cele-
brated. The Tenanken elders had been ready to let them die at birth,
but Anka had insisted they be suckled by those who had milk, and
so here they were at his feet, snoring. He despised them both, but
they were useful.

Maki prodded with his foot, then kicked hard.

"Wha—" grunted Han, somewhat the brighter and more alert of
the two. "Do we get up, now?"

"Quickly, before first light. We cross the valley this morning.
Quiet. I'll be outside." Maki pushed the tangle of branches and
thorns aside far enough to wiggle through to fir boughs covering the
cave entrance, crawling out onto a shelf traversing the wall clear to
the valley, and bypassing thick underbrush in the canyon below.
There was grumbling inside the cave, then Dorald's brute face
pushed through the branches, grimacing.

"I'm caught on something. Why are we leaving so early?"

"Never mind. You'll see why later."

"I'm hungry. I want to eat first before we—owww! What are
you doing back there?"

"Shut up! You're pulling a tree after you. There, I've got it,"
mumbled Han.

"Hurry up," said Maki, and in a moment the other two had tum-
bled out into a heap on the shelf.

"Where do we go?" asked Han.

"We hunt some more. Father was pleased with the meat we
brought back, and I want to keep him that way. We'll go to the next
valley; I want to try and find Hidaig and his group, and see if I can
talk an alliance. We'll be out two nights."

"I should bring my throwing stick," said Han.

"No, leave it. Your hands must be free for carrying, and my
sling is all the weapon we need. Come on, let's go!" Maki moved
off along the shelf, shivering a little in the morning cold. It would
not do for them to see him shivering, for their skin fat was so thick
they did not feel the cold while his was thin, poorly insulating the
lithe body and delicate features he hated.

The shelf remained wide down to the valley, and they moved
quickly in a line: Maki, then Han and Dorald following, stomachs
grumbling. At the end was a shear drop of a hundred paces, but a
chimney big enough even for Dorald. They squeezed into it, backs
against one side and feet pressing the other, quickly wriggling their
way down to ground level. In a few minutes they reached the edge
of tangled underbrush, and stared out at open slopes leading to the
valley and forests beyond. This traverse was always dangerous, the

place where they were most easily seen. Maki instructed the others, "Stay right behind me, and do exactly as I do. Don't stop until we reach the trees."

They nodded gravely at him, so he knew they understood the danger. Maki hunched forward to keep a low profile and moved off at a dog trot, pacing himself so Han and Dorald could keep up and he could be comfortable, for although he had considerably more speed than his companions he did not have their endurance. Under no circumstances could he allow them to see a weakness of any kind in him.

The jog was downhill at first, exhilarating in morning cold, then leveling out on a grassy plain leading to cultivated fields ready for harvest. The Hinchai fields were full of food, and he heard Dorald's stomach growl at the sight. Better to stop a moment and satisfy the Tenanken's hunger than to risk a foul temper later in the morning. Maki angled towards the field of thick, tall stalks where they could hide while eating. From there it was only a short sprint to the trees. In a moment they were surrounded by food hanging in silken pods attached to thick, yellow stalks. Vegetables crunched and popped as strong jaws of Tenanken hunters flexed. As they ate, Maki crouched alertly at the edge of the field, his eating style dainty compared to the others. Dorald's loud belch was a signal to leave, and Maki led them across a plowed field, vaulting a short, wire fence which the others scrambled over clumsily, and then they were hidden from view in the trees.

They kept to the trees all day, climbing out of the valley to a high hill beyond which was solid forest without the stench of Hinchai, an untouched land as in The Memories. Near dusk they came to a hill thick with trees and scattered outcroppings of pegmatite, where they found a small cave littered with tiny bones from which the marrow had been removed. Maki sat at the cave entrance for several minutes, eyes closed, casting a vision of caverns filled with Tenanken and then of a hunter posing with a long spear and a sling, an idealized portrait of himself. There was nothing in return, no gentle, instinctive tuggings to point him in a particular direction. Dorald and Han watched him quietly until he opened his eyes.

"It appears they've moved on. I'm sure their caves were near here."

"I'm hungry again," said Dorald.

"Of course you are," said Maki. They hunted until darkness, taking two bushy-tailed tree climbers, partially cooking them over a tiny fire started with Maki's fire-stones and tinder soaked in sap.

In the morning, after a fitful night crammed together in the little cave, all of them were hungry. Dorald was ravenous.

They followed the forest for hours, watching for game and seeing none, searching each cave for signs of habitation. Privately, Maki worried about the move of Hidaig's band, small in numbers, but proud and fierce. If they were still around, a welcome would have been sent by now, for Maki's tall, slender form was easily recognizable at large distances. Why had they moved on?

A few minutes later, Maki had his answer.

Even Han's stomach was grumbling, now, and Dorald had ceased complaining, eyes glinting dangerously. It was a bad sign; they had to find game soon, or the stupid one would go completely mad, attacking anything or anyone around him. Maki felt both fear and desperation, searching for movement in the trees, but even the birds were still. And then, faintly at first, he heard a sound: grinding, then rapid, clanging beats close together, then again the grinding. It was beyond the trees, and he turned towards it, the others dumbly following. The sound grew louder and louder until Dorald and Han both stopped, eyes wide, and Maki knew he must go on to show his courage and leadership. Tales of his strength and boldness in the face of the unknown had already been told in the caverns, and committed to The Memories forever. His companions were far behind when he reached the brow of a hill, and looked into a shallow valley devastated beyond belief.

Hinchai were everywhere.

Uprooted trees were scattered in all directions, a wide gouge in the earth stretching nearly to the foggy horizon. Hinchai males rode animals pulling huge, shiny monsters spewing white steam and noise, destroying everything in their path. Maki stepped behind a large tree, trying to escape the noise, but it seemed to be coming from all directions, crushing him. He breathed deeply, fighting back panic, then walked back crouched over to where the others waited nervously for him.

"The invasion has begun," he told them breathlessly. "The main Hinchai force is below, destroying everything in its path. Now perhaps my father will listen to me, and begin to kill our enemy. We must hurry to warn him, and prepare for war!"

"How can we fight so many when they can even destroy the land? We have to move like the other bands, Maki." Han was nearly pleading. "We can't go back, now. Let's find Hidaig's band, and take some females to make our place where the Hinchai can never find us."

"And where might that be?"

"To the west. The hills are solid trees to the west, and there are only scattered Hinchai, alone and unprotected. We could make dominance there."

"You forget that our ancestors *came* from the west. What do you think *they* were fleeing? I'll tell you what; thousands and thousands of Hinchai, and their noise, and destruction of the land. To return west is to die; it is a stupid suggestion. We must make a stand here, or a little north. It is our last place."

"Your father will send the Tenanken out to live among the Hinchai. He says they are our cousins, that we are of them in most ways, and can—"

"My father is a foolish and feeble old dreamer who lives with memories of past days *without* Hinchai, and keeps his eyes closed to the present. He has the affliction of the old, and it is up to *our* generation to preserve the lives and dignity of the Tenanken, even is it means war! We will not be forced into Hinchai subjugation, I tell you, and we will retain our identity or die! Do you stand with, or against me in this?" Maki's voice seethed with the passion of a zealot.

"We follow you where you lead us, Maki," said Han quietly. Perhaps he actually understood, but Dorald was hopeless, his brain operating at a level only high enough to obtain food and defecate. His usefulness would be limited, although around those who didn't know him his physical presence was usually intimidating, and Maki could make good use of that.

"For now, we return to the caverns, and try to organize those few who might be willing to fight. Come on." Maki turned on his heel, and marched away from the noise and steam. The others followed silently until Dorald suddenly giggled, and said, "I kill Hinchai." Han shushed him, but Maki called back over his shoulder, "Follow me, and you'll get your chance, but you'll do it when the time is right." What kind of fantasy was playing in the big Tenanken's feeble mind?

They marched until the sun was again low in the sky, and the changing direction of the wind told them evening was fast approaching. Their route remained high on the hills, where Hinchai rarely ventured, and they could see far in every direction. It was Han who first spotted the stream of smoke coming up from the trees. An open fire, or another Hinchai settlement? They were only a half-day march from the caverns, and this was something new. Han pointed it out to Maki.

"It's on our path, so we'll look," said Maki. "I hope it's a settlement, and they have animals. The Hinchai have scared much game away, and I don't intend to return empty-handed on this trip."

They kept to the trees, and descended the hill until they saw a small clearing. Nestled at the edge of it was a substantial cabin, and a small shed with an attached log fence penning in several tusked animals related to others in The Memories.

The men sat on their haunches and watched the place for several minutes. There was no sound except the snorting of the animals. It seemed whoever lived there was away for the moment. They moved in cautiously, following Maki's hand signals, coming up on the cabin from the nearby trees to give them a quick retreat. They pressed against the wall of the building, listening, then Maki stood up and peered cautiously inside. Nobody there. Three rooms in the structure, and a fireplace, and something else, something he wanted badly. He motioned for the others to come near, and whispered, "There's nobody here, so we work quickly. You two kill a couple of the smaller animals we can carry away. I'm going inside."

Dorald was grinning broadly, eager as usual for bloodletting. Maki left them and went to the front of the cabin, pushing, rattling, fiddling with a knob on the entrance cover until it suddenly opened. He studied the mechanism, quickly seeing how the door held shut when unattended, then went inside and shut it behind him. The room was warm, and a pot of food was bubbling over the open flame of an enclosed cooking fire in one corner. Maki only sniffed at it, then went straight to the fireplace over which the long pointing weapon was hung on two wooden pegs. He lifted it off gently, caressing it as he worked the lever until he saw the yellow projectile inside. There were ten others strapped to the broad part of the weapon that went against the shoulder.

It was a weapon he was familiar with, one that had nearly killed him and Dorald in a previous raid. But without projectiles to throw, the weapon wasn't even a good club. He looked for more projectiles, at last finding them in a box on the ledge above the fireplace. As he took them there was a squeal and a scream from outside, and a sound like the smashing of a gourd against a rock. Dorald laughed loudly, and Han was telling him to shut up, but the laughter continued until there was another pitiful scream, then silence.

Maki searched the rest of the cabin, but found nothing more he wanted. He opened the cabin door and emerged triumphantly, clutching the weapon in one hand over his head. Dorald and Han, blood-spattered, were dragging two carcasses across the ground, stopping when they saw him. "Aieeee, look what *you* found," cried

Han, greatly impressed with the new power his young leader now possessed. "We've done well, too. These young boars will make a great feast." He prodded one carcass with a foot, but was pushed aside by Dorald, who like a child wanted to show off his new treasure as well. The hulking Tenanken held up a new metal axe, now covered with blood, and swung it one-handed around his head with a whirring sound. "With my new club I will split Hinchai skulls, and eat their brains," he growled.

"You've done well, and luck is with us. Let's go, now, before anyone returns." Maki closed the door to the cabin as the others hoisted the carcasses on their backs. Maki took the axe from Dorald, and carried it with his pointing weapon. In a minute they were back in the safety of the trees with a half-day march ahead of them, and darkness was coming fast. They would have to spend one more night outside, and return to the cavern in the morning. Han and Dorald both grunted under their burdens, and before long Dorald was complaining about being hungry again. It was going to be a long night for the three of them.

It was after dark when they reached the field they had eaten from on the way out, but noise drove them back to the shelter of the trees, and they watched fearfully as a great Hinchai machine chewed away the field illuminated by its dim light, spewing out a cloud of pulverized stalk behind and leaving nothing else in its wake. Fortunately for them the destruction was not completed.

The machine stopped suddenly, the light disappeared, and in seconds a lone Hinchai was walking two great animals across the now barren field towards a distant structure they had not noticed before. A single Hinchai had controlled the entire machine! Maki gained new respect for the power of the enemy; still, without their machines, they were no equal to a Tenanken warrior.

Maki turned to Han and Dorald. "It's safe, now. You go down and eat your fill. I'll stay here and guard the meat if you bring something back for me."

The others nodded, grinning, and left without a word, frolicking downhill in the light of a rising moon, like children at play. Maki felt relief at being left alone to think. The disappearance of Hidaig's band bothered him deeply, for he had counted on them for support when the time for his father's overthrow came, and that would have to be soon. If only Hidaig was at his side now, then he wouldn't have to put up with dim-witted Tenanken who thought only of their stomachs. His own stomach was cramped from hunger, but he ignored the pain. Food was only necessary to sustain life, but the survival of the true Tenanken was everything to him. He vowed to venture out again very soon, and find the new Hidaig encampment.

Maki watched for several minutes while Han and Dorald greedily stripped vegetables from their stalks, eating most, but dropping some in a little pile to take back up the hill. And when things began going wrong, it was subtle at first, Han eating, back turned to Dorald, the big Tenanken suddenly wandering away through tall stalks, the axe in his hand, heading towards the Hinchai cabin.

When Maki noticed it he wanted to yell, because Han just sat there munching contentedly. Dorald was swinging the axe in his hand, heading straight for the house, then veering towards the right, out of sight behind some trees and soon there was a crash and a babbling chorus from eating birds kept by the Hinchai. Maki shuddered. So close to the cabin, and all that noise, Dorald's hunger could cost him his life.

Han had heard the sounds too, stretching to peer over the stalks, then looking back at Maki who motioned at him frantically to return. Han started up the hill at a run as the door of the cabin burst open, spilling light onto a stump, woodpile, and something moving in the trees. Dorald was carrying a thrashing bird. He raised the bird to his face, biting down on its neck until the bird was still. Maki could see him clearly, but trees obscured the view from the cabin. The Hinchai male appeared in the doorway, a pointing weapon in his hands, aiming at sounds among the trees and screaming in the language Maki was regrettably becoming familiar with.

"You Goddamn kids! This is the last time you raid my hen house! Pick *this* out of your ass!"

The explosion split the stillness of the night, a sheet of flame the length of a spear belching from the end of the weapon.

Dorald screamed, a loud, piercing scream of agony, but kept running.

The Hinchai jumped backwards. "What the hell was *that*?" He jumped again, into the cabin, and slammed the door behind him

There was shouting behind the door, and then—something—probing—passing through Maki's mind like a wisp of wind—a vision of the caverns—Anka and Tel—his parents, grieving over something, a body lying before them. It was Maki's body, face covered with blood.

Maki forced the vision away, closing his mind to further intrusion. *Who's out there?* He looked around warily as Han reached him, out of breath, and Dorald was scrambling up the hill, holding one side with a hand.

The door to the cabin flew open again, and now there were two figures in the light. One was tall, the one with the pointing weapon, while the other was shorter but broad, nearly filling the doorway. "Second time this month," came a shout. "These damn kids have no respect for a man's property, and I swear to God I'll blow them to pieces if they come back."

The second Hinchai's voice boomed in the night. "Come on, Ed, losing one chicken ain't worth havin' a heart attack over, and besides, the kid's probably out there in the woods now pickin' buck-shot out of his ass. If it happens again, we'll get some folks together for a search party, and then we'll have some real fun!"

The two Hinchai went back inside again, and slammed the door. Ham flopped on his back, breathing deep. Dorald slowed down as he reached the top of the hill, head down because he could not endure Maki's withering glare of anger and disgust. Dorald's side was on fire, and blood oozed between his thick fingers, yet he knew he was not seriously injured. He walked past Maki and sat down next to Han, who examined his wound and said, "Many small punctures in the skin, but not deep. It should be washed, and salved."

Maki stood over them, hands on hips. "All for a bird," he said disdainfully. "You could have gotten us all killed over a bird."

"I'm sorry, Maki," said Dorald mournfully. His eyes were pleading. *Don't throw me away like all the others have. I have no place else to go.* The giant child began to cry.

Maki smiled. *A true leader is understanding, and merciful.* "So you perceive your error. It was a stupid mistake, but one I hope you will learn from. You see how we must stay together in everything we do, and if you can learn this I promise the day will come soon when we drive out the Hinchai, and I will bring you back here with your club to crush the skull of the one who hurt you tonight."

Both Han and Dorald were grinning, now. Maki slapped their shoulders affectionately, and walked away as both of them scram-bled to their feet to follow him.

The night was half over when they reached the caverns, picking their way along the narrow ledge in total darkness, and squeezing into the entrance to find welcome torchlight. Maki stored his point-ing weapon and Dorald's axe by his sleeping place near the en-trance, and the three of them disappeared down a tunnel to find wa-ter and salve for Dorald's wound.

For a moment it was quiet in the vestibule they claimed as their own, and then a tiny face appeared in the flickering torchlight. Baela. The caverns had been humid that night, so she had slept in a fumarole near the entrance, awakening when Maki's little band moved near her in the tunnel. She peered down the tunnel, head cocked to hear the slightest sound, eyes flashing mischievously in yellow light. She crept over to Maki's sleeping place, and pulled aside the fur covering the axe and pointing weapon.

She touched each one, running her slender fingers over them, wondering at the smooth, cold and unfamiliar feel of metal, and then her eyes were attracted to the shiny metal projectiles strapped to the butt of the weapon.

Baela hesitated a moment, hand poised, then smiled to herself and removed one of the projectiles from a leather loop. Holding it tightly in her hand, she covered Maki's possessions with the fur again, and hurried quickly away to her hiding place.

CHAPTER FOUR

PETER PELEGEROPOULIS

The Athens Bar was jammed with miners from out of town, and it was getting loud. Sid Henderson, a tall, skinny man with the face of a predatory bird was working frantically to keep up with the thirsty men and their few women, but he was running out of glasses again. Sid hated weekends: Jake was getting drunk and belligerent at the end of the bar, and any second some hard-rocker was going to put his body through a wall, and then Sally came out of the kitchen, crying, and covered with soot. There had been another grease fire, and she had used the sand, so now five orders were burned beyond recognition, and another four were covered with grit. Nine hungry miners was a bad situation, which Sid temporarily saved by pouring nine drinks courtesy of The Management, who was upstairs in the apartment over the bar, eating dinner with his pregnant wife.

"Sid! Goddamn it, I'm empty again! C'mere."

"You've had enough, Jake. Coffee, or nothin'."

"Fuck you! I'm the best customer you've got here. The rest of these dirt diggers come to diddle the women. Me, I'm takin' no chances; locked up my cows, too. Hee, hee, hee."

"Shut your face, rummy, before I push it in."

The voice of doom had emanated from a hulking miner whose buttocks reached to the stools on either side of him, a man-ape with red cap and plaid shirt. The man neglected his half-empty beer stein and drank straight from the pitcher. He gave Jake a baleful stare.

Jake Price was offended, and not the least bit frightened. "Ohhh, what a big man you are! Why don't you threaten me when I'm sober?"

"You name the time and place, big mouth, and I'll be there with a pick."

"You'll need more than that if you expect to—"

"That's enough from you, Jake! One more word, so help me Christ I'll never serve you a drop again, and Pete will back me up. We're *both* tired of your shit!" Sid leaned over the bar and grabbed Jake's glass, sweeping the place clean in front of him. It got quiet for just a minute, people looking to see what Jake would do, but finally the man just put his head down on the bar, and started to cry.

"Oh shit," muttered Sid. He washed Jake's glass in the suds, then filled it again for Sally, who had given up on the cooking and was now waiting tables. People were banging glasses on those tables, and Sally couldn't move fast enough. That was it, Sid decided. Time to yell for help. He grabbed onto the rope hanging from the ceiling at the back of the bar and tugged on it frantically in Pete's prearranged code for help. Just as he finished tugging, there was a crash and Jake's head disappeared beneath the bar. Sid moved fast and pulled him up woozily from the floor, holding him from behind long enough to get him back on the bar stool and hoping he wouldn't puke on the bar. The smell of booze, sweat and even hair on the animal heads mounted around on the lacquered pine walls didn't help any, and there was no other place to put him because the dozen tables in the place were all filled up.

It was getting ugly: glasses pounding on tables, big men yelling at Sally for service, and the stink of grease smoke in the air when suddenly the front door swung open so hard it slammed back against the wall, and everyone screamed in unison at the man whose huge frame filled the doorway.

"Pete!" they all shouted.

Peter Pelegeropoulis flashed black eyes and a heart-softening smile from his wide, square face, raised two massive arms above his head and did a little twisting, swaying dance into the room. Humming to himself, he passed close to each table, picking up women like a magnet, two of the bigger, more aggressive ones attaching themselves firmly to his wrestler's body by the time he reached the bar. Everyone now hummed the familiar tune, a subtly wild thing that got faster and faster. Pete danced the women around and around the room until they were a blur, and the miners were chanting and clapping to the beat of Greek music that was nowhere except in their minds. In the meantime, Sally was scooping glasses off the tables, and Sid was buried in soapsuds behind the bar.

A few moments later the crisis was over. Pete staggered around like he was ready to fall over, then dumped two exhausted girls into the lap of a delighted miner and kissed all three of them. Everyone was still laughing at the embarrassed miner when Pete turned and lumbered to the end of the bar, squeezing himself onto the stool next to Jake, who had started to cry again. It got a little quieter, then, people wanting to see what would happen with Jake. To most of the out-of-towners he was just an obnoxious drunk raising hell in a workingman's bar until the owner showed up. But now Jake rocked back and forth on the stool, tears streaming down his face, and stared down at the cup of hot coffee Sid had shoved in front of him. It was amazing how a man could be ready to tear the place to pieces one minute, and cry like a baby the next.

Sid brought Pete a shot of whiskey, which disappeared in a gulp. "Thanks for coming, Pete. I guess I panicked."

"No problem. I was wide awake, and horny, and Bernie needs her sleep." Pete smiled at his little joke, and put an arm around Jake. "Besides, I like to be with my friends."

Jake bawled pitifully for ten minutes after that, then all the deep breathing and shaking finally took its toll, and he was sick. Pete got him to the inside privy just in time, and held his head while he emptied the contents of his offended stomach. This took a while, but Pete was patient, and when it was finally over he cleaned Jake up, then guided him across the room towards the door, holding him like you'd hold a little brother who'd been hurt by the town bully. On the way, Pete was patting shoulders and touching faces. Smiling faces. The big Greek took care of his customers. In fact, he took care of everyone.

The night was cold, and Jake began shivering as soon as they were outside, walking across the dirt main street of town towards a two story wooden structure garishly painted red with white block letters proclaiming it to be The Cardinal Hotel. A joint venture between Pete and Sid, the hotel interior was not complete, but a few rooms were rented out, and one set aside for business meetings or high-stakes card parties. It was also a place to sleep for special friends who weren't fit for riding or walking. And Jake Price was a special friend.

Pete dragged him past a surprised desk clerk named Ned Olsewski, who only nodded a greeting and tossed him a key. Jake's legs seemed to go numb as they reached the unpainted stairs, and his feet went bumpity-bump behind him as Pete hauled his half-alive body up to the second floor. Pete leaned him against a wall while he opened a door and got a lamp going. He laid Jake cross-wise at the end of the bed, pulled back the covers, then undressed his friend as he would a little child, and tucked him in.

Jake's eyes fluttered open then, and he said tearfully, "Sorry for fucking up your evening, Pete. I don't see why you bother with a piece of shit like me."

"Stop it. You're feeling sorry for yourself again."

"I mean it. I'm not worth messin' with."

"Bull. You think I waste my time with people? You've got a drinkin' problem, Jake. I'll serve you coffee, or milk, but no more booze. Not in my place. You want to kill yourself, you'll have to do it alone at home."

"Yeah, alone. You ever been alone, Pete?"

"Lots of times. It's okay, because I like myself."

Tears welled up in Jake's eyes again. "You never had anyone leave you like that. You told me so."

"A million men have been burned by women. Ester's a tramp who latched hold of a lonely bachelor with property, and moved on when she found something wealthier. She's never loved anything in her life."

"But I loved *her*. I *still* do." Tears were streaming down Jake's pinched face, his hands twisting the edges of the bed covers.

"You'll get over it, and there's plenty of good women out there, women not pretty, maybe, but decent inside, and a lot of them get overlooked. Like Bernie, you know? She'll never be a dance-hall queen, but I'll tell you I've got me one hell of a woman, and if an ugly hulk like me can do it, you can too."

Ordinarily Pete's grin would have made anyone smile, but Jake remained wet-faced somber, and his eyelids were getting heavy again. Pete smoothed his hair with a big hand, then stood up. "Remember, you're welcome in my place anytime, but no more booze. You put a cork in the bottle, things are gonna look a lot different to you. I gotta get back to Bernie. You stay here as long as you like, but get some sleep." Pete opened the door, and started to leave.

"Pete?"

"Yeah, Jake."

"Thanks for all this."

"Nothing. You're a friend, Jake." Pete closed the door, then let out a big sigh when he heard Jake's sobbing begin again. He went downstairs and straight outside, crossing the street to the log structure that was his first business and made him a part of society. Stairs led up the side of the building to the apartment on top. Smoke was coming out of the chimney, so Bernie was cold again. He climbed the varnished steps quickly, wood groaning beneath his big feet, and when he got to the landing he smelled coffee and heard rattling sounds in the kitchen. She had been sleeping so peacefully when he'd left, and he'd hoped he wouldn't wake her.

When he went inside he found Bernice Pelegeropoulis sitting at the kitchen table, drinking milk and eating an enormous cucumber sandwich. "Coffee for you, and milk for me," she said.

"I didn't want to wake you up." Pete pulled up a chair, and sat across the table from her.

"This kid of yours woke me up," she said jovially, putting one hand on her swollen stomach. "The little animal's been using my bladder for a punching bag all night. Seems like I have to pee all the time."

Impulsively, Pete stood us, leaned over the table to kiss her firmly on the mouth, and licked his lips.

Bernie smiled. "Cucumbers—and sour cream. I was crazy for it when I woke up."

Pete poured himself a cup of coffee, then sat down at the table again and took a couple of scalding hot sips. "Had to bed down Jake drunk again tonight. Seems like he's been that way ever since Ester left."

Bernie grunted with a mouthful of sandwich, and said, "Hell, he's better off without her. Jake isn't the first guy that little whore has messed up. Been doing it since before you swept *me* off my feet."

Pete sipped his coffee slowly, looking thoughtful. "She must have her problems, too."

Bernie laughed, reaching across the table to lay a big hand on his. "My darling, big bear of a man, one of the things I love about you is the way you try to see good in people. Ester's only problem is finding a way to acquire and spend all the money in the world. Believe me, she's just pure bad, always has been and always will be. Some folks is born that way."

Pete looked doubtful. Bernie patted his hand, got up slowly and shuffled to the sink to clean off her empty plate. Pete watched her admiringly. She was a big woman: big-boned, large, firm arms and muscular legs matching her hips and frame. A good face: generous mouth and prominent nose framed by a billowing mass of blonde hair. Swedish stock, and not pretty by the usual standards, but striking and honest and generous and loving and funny as hell, and Pete was crazy in love with her. Their baby was going to be very large, and when Pete once worried about it she'd told him, "Daddy said if us girls were like momma we could give birth to a heifer. And we're *all* like our momma."

Pete wished he'd known Bernie's parents, but they were gone before he'd arrived in town, and so now on occasional Sundays he took her to visit their graves in the little cemetery at the tree line below the cliffs. He still remembered the first visit together, when they stood before the two, simple head stones. Bernie hugged him, and said, "Momma, Daddy, this here is my man Pete. He's not a Swede, but I love him anyway. We're gonna be married soon, and have lots of babies, and raise 'em up right here in town." She went on to tell them all about Pete, tears streaming down her face, and Pete trying hard not to cry, biting his lip so hard it bled. Her four sisters had all left town and married elsewhere, two in California, one in Texas, another in Chicago. A sleepy little town like Crosley was not for them, and they would never come back, even for a visit.

Bernie pushed against the sink, arching her back and stretching it, then turning to show Pete the movement inside her. "I think he's doing something Greek."

Pete laughed. "How do you know he isn't a she?"

"You're right, what do I know about these things? What we probably have here is a boy *and* a girl, and they're fighting already." A big ripple passed across her stomach, then back again, and she slapped at it gently. "Hey, quiet down in there!"

Pete grinned at her, and then she walked over to stand behind him, putting her arms around his thick neck. "I could sure use a back rub," she said softly.

Pete didn't answer, but rose from his chair and led her through the neat little sitting room, filled with overstuffed furniture with doilies on the arms, and a fireplace mantel covered with family pictures. Beyond that, and a heavy curtain, was the bedroom and a brass bed, and beside it the tiny crib he had finished painting white the day before. Bernie lay half on her stomach, half on her side while Pete kneaded the hard muscles in her lower back, big hands moving gently yet firmly over her. She moaned, then said, "Ohhh, that better'n sex."

"What?" Pete kneaded a little harder, and Bernie giggled.

In a few minutes she was totally relaxed, and nearly asleep. Pete helped her slip under the covers, then turned out the lamp and undressed in the dark. Wearing only his under-shorts, he slid cautiously into bed beside his wife and draped one arm protectively over her so that she snuggled up against him and pulled his hand over to rest on her stomach. Her breathing slowed and deepened. From beneath the flesh of the mother a foot moved, dragging a heel past the resting hand of the father. Pete grasped it briefly, closing his eyes with his forehead against Bernie's back and sending out a feeling of love, contentment and belonging. The movement slowed, and a moment later the three of them were asleep together in the darkness.

* * * * * * *

The sun came up on a clear Monday morning, a day of leisure for Pete because on Monday he kept the bar closed until seven in the evening. It was the only day of the week he had a chance to work on the ranch, and because of this it was also his favorite day of the week. He kissed Bernie goodbye at six in the morning, went down the street to the livery where two horses hitched to a loaded wagon were waiting for him. As he climbed on, there was a shout. "Hey, Pete, one minute!" and Tom Henley came sauntering towards him from where he'd been standing across the street.

"My Gawd, Tom, what you doin' up so early? This is the quietest day in town."

"The law never rests, citizen," drawled Tom, and they both laughed.

Pete liked the big man, as did everyone. You didn't mess with him, but he was the gentlest human being Pete had ever met. Tom leaned on the wagon, kind of intimate, smelling of coffee and bacon. "Goin' out to the ranch?"

"All day. Just about finished with everything except painting, and that won't take long."

"When they comin' in?"

"Oh, a couple weeks, yet. Some of them are still waiting for papers."

"Yeah, well, the whole town's pretty excited about the big arrival. You be sure to let us know if we can help get 'em settled."

"Thanks, Tom. Really, the main thing you all can do is relax, be yourselves, and have some patience. Their English is lousy, and this is going to be a whole new world for them. It'll be tough, at first."

"No problem. Hell, if you go back far enough we're all emigrants. Just remember the folks in town *want* to help. Know what I mean?" Tom winked at him.

"Sure. I'll find some things that need doin'."

"Oh, another thing. We've been havin' some vandalism problems the last few weeks. Probably kids raisin' hell, stealing, and property destruction kinds of things, you know. If you see any strange riders, or people on foot, especially kids, let me know so I can check it out quick. Some of our folks are gettin' pretty riled up about it."

"I'll keep my eyes open. Oh, by the way, I put Jake up in the hotel again last night, but it's the last time, and I told him he gets nothing but coffee or milk in my place from now on."

"Glad to hear it, Pete. Poor Jake and his critters. I keep tryin' to get him to see Doc, but he won't listen, and I guess you can't run people's lives for them. You have a happy day, Pete." Tom banged the wagon sideboard with one hand, and stepped away smiling. He was still standing in the street, a big smile on his face as Pete drove away.

It was the last time Pete saw him alive.

The drive to the ranch was short, less than two miles outside of town to the south fence, then four hundred acres of prime grazing land and stands of corn, and access to thousands more acres of the federal land at the north end of the valley. The place had been abandoned for years, dating back to gold rush days, and falling down when Pete had bought it for back taxes, paying cash on the barrel to a pleased and surprised banker in nearby Quincy. The banker would have been even more curious about Pete if he'd known that the cash, and more like it, had come from the sale of a considerable hoard of solid gold nuggets ranging up to a few ounces in weight. It was a secret Pete kept from everyone, even Bernie. All they needed to know was he was a successful business man with money, who came to town looking for a new and simple life, and a place big enough to settle a town full of relatives now living in Greece, packed and ready to travel. Over the years, he *had* told them some tales about his life with Savas, but at least part of that was true.

He'd rebuilt the big house and barn with Sid's help. Sid had all the carpentry skills, but Pete learned fast. He learned everything fast. A little shingling and painting left to do, and that was it. All the place needed now was people. His people.

A buck deer was standing by the barn, bolting away in a leap as Pete pulled up in front of the house. A few minutes later he was pounding shingles on the roof, sweating under a hot sun, singing while he worked. Time flashed by. In the afternoon he lacquered the walls in an upstairs bedroom, mood changing, becoming more pensive, somber. His next task was unpleasant, but necessary, and best done quickly. He finished his painting first, then cleaned the brush.

It was less than a mile to the head of the canyon, and so he walked there, crossing his own property first and leaning over to slip between strands of barbed wire along the boundary fence. Soon the cliffs of slate were looming above him, and he was climbing a short ridge to a long shelf of ascending slabs that disappeared around a cornice. Each step was familiar, yet he hesitated, each moment taking him closer to a confrontation he didn't want, and twice he had a strong urge to turn back. No time to consider feelings, he decided, and pressed on.

Halfway up the canyon he came to the entrance of a small cavern leading nowhere, but it was cool—private. He bent over double to step inside, and sat down on a rock, facing the entrance, sunlight warming him for the moment as a blinding sun neared the top of the canyon wall opposite him. He closed his eyes, focusing inward for a moment, then sent out a vision of himself sitting there, arms outstretched, palms up. Instantly a wave of happiness passed through him. He opened his eyes, feeling guilty since he had not revealed his reason for contact. He waited patiently until the orb of the sun reached the canyon wall rim, then heard the shuffling steps coming along the shelf, the heavy, labored breathing of the one he regarded as older than time, one who had been like a father to him after the brother had died and left a grief-stricken mother to raise a tiny baby. Devastated by her grief, and weakened by a difficult birth, the mother had died within a year. The child was now a man.

The large, square and familiar face appeared in the cave entrance. Amber eyes twinkled, though the big shoulders sagged from the weariness of many years gone by. "Pegre, it is good to see you again. Come to me." Anka held out his arms, Pete stepping up to him eye to eye, and they embraced stiffly like acquainted emissaries from different planets, the true depth and warmth of their greeting sensed only in their minds.

"I think of you often, but the preparations have taken all of my time, and my woman is now heavy with child."

"Ah, you still speak the old language well, though you now cut your words off short." Anka smiled, and sat down on a rock. "I try to speak the new speech, but it only makes the children laugh. My tongue is forever in the wrong place."

"I'm sure you do well," said Pete, sitting down beside the chief elder of the Tenanken. "It will be quite soon, now, and those you have taught will be well prepared as was I."

"Yes, but with you I needed only to mold the genius your father gave you through our mother. Our dear father, your grandfather, was a great hunter, but a genius, no." Anka chuckled at the memory from long ago, and then there was a long silence between them. Finally, Anka leaned over and put a hand on Pete's knee. "I'm thinking, Pegre, that your visit here has a serious reason behind it. We are not here to exchange pleasantries."

"No," said Pete. "I fear my reason for coming here may seem threatening to you. I hesitate to talk about it, but I must do so."

"Since when could you not talk to me about *any* problem? You are like my own son."

I'm afraid not, dear Teacher. Pete paused, then looked directly into Anka's amber eyes. "Very well, then. In the past few weeks there is suddenly trouble in the valley." There, the plug was now out, and the words could flow.

"Trouble?"

"Acts of violence, theft, destruction of property, reports of strange creatures attacking people and their animals, mischief of many kinds."

Lines appeared in Anka's forehead. "Strange creatures, you say? You think of someone from our group here?"

"Not necessarily in all instances. There is no doubt in my mind that at least in one case a townsperson was physically attacked by three Tenanken, and in another I personally witnessed, the minds of the thieves were filled with visions of flight to these caverns. I heard a Tenanken scream when the man I was with fired at him with a shotgun. *Long-range pointing missile thrower.* He may, in fact, be injured, and that's easy to check. *And include your son.* We have troublemakers to deal with, very likely Tenanken who oppose The Plan, and work to disrupt it as the time for resettlement approaches. The townspeople are irritated, and crazy rumors are circulating about monsters or even their own children causing the damage. We do not need search parties with weapons coming into the canyon, and suspicions against every new person who comes to town. Especially not now." Pete felt his voice rising in pitch, struggling to control his anger and frustration.

Anka put a hand on his shoulder. "I understand. You've worked long and hard, and now all is ready. The Tenanken have agreed to it, and work with you. Those who disagree must follow the group will."

"You might have to remind the dissenters of that in harsh terms they will respond to. We could also have detractors from other bands across the hills, or to the south. I've had no contact with them in years, and Hidaig in particular I've never trusted since his expulsion. Beware of alliances against you, Anka. There are those close to you who have ambitions."

"Do you not have ambitions, Pegre? The Plan has been your life for several years. Your ambition. You are as close to me as any, but I don't fear you, and we both know who has opposed The Plan most vigorously. Why don't you say his name? Why don't you tell me Maki is the one I should fear?"

"I believe you close your eyes to many things your son does that are not in the best interests of the Tenanken, and I've heard Tel comment on his attitude problems in your presence."

"Your rivalry with Maki has extended to adulthood. I hoped someday you'd get along."

This has nothing to do with childhood rivalries. You treated both of us with love and understanding, yet spoiled neither of us. But Maki and I have diverged on all matters concerning the future of the Tenanken. I accept The Plan as the only way to survival. Maki plans war, stupidly believing he can destroy the Hinchai, and return us to dominance in the outside world. It is a childhood fantasy he has never given up, seeing himself as a great warrior king. I see it as a nightmare, with much blood, most of it Tenanken. I have lived with the Hinchai for fifteen years, and they are as tough as us in every way. They outnumber our bands a thousand to one, and their weapons can destroy us in a day if they choose to do it. War will destroy Tenanken, not Hinchai, and The Memories will be gone forever!"

The light on Anka's face vanished as the sun dropped below the rim of the canyon. Pete breathed heavily from his passionate outburst, his mind a blank as Anka shielded himself. They sat in darkness for a moment.

"I will talk to Maki, and remind him of the group will to support The Plan."

"And the trouble in the valley must stop. Tell him—"

"You have no evidence my son is involved with any raids on Hinchai property or persons! Didn't I raise *both* of you to respect others? Your suspicions are not founded on evidence, but speculation."

"I will not argue," said Pete firmly. "I ask you to tell him the trouble must stop, or I will deal personally with it." He stood up, and started to leave the little cave.

"Pegre. We must not depart angrily. Not now."

"I'm not angry. I'm frightened. Of war—of death. I want the Tenanken to live—and I'll destroy anything that gets in the way of that."

"I'll talk to Maki; you've nothing to fear from him. When do we see you again?" Anka's voice was soft, soothing, a model of control so that Pete felt himself calming, yet in his mind was a dark shadow, foreboding, a warning about the future.

"In two weeks I will come to lead our settlement south, then north again to the town. Please do not tell anyone this, even Tel. I want no planned interference or anxiety."

"So soon. It seems only yesterday when The Plan was approved. The years race by when you're old." Anka stood up and once again embraced Pete, but his eyes were sad. "The Tenanken will soon be in your hands, Pegre. Be gentle with them; they trust you without really knowing you. I fear for them as much as I fear for those of us who are left behind, even though I know it is the only way to our survival. I fear also for my son."

"I wouldn't expect otherwise," said Pete, hugging Anka tightly, and then stepping to the cave entrance. "We all do what we must do." He stooped over and left the cave, Anka still standing with his back towards the entrance, concentrating on his shielding of a mind screaming in pain.

* * * * * * *

From a cornice near the main entrance to the caverns, Maki watched his Hinchai clothed, adopted older brother descend the slabs of rock towards the valley below. Han was at Maki's side, Dorald fast asleep inside the rock. "There goes a Tenanken traitor who will make us all Hinchai slaves," said Maki. "I tell you that the day is coming soon when I will meet Pegre on the field of battle and kill him."

Han growled assent as they saw Anka emerge from the little cave, and begin to shuffle tiredly up the slabs towards where they waited. "Let's see what plot they've been hatching this time," said Maki, He arose, and walked jauntily downwards to meet his father.

When Anka saw his son coming towards him, he smiled.

CHAPTER FIVE

SAVAS

Savas Parkos was an enigma, a man who'd come to the California hills north of Quincy in 1870 when he was not yet forty, buying good land with cabin and well ten miles south of the three building town called Crosley. How he arrived, or from where, forever remained a mystery. He brought furniture with him, and a dozen boxes of books which he kept on shelves surrounding the one room, neat interior of the cabin. There was a mahogany table, and three matching chairs near a wood-stove used for cooking and heating, and a mattress for a bed. The few clothes he had were hung on nails around the walls, and were always clean.

His toilet was a privy ten yards from the cabin, nestled among fir trees, and beside it a metal pan on a stand facing a book-sized mirror hanging from a tree. Lamps were scattered inside and outside the cabin, the outside lights remaining on each night without exception, often the inside lights as well, for it seemed that Savas Parkos slept little, and lightly. Even when deer came quietly to lick the salt slabs he left out for them, he would be there watching through a mica-covered window.

There were no visitors to his cabin until the boy came. He spent his days drinking, and reading in several languages: French, German, Greek, Dutch and English. His origin was Greek. The few who knew him remotely said he was from Rhodes, a businessman searching for a simple life and finding it near Crosley. He bought a horse, and each Saturday rode it to Quincy for groceries and whiskey. There, he would check into the hotel, then dine at Delnico's Basque Restaurant and spend an evening approaching quiet oblivion at the bar. Late Sunday morning he would arise refreshed for the trip home. This he did with complete regularity for nine years, until the boy came.

Savas was also a mystery in Crosley, where he did his banking, and refused all social invitations from the town residents until the offers finally stopped. The local interest in him, he well understood, related to his initial deposit of over half a million cash dollars in a bank struggling to stay afloat after the end of the mining boom. There was more money than that, some three hundred pounds of gold dust and nuggets he had wrapped in burlap and lightly covered with earth beneath the floor of his cabin. He seemed a wealthy eccentric who lived simply and spent modestly, a man who wanted little to do with people. After a while the townspeople ignored him, and Savas Parkos lived a quiet life alone, until the boy came.

It was a Thursday evening, and he was washing dishes, daydreaming about something in his past. A sound, like something striking the cabin wall, and he turned with a plate in one hand to see a face pressed against his mica window. When the plate shattered on the floor, the face disappeared. Savas rushed to the door in time to see a figure crash into the brush by the privy.

"Hey! You want see me, you come back and we talk!" he yelled.

No answer. Nothing moved.

"Nothing here to steal, but I have coffee and bread. You want to eat?"

Nothing. He waited several minutes, then went inside, shut the door and watched at the window until his eyes were too tired to focus, and so he went to bed with all the lamps burning.

The next day he watched from the window, and saw nothing.

Three days after that he put some food on a plate and left it on the washing stand by the privy. The food soured, and dried.

He baked bread, leaving the cabin door slightly ajar, putting one loaf to cool on the washing stand, and forcing himself to stay away from the window all day. When he went outside late in the evening, the loaf was gone.

The next day he baked bread again, leaving the door wide open and singing every Greek song he could remember. When the bread had cooled, he took a loaf outside along with butter and a small wheel of cheese, and sat by a packing crate which served as table, putting the food on top of it. He broke bread, spread chunks of it thick with butter and cheese, and ate noisily.

Near dusk, the boy suddenly appeared.

Savas was first aware of a watchful presence, and then there was movement to his left. He turned his head slowly, eyes moving back and forth. The boy, not much more than a child, was crouched in bushes near the privy, eyes dark and wide like those of a doe, mouth closed tightly in a grim line. Savas picked up the other half of the bread loaf, beckoned to the boy with it, then broke off another piece, stuffed it into his mouth and chewed noisily with obvious pleasure. The boy swallowed hard, but remained where he was. Savas smiled at him, ate some cheese and beckoned again. This went on for half an hour before Savas leaned back in his chair, pointed to the food and said, "Why don't you join me, before I get sick from eating all of this?"

The boy seemed to understand. He stood up, short, but big-boned, heavy features and thick, black hair. No injun for sure, a kid who could pass for Greek. How old? Fourteen? Husky kid. His eyes never left Savas as he walked slowly forward, clothes hanging from him in tatters, feet bare. When he came close, Savas could see the clothing was animal skins and cloth remnants carelessly sewn together. The end of the gold boom has been tough on some folks, he thought.

"You from around here?"

No sound. The boy picked up a slab of cheese, tasted it, and popped the whole thing into his mouth. Pleasure showed in his eyes, but he didn't smile.

"Maybe you don't understand my English. Greek still easier for me, but I get better at it. Don't have much practice, though. You live in these hills?" He gestured at the surrounding mountains, and the boy's eyes followed his hand silently.

"I'm Savas," he said, thumping his chest with two fingers, and pointed. "You?"

The boy nodded, recognition in his eyes. He picked up another slab of cheese, then pointed to himself and said something unintelligible.

"Well, have some bread, whatever your name be." Savas pushed food across the makeshift table as the boy sat down beside him. Later, Savas couldn't quite remember what he talked about that early evening, but was certain a bitter, desperate loneliness had crept up on him, and the boy was the first visitor he'd had, eating and listening quietly while the host babbled on and on in both English and Greek. But at sunset, the boy suddenly arose, nodded at him, and curled his lips into a vague hint of a smile before turning and walking into the deep shadows of the trees and brush without looking back.

"Come back," called Savas, "anytime you want to. I'm always here!"

The beginning was that simple, the beginning of an association that would last nine years and alter the course of a culture older than history. Savas had no way of knowing that, of course. To him the boy was a relief from the loneliness and boredom of his chosen life, and after that first day the visits became regular, usually in late afternoon and rarely on weekends, for his trips to Quincy continued as usual until the day he died.

At first they simply broke bread together, Savas talking in Greek, the boy listening, eyes alert. It was soon obvious the boy didn't understand English or Greek, and would not respond to questions about himself. Savas became his teacher, pointing to things, naming them, using simple phrases for each of his actions. The boy made no attempt to repeat anything at first, but there was intelligence in those dark eyes, and occasionally a faint smile, like when Savas dropped an egg splat on the floor and cursed. Mostly, the boy was somber, as if life had been hard and he would not entrust a show of emotion to anyone outside himself. He learned with extraordinary speed, at first helping with the making of bread, then doing it without aid, measuring flour, milk and salt with precision. Then, one memorable day, he walked over to the newly arrived gramophone now playing a forlorn song, pointed to it, and said in perfect Greek pronunciation, "Where music come?"

Savas laughed. "New York, I think. Doubt if I'll ever see it again."

"Music come from far?" asked the boy.

"Yes, very far. This is a big world, with many, many people. I guess around here is the only place you know."

The boy looked at him sadly. "We—few."

"We?"

The boy didn't answer, and turned away. Savas didn't press, figuring eventually the boy would tell him who his people were, and where he came from.

He was still waiting for an answer the day he died.

At first they made bread, ate it and listened to the gramophone. Conversations lengthened, in both English and Greek, and when Savas finally coaxed the boy onto his horse for a ride, that also became a part of their routine. They bounced along rough trails, never going on the town road, the boy sitting rigidly erect, a faint smile the only sign of youthful excitement. So controlled, a near dignified bearing for someone far from being a man, thought Savas, a contrast to his own volatile nature now safely hidden in the hills where it couldn't hurt anyone. When he was around the boy, the violent part of him seemed to shrivel, leaving him peaceful and content with a life that hadn't turned out the way he'd planned. It didn't seem important the gold was beneath a cabin floor, still waiting to be spent in some distant, exotic place free of rattlesnakes and biting flies, or on a woman who could relieve the ache he still felt when the moon was out and he was lying on his hard mattress alone, sweating. Nothing was important except the boy, and what he might become. As the days, and then the years, went by, the boy was like a son, replacing the one he had left far behind, perhaps dead now, the son he could not go back to ever, because others would be waiting for him and then he, Savas Parkos, would be a dead man.

The boy's name remained impossible for him to pronounce. It was something like egg, only drawn out with a complex, guttural thing at the end, and the best way to get a smile from the boy was to try and pronounce it. After one abortive attempt that came close to producing an actual laugh from the boy, Savas had had enough. "I'm going to give you a name I can say," he said. "It will just be between us, if you don't mind."

"Is good," said the boy, in English.

"Something simple, and Greek, because you look Greek. We will pretend you are, and this is your christening. Stand still, now." He put a hand softly on the boy's black hair, and closed his eyes, thinking. The name of a cousin came to mind, a cousin who had been a drinking companion when they were young, and not yet scarred by money or politics, a man who had loved to sing and dance and drink and screw, before the world had destroyed him. Savas pressed firmly on the boy's head.

"I will call you Peter," he said.

CHAPTER SIX

MAKI'S CONFRONTATION

Maki slept restlessly that night, mind a jumble of things he would say to the council. His opinions on The Plan were well known, but now he could tell them of the invasion underway, as seen with his own eyes. There would soon be nothing left for the Tenanken, and thus a chance the group will could be turned. His father had been most solicitous, encouraging his request for a hearing, and now the hour was nearly at hand as he tossed and turned and fondled the weapon he kept hidden beneath his sleeping furs.

He arose early and squatted on the floor of the meeting place, chewing a piece of dried meat and calming himself to a state of dignity befitting his status. After the morning meal, the main cavern had emptied out, Tenanken retiring to more remote quarters during the hearing, since it was a private affair for the elders. The old ones had delayed the event by two days to check on the invasion report, and now they were in conference. When the six of them filed into the cavern, Anka and Tel in the lead, Maki's patience was worn thin, but they all smiled pleasantly at him and arranged themselves close together on the first slate tier above the amphitheatre floor on which he stood to greet them.

Anka looked around at the others, and when he spoke his voice echoed hollowly from the walls. "My son, we thank you for the warning regarding a sudden influx of Hinchai from the south, but our investigation shows it to be a temporary situation which will end in the near future. A major travel-way is being built so heavy supplies may be delivered to the Hinchai village. Within the next several days all workmen will be gone. Because of the formidable building machines they use, it is easy to see why you thought an invasion in progress, but as you can see now there is nothing to fear."

Maki felt his face flush with anger. His report had been casually dismissed, and he was in the presence of fools. "I disagree with your assessment," he said hoarsely. "The way is now open for hoards of Hinchai to come in, tearing down the forests and eliminating our food supply."

"This is unlikely," said Anka. "The Hinchai have so far lived in harmony with the forests, and even if the animals begin to move in numbers it will take little to feed the few of us who remain here. All the rest will be integrated with the Hinchai, and under Pegre's care." Anka's voice was firm, and Tel's mouth was suddenly pressed into a thin line. The rest watched silently, for the hearing was becoming a public argument between parents and son.

"You insist on destroying the Tenanken life and identity by in-corporation with the Hinchai. You are all afraid to fight." Maki's lips curled in a sneer of disgust with those who sat around him.

"We have had this conversation before," said Anka. "All argu-ments have been heard, and the group will has prevailed, as it must. It is a matter of personal choice, and most have chosen to leave the caverns for a new existence. That is their right. Some of us will re-main, also by choice. We will all survive in our own way, and you are free to choose yours."

"What surprise we've been forced to live in darkness for a gen-eration! The Tenanken are led by old women who do anything to save their own skins. One more generation, and The Memories will be gone, the mind-touch unused. There will be no more visions, Fa-ther, and *you* will be responsible for that. *You* will be the destroyer of the Tenanken!"

Maki was gratified to see Anka could not stand up to his fervor, was now looking down at his hands, but then his mother, eyes blaz-ing, began to shout at him.

"My son is an ignorant fool! Hinchai! Tenanken! You con-stantly distinguish, and on what basis? Appearance? Size? Speech? A way of living? I'll tell you again, carefully, as I did when you were a little child complaining when a heavy-browed Tenanken pushed you down and called you pretty. We are all *one* animal. Tenanken and Hinchai. Our ancient ancestors are in common, our only difference the time of crossing over the frozen waters. The Hinchai are there in the first Tenanken Memory, and now they are with us again. It is natural that we live together, yet you refuse to accept it. Look at yourself in a pool of still water, my son. What do you see there? Oh, Maki, in your heart you are Tenanken, but in ap-pearance you are a young Hinchai adult!"

"Tel, that's enough!" growled Anka.

"No, this is my time to talk. Maki, don't you see that Tenanken and Hinchai are but two strains of one people so close in appearance they can intermingle without discovery? Rather you should talk of Tahehto or Hanken, for *they* are the first peoples of The Memories. I look at you and see Hanken. You look at your father and I and see Tahehto with The Memories which you also have inherited. And the mind-touch, which springs from Hanken, not Tahehto. It is the union that makes us Tenanken, the same union which through liberal breeding practices has brought forth the Hinchai. Your discrimination is selective, ignoring the physical differences between yourself and your parents. Do you hate *us*, Maki? Our opinions? You talk as one who would protect the purity of the Tenanken people, but I will say what I think you really want. I think you seek power, and war with the Hinchai is only an excuse. You fail to see that elders exercise no power, no influence. It is done through concern, and love. You must learn to love, Maki, Tenanken and Hinchai alike. Or you will never be a leader. There, I've had my say."

Maki blinked back tears of embarrassment, his limbs shaking, anger at his mother coming with a fierceness he had rarely felt before. At the same time, he had never known such humiliation. His hands clenched and unclenched, and he saw fear pass over the faces of the elders sitting by his parents. In a dark flash of thought he wondered what would happen if he killed them all and called for Han and Dorald to help control the others. Too risky, he decided, but he could stand the humiliation no longer, and made a rash decision.

"I will leave this cavern, and never return. I am no longer one of you!" Maki turned on his heel, and climbed quickly up the stone terraces towards the top of the cavern.

"Maki!" shouted Anka after him, and there was murmuring among the elders.

"Let him go!" shouted Tel. "Let him do what he must do."

Maki heard labored breathing, and glanced over his shoulder to see his father scrambling up the rock behind him. He lengthened his stride, reaching the top of the cavern and traversing it until he saw Han and Dorald waiting in an exit tunnel. "Get your things together, we're leaving at once!" Han grabbed Dorald's arm, pulling him down the tunnel as Maki plunged in behind them.

"Maki, wait!" shouted Anka, and then he was gasping for breath. He stopped at the tunnel entrance, chest heaving, and sat down on a rock. There was sharp pain in his chest and one arm, but as he breathed deeply it seemed to get better. A strange kind of paralysis had set in, the reaction of an old body to an unacceptable workload dictated by emotion. Tel and others arrived to help him to his feet. He looked into her eyes as she helped to lift him up. "Why did you do that to our son?" he asked sadly.

"He's done it to himself, my heart. This is a critical time for the Tenanken, and we have our responsibilities. The new life is open for Maki also, but if he refuses it then he must find something better for himself. For now, we have more important things to attend to. Come, now, and rest. You've overextended yourself again."

They held him up, and Anka directed them to the little alcove he used for private meditation and re-enforcement of The Memories. They covered him with furs, and slipped quietly away, but as he lay still, drowsy, he became aware that someone else was near. He raised his head.

"Who is it? Please come to where I can see you."

In the light of a small torch in his quarters, he saw the tiny face of a girl. Baela, the one who ran everywhere. "Come in, child, before I fall asleep."

She entered shyly and stood before him, something clutched tightly in one hand. "Teacher, I have a gift to make you feel better," she said in the new tongue. "See how it shines?" She smiled, then leaned over and placed a glowing object on the fur that covered him. It was the size and shape of a finger, yellowish, pointed at one end. He touched it, hard and cold, reflecting the light brightly. He had never seen anything like it before, and inspected it closely. "It is a little treasure, Baela. Thank you for your gift." He reached out to her with a feeling of affection that lit up her face with a smile. She took a step towards him, and for one horrible second he thought she might hug him, but then she stepped back a little nervously, and became a part of the shadows. Anka's eyes were heavy, yet he struggled for a moment to remain awake, thinking the girl might return. At last he drifted into sleep without noticing she was still there, sitting cross-legged in darkness, watching him. She remained there most of the day, eyes closed and chin tilted upwards, living with her teacher in his dreams.

* * * * * * *

Maki gathered his few possessions into a fur bag fitted with carrying sling. He had made a sling for the Hinchai weapon, and draped it across his chest. Han and Dorald each assembled a bag containing foot coverings, dried meat and pemmican for the long quick-march. Patience at a minimum, Maki ordered the two others to leave ahead of him, Dorald taking the Hinchai axe, Han packing a spear and three slings, both prepared for war and the destruction of any Hinchai they might encounter during their search for Hidaig's band.

The time for passive talk and meek surrender to Hinchai encroachment had come to an end with the coming of a Tenanken warrior king named Maki, he thought. Maki left the cavern near sunset and descended quickly to the valley, looking back only once to see his mother standing on a ledge, one arm outstretched in the gesture of being with him on his journey. Dorald and Han were waiting for him at the tree line bordering the Hinchai settlement nearest the canyon. A light was on in the big cabin, and two Hinchai, one a female, were there on a porch. As he watched, Maki felt something dark and dangerous probe his mind. Dorald growled, and Han tugged at Maki's arm, urging him to move on. A massive figure moved out into the porch light, staring in their direction. It was Pegre. Pegre and his Hinchai mate. So this was their dwelling place.

Maki made a promise to himself. *Soon, I will return and destroy you both.*

They walked all night, stopping only once to smash and tear at the big Hinchai machines that tore down trees and gouged the earth. In the morning they nibbled some dry meat, then covered themselves with fallen boughs and slept within a tight circle of forest boulders during the day. Sleep was difficult, Dorald tossing and turning, and giving off an odor that made Maki's eyes water. At dusk they began walking again, Maki stopping once to send out a vision of the caverns, and feeling nothing in return. Hidaig's band had truly left the area, but in what direction?

There were no signs, yet Maki felt compelled to move southward and trust his instincts. They moved more slowly the second night, because now there were scattered lights in the hills, the number of Hinchai settlements steadily increasing, and barking dogs sensing them at some distance. As night progressed it became even more dangerous as the lights flickered off, because there was no moon, and once they came out of the trees to find themselves nearly on the front porch of a Hinchai cabin, facing a large, shaggy animal. But the animal took one look at them, whimpered, and crawled under the porch while they retreated back into the trees. This far from the caverns, Maki wanted no Hinchai encounters until he had found Hidaig's band. Once again he stopped, and send out a vision. Where were they?

* * * * * * *

He found them on the morning of the fourth day.

"I hear something," said Dorald, his head cocked to one side. They had moved out after a short pause before sunrise, a light wind rustling the branches of surrounding trees.

"It's the wind," said Maki. "Keep moving."

"No it's not. Listen!"

They stood still. There was a wind sound, all right, but it did not come from nearby, and seemed to fade in and out. "This way," said Maki, and they followed the sound through the forest as it grew louder. Suddenly they were standing at a shear drop-off of a hundred paces, looking down at a river cascading over rocks. Across the river there was scree, and a wide boulder field leading to cliffs towering halfway up the sky, far above their heads. The cliff walls were rotted and full of holes, crisscrossed with networks of chimneys and shelves and crumbling at their base. On the near side of the river was a rutted road running parallel to it, and they had no sooner glanced down when a heavily-laden cart rolled around a corner, passed below them and disappeared around another corner further downstream. Another soon followed, then another. Maki drew back among the trees, his eyes closed, and said, "We must get across the river, and climb the cliffs by nightfall. We'll rest here." He plopped himself down, and fumbled with his food bag.

"Do you think they're over there?" Han had felt a fleeting sensation of presence in his mind.

"Yes. It's a perfect place, and I feel something here, but quite guarded. Relax, and think about the caverns."

They sat down near the edge of the trees and ate the rest of their meat. Later, they slept a fitful sleep because of the cascading water below, masking other sounds they needed to hear. It was because of this that as dusk approached they did not hear the footfalls on dirt and pine needles until it was too late.

Somebody rammed a foot rudely into Maki's ribs. He was instantly awake, reaching for his weapon, but stopped by the sharp tip of a stone spear that nearly entered his mouth.

"Easy, now. All stay where all are." Spoken in the old tongue. They were Tenanken, dark shadows looming over them. Maki counted four.

"I am Maki, son of Anka from the north. We're searching for Hidaig's band. We played together as children, and it's urgent that I talk to him. I know he's nearby, because I feel him here."

"How do we know he wants to see you?" The spear was thrust closer to Maki's face, and Dorald growled until Han told him to be quiet.

"You *don't* know that. It is for Hidaig to decide, and your life will be short if you don't allow him to do it. Please take us to him."

There was a long pause, and the spear was suddenly withdrawn. "Get up, but be slow about it. Your weapons will do you no good with spears in your hearts."

They scrambled to their feet surrounded by four, hardened Tenanken warriors, all with spears. Maki smiled, then slowly looped the weapon sling over his head. Han looked nervous, and Dorald's eyes blazed with anger at being threatened. "We are in no danger," said Maki. "These warriors take us to Hidaig, and I will tell him about their cleverness in capturing us."

One of the warriors grunted. "You will follow us," he said, then turned and shuffled away between the trees. The rest followed silently in approaching darkness. They backtracked for several minutes, and descended a steep arroyo to the place where Hinchai vehicles still rumbled by. All was in shadow as they scrambled along the riverbank, for the moon had not yet risen. The noise of the river was deafening.

They came to a place where the water passed through a deep channel formed by sand and scree bars, two large trees having fallen across the channel. Holding onto tree branches for balance, they crossed the river at that point, then followed a jagged course through boulder fields to the base of the cliffs, Maki searching the whole time for signs of a cave and finding several. They entered what appeared to be a small cavern at ground level, and the lead warrior climbed up on a shelf, placed his hands on the ceiling and pushed hard, grunting. A light appeared beyond a hole in the ceiling, usually covered by a thick sheet of rock. The warrior put his arms into the hole, pressing down on her forearms and lifting himself up until his feet disappeared. The others followed, Maki next to last, and he found himself in a long, narrow tunnel lit by torches in both directions. The last warrior up replaced the stone slab, and they moved along the tunnel in single file.

The walk was short, rounding two corners, and then they were in a small grotto with sparkling knobs and columns, and a beautiful, green pool with a fumarole bottom winding out of sight into darkness. Four classic Tenanken, one of them female, were sitting by the pool, eating meat and spitting gristle into the water. "Where is Hidaig?" asked one of the warriors, and the female pointed lazily towards a tunnel while giving Dorald a lecherous look that made him grin. But when Maki passed by, she turned her broad back to him.

The main cavern was a few paces further; and they came out into a half-egg-shaped area at its lowest level. Above them, sitting on ledges and knobs, were dozens of Tenanken warriors regarding them with interest but no apparent surprise. Their attention returned immediately to a single Tenanken leaning back in a cavity shaped like a throne, one leg draped carelessly over a rocky protuberance. He was eating a piece of fruit, rivulets of juice running down his ochre beard, and he was grinning from ear to ear.

A fur cloak was draped around his wide shoulders, but otherwise he was naked, and only a single feature truly distinguished him from the others. Through his broad nostrils was thrust a crescent-shaped piece of polished bone curving down on either side of his mouth, turning his face into a fierce mask to match his personality, for although they had played together as children, Maki had always regarded Hidaig as a crazy-one.

"Well, cousin," said the warrior leader. "I was wondering when Anka's band would begin crawling in here. By now, game must be getting scarce where you are."

Maki raised himself to full height, suddenly conscious of the pointing weapon draped across his chest as Hidaig's eyes focused there. "I do not come for food, but to talk about the future of the Tenanken. Our way of life, and the Tenanken themselves, will disappear if we don't do something soon. I've had no success talking to my father, but I thought that you, as a warrior without fear of the Hinchai, might understand."

Hidaig's laugh roared in the cavern, and his eyes twinkled merrily. "Oh, cousin, it has been a long time. Your tongue was quick even when we were children; how easily you could manipulate those who needed flattery or wished to be close to your father or mother. Always you had a purpose, and always that purpose was for your own benefit."

"That was true, and it is true now. What I wish to propose will benefit both of us if we can work together. I have always regarded you as an equal, Hidaig. You know that."

"How nice of you." Hidaig frowned, then thought for a moment. He looked up at the patiently waiting warriors, and waved one hand towards the exit. "We will continue another time. I have business with this representative from the valley, and we must be alone. Someone please bring meat for our guests."

The warriors filed out immediately. Maki watched them leave, then turned and said softly, "Done grandly, and with style. I think you have changed since we last met."

Hidaig chuckled. "And you, on the other hand, have not changed a bit. Now what is it you come all this way to propose?" He climbed down from his rock-throne, and they sat cross-legged together, face-to-face, on the floor of the cavern. An old female shuffled in and left them two handfuls of dried meat on a slate slab. When she was gone, they chewed some meat in silence, then looked at each other. The smiles and posturing were gone.

"The old one who served us is one of three females left in my group. Her nights are happily active, but the childbearing days are gone forever, and the other two females are only slightly younger. As a band, we are dying out."

"But you have warriors, including some who came to you from our caverns. Most of our population is females and children; come and claim what you want."

"Anka has forbidden us entrance to his caverns. He will not even meet with me outside."

"Because of your opposition to The Plan?"

"Yes."

"But I oppose The Plan as loud as I can, even in front of the elders.

"And they accept it politely, of course. You are the son of two elders, and they give you free expression."

"If I were leader, I would not make such a distinguishment, and you would be welcome in the caverns."

"Ah, now we come to it. You wish to seize power."

"My father is old and sick, easily influenced by my mother and others. He dreams about his youth, when he lived with sunlight on his face. He cannot imagine anyone not wanting to live the same way, without the Hinchai. They talk of resettlement before the next full moon. If that happens, there will be nothing left in our caverns but feeble elders waiting to die; what do they care when they only have a few years left? What will be there for those of us who wish to preserve the race in its purity and *also* live in sunlight. The resettlement must be stopped before it begins. I have The Memories as Anka's son, and my skill with the Mind-Touch approaches his. You have a fighting force. Together we can take power, and change the destiny of the Tenanken."

"An attractive idea, if it were not so ridiculous."

Maki widened his eyes in surprise. "You disappointment me, Hidaig. Of all the Tenanken, I thought you—"

"Now hear me! We could easily take power, you and I, and what would we rule? Females, children, and elders too feeble to feed themselves? Or warriors turned hunters, for lack of a war to fight?

Do you realize how dispersed the Tenanken have become? I know of three groups, including yours, between here and the great, salty waters towards sunset. All are small, and all follow The Plan. The destruction of our race nears completion, and *you* wish to rule!"

"The Tenanken near extinction only because of a lack of leadership. The race can still remain pure by dissolving The Plan and slaughtering the Hinchai. With a unified fighting force, the scattered Hinchai to the north can be eliminated, and we can live freely in the forests when the game returns."

"Still *another* happy-root dream. Do you think the Hinchai will stand by calmly, and let us push them out? You've seen their numbers *and* their weapons. It is hopeless."

Maki grasped Hidaig's arm firmly. "I do not propose that we engage a population center, but move north and clean out widely scattered settlements. There are only a few individuals to deal with. That is the least of the difficulties; most importantly, your warriors must again father children if the classic Tenanken are to survive. Our bands must be united in this, and should not live apart. The females are in my group, not yours."

Hidaig grinned at him evilly. "Oh, I don't know. I have made pleasure with the one who served us, and she seems quite willing. Want to try her?"

"Children will never again issue from those shriveled loins," said Maki disgustedly.

Hidaig laughed. "Still better than a slippery Hinchai female, don't you think? Whoops!" He pretended to slide off the rock he was sitting on, while Maki glared at him.

"I think I'm wasting my time here. I'll talk to the other bands, and the journey is far, so I'll leave now. I'd expected much more of you, Hidaig."

Hidaig whooped with amusement. "No, no! Wait a moment, cousin; oh, how seriously you take yourself. You always were so serious, so nobody could joke with you." He wrapped an arm around Maki's shoulders, and leaned close to him. "Actually, I've been baiting you. Your idea makes sense, and I wish you to present it to everyone as soon as I can get them back in here. Believe it or not, each warrior has an individual vote in this band. A good idea, when each can hit me with a spear at a hundred paces if I do something they don't agree with. I suggest you propose a coalition of our bands, with you as chief elder and Keeper of The Memories, and myself as commander. With the strength of my warriors, the overthrow of Anka's rule should be bloodless enough, except for the Hinchai purge, and then as one band we will move to the north and freedom from Hinchai contamination. It is an excellent idea. I, of course, will completely support it."

"And if the vote goes against me?"

"Then I will ask them what they intend to do for pleasure when the old ones by the green pool are dead."

Maki was finally able to smile. "If your warriors agree, we must move quickly before the resettlement begins. Pegre is in charge of that, and he will not be swayed to our side."

"Ah, your adopted brother. I remember him, a genius, strong. It may be necessary to kill him."

"It *will* be necessary," said Maki, "but that pleasure must be reserved for me. You contact the other bands, see if they will provide warriors or come with us as a whole. I'll return to my father's side, and await your readiness, but it must be soon. I will coordinate our coup as to timing. The rest will be up to you."

"If my warriors agree."

"Yes—if they agree."

An hour later Maki presented his plan to the silent assembly of brooding warriors, Hidaig at his side.

The vote was unanimously in his favor.

CHAPTER SEVEN

BAELA

All morning the scent of pine had floated down the entrance tunnel. Baela was wild with anticipation, for this was one of those sunny days when she was allowed to explore outside the cavern. She bolted down her morning meal of mash while the rest of her family watched with tired resignation. She waited impatiently for the others to finish. When Moog belched, it was a sign the meal was over, and she squirmed across the shelf to lean against her father. "May I go now?" she pleaded. Moog put a big arm lightly around her shoulders. "Be patient, Baela. The sun moves slowly, and you must be presentable."

Baela pouted, but Moog touched her mind happily and hugged at the same time, so it was impossible for her to feel badly, and she sat patiently while Deda and Ba, mother and grandmother, took turns washing arms and legs and plaiting her hair. She had inherited her delicate features from both of them, but the golden hair had been a surprise to everyone, and a rarity in the caverns, reminding the elders of the first mother of the Tenanken. Baela was proud of her long hair, preferring it hanging in a tousled mass, but today her preference was ignored.

She wore clothing Pegre had brought up from the valley for distribution to those who would soon live outside the caverns. The first time they'd looked upon themselves fully clothed they'd all fallen down with laughter, but now the novelty had worn off and they were dressed much of the time. Baela had on a pair of heavy pants and a long-sleeved shirt in earth colors so she would not easily be seen while outside. Her instructions were to hide if any Hinchai appeared, but this was unlikely since she would be exploring the forested plateau at the top of the cliffs.

Finally it was done. Deda helped her to her feet, turning her around to inspect all sides. Moog and Ba nodded solemn approval, and embraced her quickly before she could fly away. "Be back before darkness, or we come looking for you," said Moog, but she was gone, scrambling up shelves and disappearing into the exit tunnel as they sat and shook their heads. Baela: known in all caverns as the little darting one.

Tiny feet made her goat-like on the steep rock. Baela climbed straight up the cliff, using barely visible hand-holds, bare feet finding miniscule flakes to perch upon between moves, her mind ignoring the forty meters of air to the treetops below. As she neared the top she found a nest with two fluffy chicks in it, and stopped to watch them, clinging to the rock like a lizard. Their mother returned with a small, dead animal clutched in sharp talons, unfurling broad wings to make a gentle descent to the nest and her shrieking babies. First casting a wary eye on Baela, the great bird tore her prey apart with sharp, curved beak, and fed it piece by piece to her young, sharing a private moment with the girl. Somehow, there was no fear or distrust between them. After a brief rest, the mother bird soared again, perhaps to feed herself, leaving her babies behind within Baela's reach. She laughed at the cross-eyed stares of the chicks, then climbed again, and they shrieked after her as if she might feed them.

When she reached the plateau, the mother bird was circling high in the sky, and Baela felt a sudden desire to spread her arms and fly from the cliff, soaring with the great feathered predator that built nests where only the daring would climb. She held out her arms, and whirled in a circle at cliff's edge, then ran to a tree and climbed far up into the branches as little animals screamed at her intrusion. Held in a hollow formed by three converging branches, she rested and daydreamed and finally dozed as the day warmed.

She awoke, startled by a snapping sound below her.

Peering down through the branches she saw a large male with green shirt, walking near her climbing tree. A Hinchai! Or was it? She looked again: broad shoulders, square jaw, a head full of black hair and the swaggering gait that was surely Tenanken. He looked upwards at a neighboring tree.

"Pegre!" she shouted.

Pete grinned up at her, hands on hips. "And how did you fly so high, little bird?"

"I climbed up. Come see my place!"

"No, no. I'm too big for those little branches. Baela, we must talk about something; please come down for a little while."

She descended willingly, for Pegre was fun to be with, and he answered all her questions. He had also taught her new speech, and was appearing more often now as the day to leave the cavern approached. When she was a few feet from the ground, he held out his big arms to her with a grin. "Show me how you fly!"

There was no hesitation. Baela launched herself from the tree, soaring like the birds for a fleeting instant before he caught her and placed her on bare feet again. They exchanged smiles that would melt the coldest heart and Pete sat down beside her. *Wait until the young boys in town see this one.* And Baela cocked her head curiously at him as he reached to touch her mind where he wanted to be when he asked his question. She allowed him entrance, but there were no images to be seen. He sensed wariness, and absolute control.

"Relax, Baela, I only want to ask you about this." He held out his hand, and showed her the rifle cartridge in it. He felt her shock when she saw it, and the brief image that escaped her at that instant was all he needed. She knew what he had seen, and suddenly was angry, clothing her mind in darkness.

"Why ask when you know? As you see, I found it in Maki's sleeping place by the entrance."

"On the floor? Was there anything else with it? A weapon of some kind? Please, Baela, it's important."

"Yes," she said solemnly. "Maki had a Hinchai pointing weapon there, with more of those. I took the one, and gave it to Anka when he felt bad."

"I know. He didn't understand what it was, and asked me. I'll return it to him for you." Pete looked worried, his mind wandering away for a moment.

Baela brooded silently, playing nervously with her fingers. "I didn't mean to do anything wrong," she finally said. "It was pretty, and there were many others, so I took just one. And Anka liked it."

"Don't worry about it," said Pete, still thinking, "but there is something you can do for me. If Maki comes back, and I think he will, I want to know what he's up to and who he's with. Could you be my eyes when I'm not here, and watch him for me? It's only for a little while."

"Has he done something bad?" Her face was suddenly serious.

"I don't know, Baela. Not for sure. But inside—I have a bad feeling, right now. Will you help me?"

"Yes."

"Don't be seen, and don't go far from the cavern. We can talk when I come for speaking practice."

"All right." Still serious, looking at Pete intently, she opened her mouth as if to speak, then closed it quickly.

"Something else?"

"Why don't you look inside his head the way you do mine?"

"Maki can shield against that."

"So can I. Well—not perfectly, but I'm learning. I don't like it when people go in my head; that's *my* place."

"Oh," said Pete, suddenly understanding her mood. Here was something else new and different about the child who was Tenanken with Hanken purity. Bernie never objected when he probed her thoughts; she didn't even know he was there. This one did—and objected to it, yet the classical Tenanken of the Tahehto branch of the tree had difficulties in communicating any other way. How different she was, and not just in the color of her hair. Slender in stature, but that was deceiving, because he knew she was near adolescence. Perhaps this reaction was a part of her changing chemistry?

"I guess I don't know you as well as I thought, Baela. I'm sorry if I offended you."

"I just wanted you to know how I feel about this thing." Spoken like an adult, matter-of-factly, a smile returning.

They sat in silence for a moment, Pete playing with a pebble he'd found, Baela looking off at the distant trees. A light breeze cooled them, and far back in the forest a squirrel was chattering off and on.

"You know, Baela, when I see you and talk to you, everything I'm doing to bring the Tenanken and Hinchai together seems natural and right, and I can believe we're all one people. I wish a few of the others, like Maki, would see it that way, but I don't think they ever will. Here I am, a Tenanken with big features and heavy bones over the eyes, but with clothes on I'm suddenly Hinchai. I've seen men in town with features like mine; they're Tenanken without knowing it. But then there are the fine-featured ones, like Bernie, my mate. She has blonde hair like yours, Baela, and soon she's going to give me a child. A Hinchai woman carrying the child of a Tenanken? We have to be the same people, but with two ancestors that looked different physically. We're all Tenanken *and* Hinchai, and we should live together."

"When?"

"I'm not sure, but soon. First I have to teach you all a few words of the language they speak in town. You won't have to know much at first because everyone thinks you're coming from another land far away where the new language I've taught you is spoken. It's named Greece, and the Greek language was the one my Hinchai teacher knew best. Would you like to hear me say something in town language?"

Baela nodded, and looked at him expectantly.

"I think Baela is a very pretty girl, and the boys in town will soon be fighting for her attention," said Pete in English.

Baela's eyes widened. "It's so *fast*. All the words run together. Now what did you say?"

"I will tell you—someday."

"No, tell me now." Her blue eyes sparkled hypnotically.

"Remember what I said, and as you learn more you will be able to translate it for yourself." Pete repeated the sentence one more time, slowly, while Baela listened with rapt attention. The challenge seemed to satisfy her, and she was still repeating the sentence to herself when Pete stood up. "I have to go, now. Don't be late. During speaking class I have something special for all of you."

"I'll be just a little while; it's so nice out here." Baela tilted her head back, letting the sunlight fall on her face, and closing her eyes. When she opened them again, Pegre was nearly out of sight, traversing the cliff face below. She walked to the edge of the cliff and watched him pick his way gingerly along a wide shelf to the cavern entrance, disappearing inside. She found the soaring mother-bird's nest again and watched the little family for a while, her mind still mulling over Pegre's sentence in English and wondering what special thing he had planned for the class. Finally she could stand it no longer, and scuttled down the shear face of the cliff back to the cavern she was ordinarily so happy to leave.

Pegre was at the gathering place when she returned, a few children and adults, including her mother and father already sitting around him. She hurried down the shelves to join them, wedging herself between her parents and watching as Pegre placed a polished wooden tube in his mouth and blew into it. A beautiful, pure sound came from the tube, then another, higher, and his foot began tapping on the floor. The sounds were pleasing, rhythmic, stirring something within her, and she knew others felt it. Her mother was suddenly smiling, and wedged between her parents Baela could feel their bodies swaying to the rhythm of the sounds. Pegre was watching them, tapping his foot softly each time they swayed. Others came to join them, but then Pegre took the tube from his lips, and the sounds stopped.

"This is called music. It is very important in the Hinchai world, and yet not even Anka can remember such a thing in Tenanken culture. Perhaps the images of the Mind Touch have been our substitute for the pleasing sensations music gives. This is music from Greece, the land where you come from. As you listen to it your body will want to move, and you should let it happen. After the speaking lesson I will show you ways to move together with the music. This is called dancing, and Greeks love to dance. Since you are supposed to be Greek, the people in town will expect you to know some dances. I brought along a book with pictures of Greece and its people, and one of them shows dancing. These people like to have a good time." Pegre passed around the little book with pictures, and they crowded together for a look.

After the speaking lesson, during which Baela learned to say 'Thank you' and 'My name is Baela' and the names of several food items in English, Pegre played again and showed them a simple dance they did in a circle as a group, hands on neighboring shoulders, bending knees and tripping over their own feet, but in time to the music. This time the music was different, starting slowly, then building in intensity and rhythm until the cavern was a blur as they twirled in a big circle, Pegre in the center. Baela had never seen her mother looking so happy—so wild—her eyes flashing. It suddenly occurred to her that Pegre and her father looked very much alike. When the music finally ended they collapsed in a heap, laughing but tired, Deda suddenly kissing Moog full on the mouth before all of them, and the laughter became shrieks at the embarrassed male's expense.

Anka watched all of this from a perch near the top of the cavern. Music—dancing—English—books and pictures, all part of the Hinchai world. And where was the Tenanken culture in all of this? A constant chatter of words without visions, emotional displays with body and face without the Mind Touch, this was not the Tenanken way. How much were they giving up to live in the outside world? He pondered these things and tried to ignore the ominous feeling in his stomach. A major change was near, and it could bring violence as such change often did. Their cloistered life had perhaps not been healthy, but it had been safe and peaceful for many years. Could he remain in the caves when most of the others were gone? Yes, he thought, the change would be too much for him, and so little of his life was left to waste on adaptation. Better to focus on The Memories for Pegre's writings, and leave the new world to the young.

Anka brooded, not noticing the music had ended, participants in the dance again ascending the shelves to their hearths for the evening meal. Baela as usual had raced ahead, and now stood before him, looking sad. He felt something—a presence—understanding— a wisp of smoke in his sorrowful mind, and then Baela stepped up to him, put her slender arms around his neck and hugged him tightly. She darted away, leaving him stunned as a familiar presence entered his mind, and Pegre was standing before him, the wooden tube in his hand, the man now ready for the treacherous walk back to the valley.

"This has been a happy day for me. I was afraid they might not like the music, but you saw what happened. It is good, Anka, believe me. It is good that Tenanken can feel the music."

Anka held out his hand for Pegre to grasp and hold, while he made the effort to stand. "Of course it is, and I support it as long as you don't expect *me* to dance. You had better go, now, before it gets too dark."

Something golden flashed by them, and into the exit tunnel.

"Where do you suppose she's racing off to now?"

"Outside, is my guess. Baela would play in the dark if we let her. I'll remind her to come in soon." Pegre started towards the tunnel.

"I'll walk you to the exit," said Anka, shuffling along. "I want to scan the valley as best I can with these old eyes, and look for Maki. I have a feeling deep inside that he will soon return."

Pete kept a thought to himself: *Baela and I will watch with you.*

CHAPTER EIGHT

The Prodigal Son

Maki and Hidaig began the morning with a grog of fermented juices and marrow while Han and Dorald packed for the trip, Dorald grinning often and wriggling bushy eyebrows in memory of the rough delights he'd shared with the old female by the green pool the night before. Han, too, had a new treasure which he constantly carried in one hand: a long spear, tipped with a metal blade made from a Hinchai implement, and presented to him by one of Hidaig's warriors after a spear throwing contest in which his heavy weapon had gone further than any other's. Maki had never seen his two companions so happy, for it was the first time they had been totally accepted by anyone, Dorald because of his great strength and friendly grin, Han because of his skill with the spear. Now they scurried to and fro, preparing to leave, but knowing that soon they would all be together again.

"It is a good day for travel," said Hidaig. "I will leave later in the day, and travel at night, because the way following the sun is now thick with Hinchai settlements."

"I still think it's a waste of time," said Maki, wiping his mouth on the back of his hand. "How many Tenanken can you recruit from bands so far removed from our difficulties here? They will have no motivation for a fight in which lives will be lost, and if they know our plan, word may be sent to my father."

Hidaig shook his head. "I expect no cooperation from their leadership; indeed, Meandre is now Keeper, and an old friend of your father's. I will not approach him on the subject, but there are several warriors who have been privately sympathetic with my views. Up to now they have not left because their mates are bound closely to the band, but all can be persuaded if the rewards are right. The warriors I'm talking about despise the Hinchai and spend as much time as they can outside the caves. It's a return to the old life they're looking for, and our plans will promise it to them. There could be a betrayal, of course, but I'm always ready for that." Hidaig grinned evilly at Maki. "When we return, I will post warriors along the three routes to the valley. Any Tenanken sent from the caves will be killed on the spot. In the end, Maki, all bands must be unified in this. Anyone who opposes us must die."

"I agree," said Maki firmly. "So how many warriors will you have when the time comes?"

"Perhaps forty," Hidaig indicated, opening and closing his hands to count the number. "It is enough if we can achieve complete surprise. I will rely on you for the timing."

"You shall have it. We need now to set a time for rendezvous. How long before you'll be ready?"

Hidaig emptied his cup, and filled it again from a skin bag. "A few days, in both directions, perhaps a little more. I remember a deep hollow on the bluff at the near end of your canyon. We can meet there."

"I will station Dorald and Han at that place the second full moon from now."

"Why so long?"

"I need to convince my father all is well, and his plans can proceed in safety. He will be the easy one; it is Pegre I will have to work with carefully. He is neither naive or foolish, and sees deeply. He also has the favor of my father, and is revered by those who would live with the Hinchai. Consequently, I will work my persuasions when he is not present in the caverns, and remain silent, thinking of darkness, when he is nearby. Remember that when the attack begins Pegre must die, but it will be by my hand. I will have it no other way."

"So it will be," said Hidaig seriously, "and we will drink to the time." He filled Maki's cup, and they gestured to each other before drinking noisily. "To a Tenanken life in open air and sunlight, and to the new Keeper of The Memories," said Hidaig.

"And to the Tenanken commander over all the bands."

They toasted each other, and the sun was suddenly covered by a dark cloud. Hidaig frowned. "It is an omen," he whispered anxiously.

Maki smiled. "It signifies the passage of a short, dark time in Tenanken history, a time of the caves. But the cloud moves on, and the bright light will soon reappear." He lifted his cup to touch Hidaig's. "There, see—we are the sun."

The exit was a few feet from the top of the cliff face, the river below a shining snake hissing up at them. Hand and footholds were small but plentiful, and Maki danced up the rock to a field of tall grass and flowers. Dorald froze at first, staring at the miniscule boulders below. Even with Maki's gentle directions and Han's prodding of his buttocks with a spear it was several minutes before he dared to trust his life to the grip of fingers and rough toes on the rock. By the time he reached the top, the big Tenanken was hyperventilating so badly he had to lie down on the grass while Han scrambled up to join them. Both waited for Maki to begin shouting at them about their slowness, but today their leader seemed patient, even kind to both of them so that at least their journey was beginning as a happy adventure of three comrades-in-arms returning home.

They marched until nightfall, keeping to the trees and traversing hillsides rather than climbing up and down, since Hidaig had sketched for them the direct route his little army would follow to reach the caverns of Anka's band. The route was far from Hinchai machines, but as darkness came they saw occasional lights on distant hillsides, reminding them they were not alone and were still vulnerable to observation during the day. Han collected fir boughs, and made beds for the three of them under tall trees. They relaxed, ate dried meat, and got a little drunk while emptying the skin of grog Hidaig had sent along with them. Their sleep was deep and peaceful, whatever dreams they experienced forgotten by the time sunlight awoke them totally refreshed and anxious to march again.

Ahead of them lay a vast expanse of pure wilderness: clean air, fresh springs, and game. Antlered creatures watched them carefully from thick stands of trees and brush in hollows between rolling hills, and birds flew near their heads when they passed by a nest placed on a tree-limb within easy reach from the ground. Without the Hinchai, it could all be like this again, thought Maki, and his resolve increased with each step. His father would be spared to see it happen; he could not be punished for the frailties of old-age, and would perhaps be useful as spiritual advisor in his last years. Pegre was another matter, and all his accomplices in the caverns. To begin anew it would be necessary to purify the race, but in keeping with The Memories it would be done mercifully. In ancient Memories the Hanken-featured newborns had been dispatched with a single blow to the head. Was this merciful? Did pain have a chance to register in a child's tiny brain? Surely they were not spiritual in any sense, for they lacked The Memories. But they were self-aware. How does one kill such a being mercifully? Maki pondered these things moodily to himself as Dorald and Han frolicked ahead of him.

When the sun was high they stopped to drink from a stream cascading down the hillside. Below them was another streambed cut deep into the ground, a wash of pebbles left over from the rush of some ancient current. Maki walked down to the wash, looked around and found a polished chunk of driftwood which he placed on top of a large rock before stepping back along the stream bed many paces and unslinging the pointing weapon from around his shoulders. Han and Dorald jumped gleefully to their feet from under a tree where they'd been resting, Dorald clamping his hands over both ears and grinning broadly. They rushed to stand at the edge of the wash, looking down at Maki as he tentatively fingered the weapon.

"It makes much noise," said Han nervously. "We'll be found."

"Not here," said Maki, "and it's time I learned how to use this." He searched The Memories, and found an observation to imitate while he explored the thing in his hands, pushing and prodding and finally pulling down a lever carefully to reveal the projectile inside. He pulled the lever up, watching the projectile disappear inside the weapon, then pressed the butt to his shoulder and looked along wood and metal towards his driftwood target. One finger curled around a lever on the underside of the weapon. He was looking at two blades, one at the end and a shorter one with a groove in it towards the rear. He wiggled the weapon up and down until the blades were nearly superimposed, and the target just visible above them.

He pulled back on the lever, and felt something give inside the weapon.

Sharp pain knifed through his head as the weapon exploded in his hands. Han and Dorald screamed simultaneously. It was like the time he'd run blindly into someone in a darkened tunnel, the weapon slamming horribly into his shoulder, breath leaving him with a grunt, and he felt a burning sensation throughout his entire body. When he looked, the target was still there, but somehow different. Han jumped down into the wash, and inspected it, pointing to a place near the top.

"See, you hit it! A piece has been removed at this point."

"It is high," said Maki calmly. Using The Memories, he levered a spent projectile case from the weapon, chambered a new one, then aimed again as a startled, frightened Han scrambled frantically out of the wash. This time he lowered the front blade until it filled the groove in the second, and the center of the target was sitting right on top of the combination. He took a deep breath, and let it out slowly, struggling to control his fear of the impending explosion, and forcing all attention on the sighting picture so that the weapon seemed to go off by itself.

The pain in his head was even sharper the second time, though Han and Dorald didn't scream, having clamped hands tightly over their ears. The target seemed unchanged, and Maki felt a surge of disappointment, but when he walked over to inspect it he found a finger-sized hole in the very center, and a larger hole in the back where the projectile had exited. "See what this does to hard wood," he said proudly, "and imagine what it will do to bone, long past the range of a spear. We must obtain more of these before the battle begins, and a good supply of projectiles. Their pointing is easy to learn." Enthusiastic, he quickly levered a new projectile into the weapon, with a snap, and reslung it over his shoulders while Han and Dorald looked at him fearfully. It occurred to him that these two, with their simple minds, would never dare to fire such a weapon. Perhaps he could teach Hidaig, or one of his warriors, so they could fight the Hinchai with their own weapons, and insure a quick victory.

Maki left the empty projectile cases where they had fallen, and climbed out of the streambed. Dorald had stretched out again under a tree, but Han was squinting towards a distant hillside, a hand shading his eyes.

"There it is again," said Han.

Maki turned to look over his shoulder.

"A bright flash—on the hillside where the trees come down to a point. That's twice I've seen it since you made the loud noises—there it is!"

Maki saw it this time, a bright flash of light from a far distance, near the ribbon of crushed rock where the Hinchai traveled. He dismissed it as unimportant. "Light reflected from something on a Hinchai traveler. Move on, so we sleep near water tonight. We have little to drink." He walked away jauntily, happily unaware of a serious error in judgment, an error he would regret in the days to come. Han's concern evaporated with Maki's, and Dorald had no concern to begin with, the two of them following their leader like obedient children.

The remainder of the day was the beginning of a nightmare from which there was no awakening.

Their route kept them in the trees, traversing hillsides into a long, brush-choked gully leading to a shallow valley filled with grass and scattered boulders. A small stream meandered through the valley, and they camped by it, a circle of three boulders sheltering them from wind and hiding them from Hinchai who might pass by on the distant road. They filled themselves with water, and ate the last of the dried meat, knowing they would reach the caverns the following morning. Appetites satisfied, and feeling secure, they lay down in the grass for a carefree nap, but each sleeping with his weapon in the custom of a Tenanken warrior. The air was cool, and they slept deeply at first before moving into dreams unremembered, and a shallow sleep near consciousness.

Maki awoke with a start. He kept his eyes closed, willing stillness, sensing the alien presence at a level he did not understand, a subtle presence, quiet, watchful and vaguely hostile. Nearby. All senses heightened, he felt for movement in the ground, sniffed the air, and listened for the slightest sound, hearing at first only Dorald's quiet snoring next to him. The first sign was a sweet odor, which he recognized as the smell of Hinchai flesh, and then a scratching sound. Maki dared to open his eyes to a slit, remaining absolutely still despite his pounding heart. He closed them again, willing calmness, but feeling the sudden beads of sweat beginning to evaporate from his face.

A Hinchai male was with them: large, dressed in earth colors, lounging on a boulder and watching them sleep, and on a hip was strapped one of the smaller pointing weapons Maki had seen fired with one hand. Maki visualized his position, and the weapon near his hand. With a distraction he could—

"Okay, Boys, sleepy time is over. Time to get up."

Maki groaned softly, as if bothered in sleep, but Dorald's snoring cut off sharply and he grumbled.

"Jeezus, God, if you aren't a sight. I thought all the injuns had cleared out, if that's what you are. COME ON, GET UP!"

Dorald and Han awoke with a start while Maki opened his eyes to stare balefully at the stranger and roll slightly to one side to cover his weapon lying in the grass. There was no reaction; the Hinchai hadn't seen it. Now Maki's companions were on their feet, grasping weapons, and the Hinchai's hand moved in a blur, appearing with a black weapon leveled at all of them.

"Don't do anything stupid, fellas, or Mister Colt here will give you a terrible bite."

Maki spoke harshly in the Tenanken tongue. "Relax your weapons before he kills us all, and move apart from each other. My weapon is hidden beneath me, and when I move to shoot it is a signal for you to strike!"

"Shut up! White renegades actin' like injuns, Christ, those people take baths. Your stink is enough to knock a man out! Tattered rags and spears and—hey, big guy, where did you get that nice, shiny axe? Seems to me I got a report about that, along with a missing rifle. Any of you see a nice, new rifle around here? Henry, I believe it was—lever action. What about you, yellow eyes; seen any-thing?" The Hinchai looked straight at Maki, and slid down from the boulder he's been sitting on, weapon level and steady.

Maki shook his head, leaning on one elbow, the weapon hard against his side.

"No? Sure ain't talkative, are you? None of you? Well, we can get into the details back at the jail, if you'll just follow me, gentle-men. My wagon is waiting, and thank God you can ride in back and not up with me. Whew! We've just *got* to get you boys into a tub and scrub you up. I keep a clean jail."

Han had moved away from Maki a couple of steps, and Dorald a few steps beyond him, the axe hanging limply in one hand. His teeth were showing in a kind of death-grin, and the dangerous glint had returned to his eyes, telling Maki the big Tenanken had reached the limit of self-control. Dorald took two tentative steps towards the Hinchai, and the blue-black hand weapon swung around to point di-rectly at his stomach.

"Now don't get stupid, man! This here's a forty-four, and your size won't do you a bit of good. One shot, and you are a dead per-son. Now you all quit your movin' around, and get together again." The Hinchai's voice was low and ominous as he motioned them to-gether with the hand weapon. "It suddenly occurs to me I'm lookin' at Jake's critters, and damned if'n he wasn't pretty accurate. All the thievin's been goin' on around here, and it turns out to be white folk; I think you have a lot to answer for, so let's get on with it. Over here, now, all of you." The Hinchai turned slightly away from Maki, motioning them to one side.

Maki slid his weapon out from under him in the tall grass, grasping it in one hand and sitting up as if to stand.

Han's hand slid down the shaft of his standing spear, grasping it lightly with two fingers.

The muscles in Dorald's right arm suddenly knotted as he gripped the axe tightly. He took another step towards the Hinchai, staring into the black maw of the hand weapon.

"I'd rather take you in alive, but I'm not particular in your case, mister," said the Hinchai.

Han's arm moved in a blur, straight up, then over in an arc, the spear appearing as if by magic in the chest of the Hinchai. The man grunted, surprised, turning to face Han as Maki pulled his weapon to his shoulder and fired in one motion, gratified when the man's body slammed back into a boulder and blood exploded from his mouth in a bright gush splattering his clothing in red. Dorald moved in for the kill, swinging the axe high over the wide-eyed Hinchai who looked up at him and gurgled, "Who the hell are you people?"

The axe descended, the impact a sickening crunch simultaneous with the explosion of the Hinchai's hand weapon.

Dorald leaped backwards, leaving his axe embedded in the shattered remains of the Hinchai's skull, turning slowly to face Han and Maki, clutching at his stomach with one hand, eyes sad. He held out a hand to them, saying nothing, taking one staggering step, and then Maki saw the blood oozing out between his fingers. Another half step, then Dorald groaned, and sank to his knees, grabbing his stomach now with both hands. Tears trickled from his eyes and down his face as Han and Maki knelt before him, helpless in the sight of a horrible wound, putting their hands on his shoulders. Before their eyes, his skin was suddenly ashen and turned cold to the touch.

"I'm sorry," said Maki. "You fought well, and killed our enemy. This is committed to The Memories, and the Tenanken will remember your deed in the Visions. Forever."

Dorald grinned weakly, eyes glazing over as he whispered his answer. "I crush Hinchai skull good," he said, and then his eyes rolled upwards, a belch of black blood issuing forth from his mouth as he toppled forward so quickly they could not hold him up. His face hit the ground with a thud, and it was only then that Maki saw the fist-sized hole in Dorald's back, streaming blood past a shattered array of bone and nerve fibers that had once been a spine. Maki turned his face from the sight as Han moaned softly.

"The Hinchai has killed him. My friend is gone." Han's voice was filled with grief, and Maki felt sudden guilt at the times he had wanted to be rid of the big Tenanken. He put an arm around Han's shoulders, and they sat by the body for a moment. "He was my friend, too," said Maki, partially believing it. "He wanted to be a warrior, Han, and at the end he was, with us at his side. Now he is in a better place. We will grieve for him, then do what we must do. Whatever happens, Anka or anyone else in the caverns must not know about this. We must bury the bodies quickly out of sight, with no evidence of digging."

"I have no ochre," said Han.

"There's red clay near the canyon rim, and flowers. I have a little food left."

"We'll have to move him there."

And the Hinchai. We dare not leave anything here."

Han jerked the axe from Hinchai bone, then his spear. "I will cut the branches." He scurried away towards the trees.

Maki surveyed the disaster site. The big Hinchai was sprawled over a boulder, the contents of his skull splattered over the rock, eyes open and staring at the sky. Maki twisted the hand weapon from his fingers, fiddling with it until he understood recent Memories, then removed the belt and holster from the body, replaced the weapon protectively and buckled the assembly around his own waist. He dragged the Hinchai from the boulder, and used a bunch of grass to wipe away the trail of goo left behind, while Han chopped furiously to bring down four, small trees.

It was late afternoon before they had finished making a simple travois for each body out of limbs and soft roots covered with fir boughs. Han insisted on pulling his friend, and started out before Maki was even ready. Maki dragged the Hinchai unceremoniously to the travois, flopped him on it, chambered a new projectile into his pointing weapon and began the long pull back to the canyon.

There will be consequences, thought Maki. *The Hinchai will be missed, and then a search party. They must not find the body; Pegre will relay the story directly to Anka, and a connection can be made to the return of his son. There must be no suspicion before Hidaig's arrival. Put the bodies in different places, under rock where they can never be found. The Hinchai has simply disappeared, gone away for a while to another settlement. By the time they look for him, it will be too late.*

Maki felt assured by his analysis, but there was an important flaw in the logic, for he had neglected to ask himself how the Hinchai had found and then intercepted them in their camp. Back near that camp, the Hinchai's wagon and two horses still waited on the road, a telescope pulled out to full length across the driver's seat.

* * * * * * *

They reached the edge of the canyon near dusk, panting from the uphill pull, and near exhaustion. A spine of rock ran up the hillside like the dorsal of some great, buried fish, rotted and falling down in places, the ground around it covered with debris. They dumped the Hinchai body into a wide crevice, and threw rocks in after it until the crevice was filled. But Dorald was special, and they searched carefully for a place until Han called out, "Over here, and I can see the canyon. Maki, it's perfect for him."

Maki climbed the hill. Near the end of the rock spine was a deep depression shaped like a tub, bottom covered with a thin layer of soft earth washed in by rains. He studied it, then said, "We can build a roofed cairn over him, then cover it with rocks. We'll lay him thus, so he faces the rising sun and his spirit can meet it for the last journey. See, those flat rocks there for the roof of the cairn."

Han nodded solemnly. There were no tears, now, as he helped to prepare his friend for a transition to the everlasting life of a spiritual world without earthly pain and suffering. He struggled with Maki to pull the travois up the final hill, and unloaded the big Tenanken gently into the rocky depression. Using red clay and saliva, he decorated Dorald with the marks of a warrior, and crossed his arms over his chest with the fingers of both hands curled around the big axe. Into the depression they put two small bags of food within easy reach, then covered their companion with flowers picked from the hillside. The cairn went up quickly, rectangular-shaped with a flat roof nearly touching the thick chest, a miniature tomb for one warrior, and then they piled rocks in random fashion until the depression was filled to the brim, as one with the entire outcropping.

The sun was setting when they finished, and they went to bed hungry and sorrowful.

When they awoke in the morning, it was with sudden knowledge that the spirit of Dorald had flown into the sun. Han wept. Maki stood with him a while by the rock-covered tomb, and then they packed, the Hinchai weapons going into Maki's long pack. They made the short walk to the caverns along the bluff and down steep shelves past the place where Baela perched in a tree, watching them. The sky was dark blue, a gentle breeze cooling them along the canyon. A day Dorald would have loved.

When they neared the entrance, Anka suddenly appeared and hurried to meet them, opening his arms and emotionally embracing his son. "You've come home," he said, choking back tears. "I thought I'd lost you, but you've come home. Let me get you something to eat, and then there is much to talk about."

As they went inside, scavenger birds had begun to circle above the bluff at the end of the canyon.

CHAPTER NINE

SUNDAY

Pete kept nodding off during the sermon. His head would droop, then snap up, eyes darting around to see if anyone had noticed. Bernie noticed. When the service was over, they filed out of the little, white church, said their good mornings and made polite conversation about the weather before returning to the wagon. Pete boosted her up, and Bernie clambered in grunting, fanning herself with the church program in noon heat. They drove out of town, staying on the road for a mile before turning off into two ruts for a rough, uphill ride, the wagon bouncing so hard at one point that Bernie turned and said, "One more like that one, and you can deliver your own child right here." Pete grinned at her, and slowed a little.

When they reached the top of the hill the ruts became a road again, for they had taken a shortcut that would soon be graded as well. It was the view from the top of the hill they had endured a bouncy ride for: the little valley below, surrounded by a ring of trees, and beyond that the cliffs and brush-filled canyons leading to a high plateau covered with grass and flowers. The ranch was centered within the trees, buildings made from rough-hewn logs, the first poles in place for a fence.

"Ours," said Bernie.

Pete took her hand. "Wish your folks could've seen it. You said they always wanted a place like this."

"Daddy'd be satisfied that one of us got it. He never really wanted anything for himself, but momma did. I don't want to think about it. Let's get down there, and get some work done. You hungry yet?"

"Didn't you hear my stomach in church?"

"Nope. The snoring was too loud for that. How does biscuits and sausage sound?"

The wagon lurched forward. "Good enough for a fast ride downhill. Hang on!"

Bernie yelled all the way down the hill.

They unloaded cans of varnish and large brushes from the back of the wagon, and hauled it all inside the big house facing west. Pete varnished a floor while Bernie cooked breakfast over the big cast iron stove, and they ate together on a small table in the kitchen. The rest of the afternoon Pete varnished while Bernie sewed and hung curtains in the upstairs bedrooms. Supper was cold meat, potatoes and coffee, and as the sun was setting Pete lit the lamps before they went out to the porch to sit in matching rocking chairs, custom ordered from Quincy, and watch the evening come.

Bernie sighed. "Look at that red, red hill. Did you ever notice how the birds get quiet just as the sun turns red? I wonder if the color has something to do with it?"

"Who knows? For some people it means drinkin' time. Business usually picks up about now." Pete rocked in his chair, and took a big swallow of coffee.

They sat in silence for a minute, then Bernie said, "Did you ever think you'd have something like this? You know, when you were living with Savas, or even before, in Greece? Did you ever think you'd have a big house in a valley all to yourself?"

Rocking together in growing darkness, watching the stars come out, Pete considered the lie he'd lived, and decided to continue. "We talked about it some. The old man told me I could get whatever I wanted or be whatever I wanted to be if I worked hard enough. After a thousand times of hearing it, I guess I believed him. Sure, I wanted a nice house someday."

"Momma dreamed about having a place like this, but daddy was never able to give it to her. Poor daddy, he tried so hard and loved us so much, but he never did very well. He just didn't have the business smarts like you do, Pete."

"But he was a good man."

"Oh, yes, he was a very good man, and I learned a lot of things from him, like how to respect everyone's dignity and never look down on anyone."

"Good thing for me he taught you that."

Bernie looked at him curiously. "What do you mean?"

"Oh, just the way things happened when I first came to town: the stares, the jokes about the way I looked and talked, the way the women hugged their kids to them when I came near. Then I saw you in the store that day, and you were laughing with the clerk about a potato with a strange shape. I thought to myself you were the prettiest thing I'd ever seen, and my heart nearly stopped when you turned and smiled at me."

"It was easy; no man had ever looked at me that way before. Your face lit up like a lantern. By the way, that potato looked like a giant penis."

"All I noticed was you."

Bernie reached over, and grabbed his hand. "Still feel that way?"

"You bet." He squeezed her hand and held it until darkness fell, and he went inside briefly to get a cup of coffee. When he returned, Bernie was rocking gently in her chair, both hands on top of her tummy, smiling the contented smile of a woman feeling the stirrings of life inside her body.

"What was Savas really like? Everyone in town was kinda afraid of him, and wouldn't go near that old cabin of his. If anyone'd know him, you would. I only saw him a couple of times when he came to town.

"Well, he was Greek, and he took me in. *So far, the truth.* He wasn't what you'd call an admirer of the human race, and wanted to live an uncomplicated life as much as possible in silence." *Also true, but after first coaxing me out of the bushes he spent two years teaching me how to read and write both Greek and English.* "He taught me English, and had a lot of books. I read them all. Otherwise, he didn't say much, and I tried real hard not to bother him." *He was half-crazy, with dangerous corners in his mind, yet there came a day when he thought of me as a son.* "I can say we were friends, and I felt bad when he died. By then I'd bought his nephew's bar in Quincy. He's the one who taught the business to me. I was doin' pretty good, but when I came back to give Savas a nice funeral it was the first time I'd really seen the town of Crosley. Loved it—sold the place in Quincy—moved here." *With enough cash and gold to pay for a business and a ranch, and a way out for others burrowing in those cliffs behind us right now.*

They rocked in darkness. "And then I met you."

"Yes you did, and now *your* child is kicking again. Oh, oh, who's that out here after dark?"

Lights had suddenly appeared at the top of the hill, moving towards them, jiggling up and down as a vehicle bounced in the rutted road. "Sure is in a hurry," said Pete. "I have a feeling this is the end of our first quiet evening at home. Should've known."

A battered, spring wagon pulled up in front of the house and Jake Price got down, walking over to the porch with Stetson in hand, all cleaned up like he was going to a social. He nodded to Bernie.

"Evenin', Bernice. Say, didn't that road give me a scare tonight; be glad when you folks finish it."

"Cup of coffee, Jake? Got plenty." Pete started to go inside the house, stopping when the man shook his head no.

"Gotta get back, Pete. I know it's Sunday and all, but people are really riled up about all the stealin' and vandalism lately, and a bunch of the boys are meetin' tonight to see what we can do about it."

"That's Tom's job, Jake. I think we ought to let him do it."

"He's only one man, Pete. Besides, he went out of town before church this mornin' and hasn't come back yet. We're not talkin' mob, Pete, just a discussion about what we can do to help. And everyone wants you to be there."

"Of course," said Bernie. "Oh, well, we were going back a little later anyway." She pushed her chair back, and stood up, stretching her back.

"I don't think we should meet without Tom there," said Pete.

"Well, he should be back by now, and he's sure invited. We've got to do it *sometime*, Pete, before people start shootin' at shadows."

"Or critters," said Pete, and instantly regretted it. Jake looked like he'd been slapped. "Sorry, Jake, that was nasty. I just don't like having my evening messed up."

"I know what I seen, Pete. We get down to the bottom of the trouble we've been havin' and some eyes are gonna be opened up. Want to follow me back?"

"Only if you'll forget my stupid remark, and have a cup of coffee with us first."

Jake smiled, then, and they had their coffee before turning out the lamps and harnessing up two reluctant horses. It was a new moon, stars spattered across the sky in a band, and below tree level was inky blackness. The two wagons bounced and skidded on the rough road, braking together once when two deer dashed across their view, and hitting the road near the edge of town. A small crowd was milling around in front of the hotel, waving to them when they passed by. Pete made a U-turn in the wide street, pulling up by the bar, and scrambling to help Bernie down.

"No meeting for me," she said. "Don't see any women there anyway. Sounds like men's' business, and I'm not in the mood. See you." She kissed Pete on the cheek, then climbed the stairs to their apartment, puffing, and talking to herself.

Pete crossed the street to the hotel. The group of men greeted him quietly and politely, Pete shaking hands with some of them. When he got to the porch, Ned Bester, president of the bank, pumped his hand twice before asking, "Mind if we use the hotel? Tom's still out of town, and nobody else has the town hall key."

"Sure, come on in. The dining room isn't finished, yet, but it's a warm place to sit."

The men filed in behind Pete through the lobby and down a short hall to a large room with stacked chairs and tables to one side, and the foundation of a stage area to the other. Sawhorses and planks were scattered around the room, and in the center a giant crystal chandelier sparkled in the dim light. Ned looked around, and took Pete by the elbow. "Live music, and everything, huh?"

"That and good Basque cooking. I know a guy in Verdi who's the best, and he's agreed to chef for me."

Ned rubbed his fingers together. "Good business, good business. Might even get 'em over here from Reno." He smiled at Pete, then moved in front of the group while everyone was finding a place to sit, and clapped his hands.

"Let's get started, now. Working day tomorrow, and it's getting late. Thanks to Pete for letting us use this room, and remember this isn't a formal meeting, so just jump in when you want to. Several of you asked me to call this because of trouble you've been havin'. I'm a little reluctant to do it because Tom isn't here, and I don't want him to think we're goin' behind his back. I think he's been a good sheriff for us—"

"Nobody's sayin' he isn't, Ned," said someone.

"Okay, well that's good to hear. He's only one man, and there's a lot of area around here to police. If we've got injuns living back in these hills, it'll take more than Tom to take care of things."

Pete grinned. "Injuns? I thought they all cleared out a long time ago."

"Maybe not—maybe so, but whatever, someone around here is doin' a lot of stealing, particularly livestock, and Darin here lost a rifle and some shells last week."

"And two pigs!" shouted another man. Now there was an undercurrent of grumbling in the room.

Ed Duchal, tall and redheaded, turned around to face Pete. "Hell, you seen it first hand, the night they stole a chicken right out from under our noses, and I shot one of them."

"Bunch of bare-footed kids, Ed. We found footprints the next day. A bunch of kids. Before we get all riled up about injuns, we'd better look closer to home. It could be some of our own."

"Easy for you to say when yours ain't even born yet," said Ed, smiling. Pete laughed with him. "We've all checked into that, and our kids are accounted for. Besides, that scream we heard that night didn't even *sound* human to me. Admit it, you didn't think so either. We just stared at each other after we heard it. Sounded crazy—wild—like some kind of animal."

"Liquor can make you pretty crazy, Ed. God knows what kids are drinkin' it these days, but it's a fact of life, and we've got to consider it. Let's keep this realistic; what we're probably looking for is some drunken kids on an occasional rampage. They could be from any number of towns around here, pickin' on us 'cause we're so isolated. There's only one main road coming into town; all we have to do is give Tom some help so he can keep an eye on it, and screen out any suspicious folks coming in. If the raids slow down or stop, then we know what's goin' on. We might even catch 'em. Anyway, that's my opinion." Pete leaned back in his chair, and crossed his legs.

Everyone seemed to be thinking for a few seconds, and then Jake suddenly stood up and thrust his hands deep into his pockets. "Well, that's just not the way I see it, and I'm the only one here who knows what these critters really look like."

"Oh, Jake," said Ned.

"Now don't give me that 'oh, Jake' stuff. Nobody listened to me about the raids on my place until it started to happen to the rest of you. Hell, I've had this trouble for nearly a year, and only now is everyone gettin' excited about it. And I ain't talkin' monsters, or anything weird like that. I've *seen* these critters, close up, damn near died doin' it—and they're *people*. Ugliest things I ever seen, but people all the same. And they ain't no injuns, 'cause I've seen plenty of them, too. These folks had primitive weapons, and worn out animal skins for clothes, long, scraggly hair and beards, heavy features, small eyes, but white folks all the same."

Ned looked at Jake sternly. "So you're telling us we're being harassed by a bunch of white folks."

"Nobody from town, Ned, and no kids." Jake's voice was calm, serious, devoid of the pathetic self-pity they were used to. "Look, you've all known me for a long time, and you've seen me in my cups. Okay, but you also know I haven't had a drink in nearly a month, and I'm standing here cold sober telling you what I saw. Tom believed me, that's why he's been spendin' time patrolling the roads, especially in the evenings, 'cause that's when they move."

Pete sat calmly in his chair, legs crossed, kicking one foot absently.

"Another reason for Tom to be here," said Ned. "He went out so early this morning I didn't get to him about this meeting. I think we really need to hear what he has to say about all this before we take any action. But I think we can agree there's a problem, and probably a single group of people is behind it. According to Jake, they're adults maybe gone wild, but he's the only one who's seen them, so we don't really know how many people are involved."

"At least three," said Jake.

"Okay, so we have a minimum number, and maybe they're dangerous, but I don't want any of you men turning vigilante, and shooting innocent people. Bad enough y'all ride around with guns in your wagons."

"You're just not a hunter," said Ed.

"Hunter, my foot. I see a man with a rifle in his wagon, I see a man lookin' for trouble. I say let's wait till Tom gets back, and find out what kind of help we can give him. Agreed?"

More grumbling in the room, Pete only watching and listening, unusual for him, but nobody seemed to notice.

"Yeah, sure, Ned, we'll wait for Tom, but then we've got to do something. And everyone check up on their kids. Know where they are at night. If worst comes to worst, we don't want to end up shooting one of our own; we've got wives can do that." Ed laughed, but alone. Everyone had begun to leave the room, Ned in the lead.

People were still talking on the porch, and a few had gone home when another wagon rattled into town and stopped across the street from the hotel. Lyle Nygaard owned a chicken 'n' egg ranch several miles south of town, and his wife Melinda was with him. He got down from the wagon and went straight to Ned, who was talking with Pete and two other men. "Evenin', Ned—Pete. I miss somethin' important?"

Ned told him about the meeting. Lyle rubbed his jaw with a stained hand. "So you're waitin' to see Tom, huh? Well, I stopped by to tell you his wagon is sittin' on the road about three miles south of here, thirsty horses, and a nice telescope layin' on the seat just askin' to be stole', and Tom nowhere in sight. Called out, got no answer. Inky black out there, and I didn't bring a lantern. Needs lookin' into, I think."

It got real quiet on the porch.

"Any of you men got lanterns?" asked Ned. A couple of hands went up. "I'm asking for volunteers to look for Tom." Several hands went up this time, and men started towards their wagons and horses.

"I've got a couple of extra lanterns in the hotel," said Pete. "Ned, can I ride with you?"

"Sure thing."

Lyle turned towards his wagon. "I'll meet you over there. The wagon's right on the road, by the meadows. Gotta take the missus home first, then I'll be along."

"Thanks, Lyle," said Ned.

Pete came out of the hotel with three lanterns a minute later, and mounted up with Ned. A caravan of ten wagons left town that night, headed south and moving slowly. Most of them had rifles and shotguns, and the men were grim-faced. They drove slowly in the moonless night, total blackness closing in on them, apprehension heavy in each man. There was no conversation. They crossed a bridge and the road turned gently, then ahead they saw a shadow off the road to the right. Tom's wagon appeared in dull light, and the caravan stopped along the road on either side of it. Two men swung lanterns above their heads, and shouted out "Tom!" several times, and everyone else was as quiet as death. There was no answer.

"Anyone know what's out there?" asked Ned.

"Good place to see deer in the evening," said somebody, "and people have camped by some rocks out there."

"Well, let's take a look."

Everyone dismounted, a few rifles coming with them, but Ned was not in a mood to protest the presence of weapons on an inky-black night when a good man was missing. He led them into the meadows, Pete walking right behind him. Lanterns cast a soft glow in every direction. Gradually they spread out into a line fifty yards wide, moving slowly, dull light spilling on long grass and occasional wildflowers. They came to a hollow circled by boulders and smaller rocks; in the center was a small pit, and the burned out remains of a fire. Ned and several others walked around the hollow while the rest searched the fields beyond, still moving along a line. Pete stooped down suddenly, and picked up something, looking at it closely. "Found a cartridge case," he said, and Ned went over to look at it.

"A thirty-thirty, pretty common, better hang onto it." Ned took the case from Pete and put it into his pants pocket, He had started to turn away from Pete, when Ed suddenly said quietly, "Ned, you'd better come over here." Nobody else seemed to hear at that moment, and Ned went over to where Ed stood by a large boulder slab, holding his lantern down close to it. In the glare of the light, he could see something staining the rock, something dark, running down the rock and into the grass. He got down close, turning the light this way and that, and then the odor hit him. A musky, salty odor he had last smelled when watching a friend butcher a freshly killed deer. He touched the stain with his fingertips, and sniffed them. "Blood," he said.

"Some more there, too," said Ed. "Runnin' down the rock, and into the grass. See there?"

There was more blood in the grass, a big splash of it.

"Doesn't look good, Ned."

Ned thought for a minute. "You still keep those hounds of yours, Ed?"

"Best trackers in the county."

"I'll wait here with the others while you go get those dogs. They've got some important work to do."

Ed left in a hurry, without a word. Ned touched the blood stains again. Coagulated, but fresh. "Okay, men!" he shouted. "Everyone in, and gather around here. I've got something to show you—and sorry to say it's gonna be a long night."

CHAPTER TEN

INTEGRATION

"I can get you a job in Quincy, Peter. I know people. But we'll have to give you some identity."

Savas got up from his chair, grunting at an audible pop from one knee, and shuffling across the room to one end of the couch, where a small, green chest was pushed up against a wall. He carried it back to the table, and flopped back in his chair as Peter closed the book he'd been reading out loud to his teacher, in between arguments.

They argued often, now, but not in a heated way, as Peter's mind worked to absorb and analyze all the material Savas brought out for him to read. They had been discussing a journalist's book about the Indians, and Peter had suddenly vented emotion at a speculation of ritual child killing during food shortages, but Savas was tired, wanted no more serious talk for the moment, and tried to change the subject. He opened the chest, and looked inside.

"The killing of children for any reason is immoral and destructive. I don't believe they did that," said Peter. "Look at the mix of people in these books, and ask how it could happen if certain children were selectively destroyed. Whole races wouldn't exist!"

Savas piled handfuls of papers, cards, inks and pens on the table. "Human history is full of genocide, Peter. Look how close we've come with the Indians. Killing off the buffalo was done for that reason, you know. We've all tried it, Peter. Here, I want to show you some things I haven't looked at in years."

But Peter would not let go just yet. "We're all descended from common ancestors. It is in our faces. If an early race had been wiped out, would we now be the same?"

Savas opened a bottle of ink, and sniffed at it. "Oh Peter, I don't know. Maybe we wouldn't be quite as strong, or quick, or smart. The best have led to the best of us. The strongest select the strongest to mate with. Screwing selection, Peter, not killing selection. It's the best way, every time."

Peter's intensity suddenly vanished, and he relaxed back in his chair. "Yes—perhaps it's so. Now, what is this on the table? I've already shown you my writing for the day."

"These are the legalities of your new life," said Savas. "You see this? Immigration registration card, and blank. There used to be a name on this card, but I've bleached it off. Can you tell?" He held it up admiringly to the light. "I can't even find the chemicals anymore. You see how simple it is. I write your name here, so—Peter—Pelegeropoulis. This means you can work, earn money, own land, but we need other things." He rummaged in the pile of papers once more, held up a single sheet with a seal and signature near the bottom. "And here it is—a birth certificate, nicely laundered, signature intact. You will be born in Athens—parents—hmmm, we'll think of some names. They're deceased, of course, year—let's make you twenty-one—no, twenty-three, and seven years of schooling before working for me." More rummaging. "I will be your reference to start. Ah, here it is, and from the same man. I assure you he will not mind if we use it."

Leaning closely over the table, Savas practiced several times on a blank sheet of paper, then carefully scrolled Peter's name in Greek and English on the laundered documents, and held them out to admire his handiwork.

Peter was puzzled, but interested. At first he'd pretended indifference, opening his book and paging through it, but finally standing at Savas's shoulder as pen stroked paper. "Why are you doing this?"

"So you can go to work. You want that, don't you?"

"I'm not sure."

"But we've talked about it, Peter. You said you wanted to be a real part of the world, and you're ready for it now. Why wait any longer? Do you want to talk it over again with your kin?"

"I've done that, and they tell me to do as you say. I do this for them, so they can all join me someday. *But am I ready to be alone in the Hinchai world?*

As if they care, thought Savas. "I'm not saying it'll be easy, but yes, you're ready. I have the contacts, and I can get you started, but the rest is up to you. Quincy is close, and I can see you regularly, if you want it."

"Oh, yes, I would want that."

"Start with a simple job, and work your way up. Living in town will be different than here. Work hard, and save your money. You can be whatever you want to be, have whatever you want to have, if you focus on it, and believe in yourself. Some people don't believe that, but I do."

Peter took a deep breath. "It all seems too soon. I still fumble around buttoning this shirt."

"The rest of us don't? Look, you think about it as long as you want, talk it over with your people, the ones I never ask you about. In a day I'll have arrangements ready for you. You give the word, and we're out of here for you to make a start. If you can't do it, nobody can."

Peter was silent a moment, nervously fingering his book, then he turned towards the door, and said, "I'll let you know tomorrow."

* * * * * * *

In the morning, they packed some clothes, climbed into the wagon, and drove south.

It was the first time Peter had been on the big road and near the Hinchai, but as usual his emotions were tightly guarded, and he showed no reactions to new things. In three hours they reached the town called Quincy and drove straight to the bar and grill patronized by Savas for some twelve years, though two owners had come and gone since he'd started drinking there. The latest and perhaps most inept owner was Rudy Mueller, a heavy, agreeable man with a swollen nose and red tracks running horizontally across both cheeks, a man expert in the consumption of that which he sold to his many customers, mostly miners and ranchers, and drifters searching for a new life. Rudy was cook, waiter, and bartender at the time, and although service was less than fast and food more than cooked, the drinks were generous and so business was brisk. Unknown to Rudy, his liver was already nearing retirement, and in only a few years the River Bar and Grill would once more be seeking a new owner.

It was noon when they entered. The place was dark except for the lamp over a card table at the back, where two miners were playing for gold dust, two others watching, nursing beers. The four men at the bar had begun serious drinking when the place had opened at eleven, and were now well along the path to euphoria and enlightenment, one already snoring peacefully. Those conscious turned to look closely at Savas and Peter as they found two places at the end of the bar, then at Rudy when he yelled from the kitchen.

"Hey, Savas! You're early for dinner!"

"Came in on business, Rudy. Got my cousin with me."

Rudy came out of the kitchen, wiping greasy hands on an unwashed apron, then stuck a fat paw across the bar at Peter, who took it immediately and shook it firmly. Rudy grinned at Savas, who introduced them.

"Kid's got a grip like a hard-rocker. Relative, eh?"

"Yup. We came to town to find him a job. Know of anything?"

Rudy thought for a minute while he poured two shots of whiskey in a glass, and drank it down in a gulp. "Kind of slow in mining, now, and the mill is filled up. What kind of work you looking for?"

"Anything I can get," said Peter before Savas could answer. "I can read, and write—and I like people."

"Yeah? Regular schoolin'?"

"Yes."

"We brought his papers along," said Savas quickly.

"No shit? How 'bout a drink?"

"Sure. A couple of beers," said Savas, and Peter nodded. Rudy poured two of them slowly, pushed the big glasses across the bar and watched Pete sip, then poured another drink for himself.

"Hardware store may need some help clerkin' or stockin', but the pay ain't much. You can get sweepin' jobs lots of places. I can even—"

"Hey, Rudy, we're thirsty down here!" One patron, a red-faced man with a hawk-nose, and a chewed up cigar hanging from a corner of his mouth, banged down a glass at the other end of the bar. The sound registered vaguely with his companion, whose half-opened eyes suddenly showed signs of life as they moved in an attempt to locate the source.

"Now, Rudy! I ain't got all day!"

"Be right there, Mac."

But that wasn't fast enough. "Aw shit," said the man, sliding off his stool and holding on for support as he turned one corner of the bar and staggered towards them with an angry look on his face.

"Watch out for this one," said Rudy softly. "Bad fight two weeks ago in here; bloodied a guy up."

Savas stiffened, right hand going by reflex into his pocket and out again, a thumb moving, and with a sharp snick four inches of shining steel became a new finger. But then a big hand touched his gently; when he looked around, Peter's face was close, eyes fixed on his. By the time the drunk reached them, Savas had somehow closed the knife and put it back in his pocket.

As the drunk lurched around the final corner, Rudy said nervously, "This is John Macavee, men. Mac, meet Savas and Pete." And then he stepped backwards to get out of the way.

John careened into Peter, who was nearest the corner of the bar, bounced off surprised at the mass he'd encountered, then bored in on Savas, whose hand was moving again towards his pocket.

"Ain't nice takin' the man's time so's he can't even serve a thirsty customer who drops a lot of dough in this Goddamned place. Don't nobody hear so good anymore? I want a fucking drink!"

"Comin' right up, Mac, so relax." Rudy grabbed bottle and glass, and started pouring.

John watched for a second, and turned rheumy eyes towards Savas. "What're *you* looking at?"

"A man who wants to die," said Savas quietly, eyes like those of a shark, black and fathomless. He turned towards the drunk, hand coming out of his pocket, but then the man was being pulled back by another big hand over one shoulder, twirled and hugged against Pete's side so he couldn't move, and at first didn't even think of struggling.

"Good drink you've got coming there," said Peter affably. "You'll have to forgive my friend, 'cause he don't like it when people get so close up to him like that. Makes him feel closed in, you know, like bein' in a jail cell. I don't mind, though. I'm buyin' this one for you." He threw a half eagle—a five dollar gold piece—on the bar.

"Yeah?" said Mac, looking up at the wide, square jaw near his face. Peter's big arm had totally immobilized him, but he showed no fear. "Thanks," he said finally.

"You know," lied Pete, "I had a lady once who dumped me for a guy she thought had more'n me. She ended up nearly starving to death. Sometimes women have no sense, just don't know what they're losin'. You get over it, and find someone better. Here's to all the better ones out there." Pete raised his glass, Mac picked his up, too, and they drank together.

"Well," said Mac, wiping his mouth with the back of his hand, "nice talkin' to ya. Better get back to my friend, now. See you around again." He lurched away, made one turn, and cocked a thumb back at Pete as he spoke to Rudy. "Big one's okay, but the other one's a little nervous."

Rudy's breath whistled between his teeth. "Jeezus, how you handled that. One of my best customers, but he can be *real* trouble. You used to dealing with drunks?"

"No," said Peter.

"You want a job here, you've got it," said Rudy. "Be my bouncer, and tend some bar, I'll pay you better than anywhere else in town. I've been tryin' to run this place by myself, and it would sure go better with help. Ten bucks a week to start, and your meals here. Extra from customers when you tend bar at nights. I'd rather cook. What do you think?" Rudy looked at Savas for support.

"Sounds good to me," said Savas. "It's a start, Peter."

"Yeah, but I don't know anything about bars."

"Hell, I can teach you all that in a month. I been in this business twenty years one place or 'nother."

"He learns fast," said Savas.

Peter looked at Savas, and both of them smiled. "When should I start?" said Peter.

"How about tonight? And here's an address, a lady friend of mine who rents out two rooms, nice and clean, no other expenses. Just down the street. Hell, your living expenses will be nothin'."

"Thanks, Mister Mueller," said Peter.

"It's Rudy. Come back at six, I'll fry you both up some veal and my own special kraut, then Pete can get started."

"Good enough," said Savas, draining his glass. "See you then."

As Peter and Savas left the bar, John Macavee gave them a friendly wave. "See ya later."

Outside, Savas turned to Peter with a frown. "How *did* you calm that guy down? His eyes were slits. Very dangerous."

"I was just friendly," said Peter.

"Right. And what was all that bullshit about women?"

"Man lost his lady."

"How the hell did you know that?"

"He was telling his friend about it."

"At the other end of the bar? And you heard it? Come on, Peter, was it a lucky guess or something?"

"Or something," said Peter, grinning. "I guess I pay better attention than my teacher thinks I do."

Four weeks later, at the age of twenty, Peter Pelegeropoulis was the new bartender at the River Bar and Grill.

In two years he was bookkeeper, and partner.

In five years he was sole-owner of a thriving business, financed by gold once kept hidden beneath the floor of a Greek's cabin in the hills.

CHAPTER ELEVEN

Loss

"I feel your pain as I have never felt it before. It hurts deeply, yet I never knew him." Anka put a hand on Pegre's shoulder, leaving it there to warm him in his grief.

"I hadn't admitted it, but he was another father to me, responsible for much of what has happened in my life." Pegre looked at Anka with moist eyes, and saw understanding there, the understanding of someone old who had seen much death and become resigned to its inevitability.

"It isn't right, but I feel jealousy. There are things you shared with the Hinchai I could not be a part of, and somehow I feel negligent in not giving all I could."

They were sitting in the little grotto a few yards down-canyon from the main cavern entrance where they always went for private talks. Outside, the sun had risen only an hour before, and the cold made their breath a sparkling fog in the new light. They sat facing each other on a flat rock, Anka draped in a thin robe of deerskin, Pegre dressed in jeans and a heavy wool shirt. Both were shivering.

"There was nothing you could teach me about the Hinchai world, but all else comes from you."

"You are as your real father, my brother, with the feelings of your mother."

"Savas was my friend, but he never pressured me to tell where I came from, volunteered little about himself, even near the end when he realized how ill he was. I always felt his past was dark with happenings that caused him anger and fear. If he was threatened, he could be extremely dangerous, but with me he was patient and kind and openly pleased with my successes."

"I'm sure you were a son to him, Pegre, as you have been to me. You have much to give to others, and I am learning to share you. Was his death a painful one?"

"I don't think so. He had medicine for the pain; it made him drowsy. Sometimes he didn't remember to eat properly, and near the end he wasn't eating at all. I rode up every day or so to see him, and when I found him yesterday he was in bed, quite dead and already stiff. What bothers me is he died alone. I should have been there."

"One cannot predict the time a spirit chooses to leave, whether Tenanken or Hinchai. You did what you could."

"The body is being prepared in town by someone who is paid for such things. We will bury him tomorrow in a graveyard near the property he owned."

"We? You do this with Hinchai?"

"A few who knew him: a banker, those who sometimes drank with him, and two others who do the burial. I got to know the banker because Savas had considerable wealth, and left it all to me. I share it with all Tenanken, Anka, by buying land for our homes and businesses that will make our place in the Hinchai world. Wealth is important to them, and Savas has provided it for us because I told him I wanted to bring my family to live in the valley, and he thought it was a good plan."

"Ah yes, The Plan. Can such an ambition be realized?" Anka said this with some fear, for the idea of mixing Tenanken and Hinchai in one community was yet abhorrent to him. They were one species, and yet they were not. The cultures, spirituality, life ethics, all had diverged in a far distant past. How safe the Tenanken had been, isolated in wilderness for tens of thousands of years, since before the time of severe cold and great ice mountains only vaguely recallable from The Memories, and then the settlers had suddenly come, driving them fearfully to the caves.

"I will teach Tenanken the Hinchai ways, and it will not be difficult because we are one with them and should never have been separated. It is my intention that the newest generations of Tenanken will feel the heat of the sun as they work, and in this there cannot be opposition," said Pegre.

"I will use all my influence," said Anka, nodding sagely.

"Even with your own son?"

"Particularly with him. He will hear me, Pegre, and his motives are honorable. He cares only for the future of the Tenanken."

"So he says," said Pegre sharply. "I feel otherwise. Why does he dislike me so? In the years you raised us both, never did I strive to capture your affections only for myself, yet I sense a terrible and dangerous jealousy within Maki. If this is behind his opposition to The Plan I will gladly withdraw, and leave the leadership to someone else. Perhaps Moog. He has great intelligence."

Anka shook his head. "No, you will not abandon your role in The Plan. I forbid it. Maki's jealousy is a problem he must deal with, along with his ambition. I fear he expects too much as the only true surviving son of a Keeper, and I share the blame for that. But as you both grew up, I had no favorites, and I have no apologies to offer for that. Do what you must for the Tenanken, and Maki is sure to support you."

"I want to believe that," said Pegre. "I really do." He picked up a small stone from the floor, and studied it. "I remember how I used to come here as a small boy, sit by the entrance and look down into the valley, wanting to climb a tree or run in the long grass, or throw myself into that icy stream, and always there was the strict law forbidding any of us to leave the canyon wall, and I'd wonder why we had such a law. What were we afraid of? Why were we hiding in dark and cold like common animals? I was afraid to go near a Hinchai until that first day with Savas, and later I discovered the stories they had made up about the dark skins who were here after us. Their children shivered with fear of strange savages who killed Hinchai without reason. They still tell such stories about a people whose lives they have forever altered. Fear is stupid, and we are all guilty of it."

"Then prepare the way for us to be together. You have my support, and Tel's."

"I'm glad of that. We've never really become close."

Anka offered a faint smile. "The bond between mother and the last son of her body is strong. Grief for Maki's brothers nearly killed her."

"I remember. Before that were happier times."

"They will come again. You will see to it, Pegre. Get on with your destiny. Can you stay with us this night?"

"No, I have to return to town for more business with a man who sells land, and I left my animal some distance from here. If I don't return soon, someone will search for me. Fear again, you see."

"Then go, but with a promise. Promise you will never forget you are first a Tenanken, the Keepers of The Memories and The Mind Touch. We are special, Pegre. Not superior, but special. Preserve us."

"The best I can," said Pegre solemnly, "and I will never forget who or what I am."

"One more thing," said Anka quickly. "This thing you have learned from your Hinchai father, this use of symbols to record thoughts and events for others to see and understand without spoken words, I wish you to use this also for the Tenanken."

"Writing," said Pegre.

"Yes. I have concern for The Memories, Pegre. Their keeping is central to our identity, and a fragile thing. Keepers appear with increasing rarity among us, though now there are three: myself, Tel and Maki. I wish you to record The Memories for us, Pegre, with your writing. From this day on, when we meet, I will have something for you to record. Our identity is in The Memories; they must not be lost."

"I will do this," said Pegre solemnly, "but Keepers will arrive as they have before."

"Perhaps," said Anka, "but when we join with the Hinchai our blood line is certain to be diluted. We are too much alike to prevent inter-breeding with them, and The Memories could be lost forever. That is my fear."

"I will record them for you," said Pegre, "when we meet again. But now I must leave."

They stood up, embraced stiffly, then Pegre turned and went out of the grotto, leaving Anka behind for quiet minutes to recall and put in vision-form a day in his robust adulthood when he felt the long grass beneath his feet, home was an earthen work dugout in a forest filled with running animals and birds, and day was divided between darkness and light.

Before the Hinchai came.

* * * * * * *

The day they buried Savas Parkos all clouds had disappeared from the sky, and an eagle soared above them, lifting their spirits for the ceremonies, a task made easier by the fact that the dead man had lived a long if somewhat isolated life, and his few friends had all arrived to send him on his way. Peter had made the arrangements with the aid of Reverend Nate Burgundy, pastor of Faith Baptist Church, at which a closed-casket service was held at ten o'clock on a Wednesday morning. Of the fifteen people attending the service, Peter knew only three: Burgundy, whose short eulogy he found contrived, banker Ned Bester, whose interest he had sparked with a single deposit, and finally one John Macavee, up from Quincy, having become a good friend of Savas after nearly being killed by him. It pained Peter to speak of the dead man, but speak he did, and gave birth to the story of his journey from Greece and then Reno to live with his uncle, the kindness he had received, the wisdom, *et cetera, et cetera*, until he was nearly sick from the lies. He marveled that the Hinchai God did not strike him dead on the spot, wondering if it was passive like the World Spirit of the Tenanken, preferring subjects to solve their problems and suffer their consequences. He spoke simple words with affection and sadness, moving some of his audience to tears, for without knowing it he had touched them all with naked grief directly from his mind.

Peter, John, Ned, and the hearse driver acted as pallbearers, carrying the plain wooden coffin sedately down the steps, and then the little procession of wagons and horses followed the remains to the graveyard south of town, neatly clipped and surrounded by a white, picket fence with a broken gate that creaked in the wind. The graveyard overlooked a meadow where some years later there would be a murder. Nate Burgundy read some words, and the coffin was lowered into the ground while everyone looked solemn. Nate offered condolences, and Peter paid him a ten dollar gratuity for the service, then the rest of the people came by to mumble their sympathies before returning to interrupted lives. Peter stood by the grave, a light breeze blowing black hair over his face as Ned Bester came up to him and put a hand on his shoulder.

"My regrets, Mister Pelegeropoulis. Hardly knew the gentleman, but he must have been a good businessman. You never know about some people."

"Any problems with the gold?" Peter peered into the blackness of the grave.

"No, the quote is firm. You say the word, it leaves for Reno in the morning. In your position, I'd keep half at least; gold is certain to go up."

"Send it."

They walked away from the gravesite, and towards an awaiting surrey. "When can I start remodeling?" said Peter.

"Right now. The business was yours this morning, and a lot of folks are anxious to see what you'll do with it. I'll grant you it's in tough shape, but you *did* get it for a good price."

"An honest price, you mean." Peter laughed, and Ned looked at him nervously. "Oh I'll get it fixed up good, especially in the kitchen. New ovens, and fresh bread every day, Greek style. Every drink you can think of. The Athens Bar and Grill—after Savas. Greek flavors will bring them in from Quincy and maybe even Reno when the word gets around. You like Greek food, Mister Bester?"

"That's Ned. Yes, I do."

"Opening night you've got a free meal coming at The Athens. My treat, Ned."

The man laughed. "Why it's sure nice doin' business with you, Peter."

They shook hands as they stopped at the gate, then Ned turned and shouted over his shoulder, "Coming, Bernice?"

A young woman was at a far corner of the graveyard, hunched over a pair of worn, stone markers, picking grass away from them with her hands and replacing some dried up flowers that had been lying there. She looked up at them sadly. "Are we leaving already?"

"I should get back."

The woman hastily pulled more grass, then stood up. She was tall, large boned but lean-looking. Blonde hair fell down her back and around broad shoulders. She wore a long skirt cinched in at the waist, and a tight, lacy bodice that somehow made her look fragile despite her size. As she walked towards them, Ned turned and whispered, "Her folks are buried over there. Takes good care of everything."

Her eyes were blue, cheekbones prominent above a generous mouth. As she came up to them Peter suddenly realized he was staring when she looked straight into his eyes and smiled. Ned put an arm around her shoulders, and said, "Bernice, I'd like you to meet Peter Pelegeropoulis, Crosley's newest businessman. Bought the Granville place, and he's turning it into a bar and grill. Peter, this is Bernie Ekstrom, and she *is* Ekstrom lumber and hardware in Crosley. Ask her for help, and you've got it."

"Well, I'll certainly need it with all the remodeling I have to do," said Peter, fighting a dry throat.

The smile again. "Stock's limited, but I'll do what I can. Sorry about Mister Parkos. He came into the store a couple of times for little things. One of the most polite people I ever met. I'm sorry."

"Thank you," said Peter, "and thanks for coming today." He held out a hand, and she took it in a firm grip that seemed to shoot fire into his arm and chest.

"I'm glad I did," she said happily, "and I look forward to doing some business with you."

"So do I," said Peter.

CHAPTER TWELVE

DECEPTION AND MURDER

Maki arose early, moving quietly from the vestibule so as not to disturb his sleeping father after a continuous night of talking, and sharing of The Memories. His earlier anger and contempt had now dissolved to pity; he was convinced The Keeper did only what he felt was right, but suffered from the delusions of the very old. As future Keeper, he, Maki, had made the decision to be merciful; he would reinforce orders to Hidaig that his father should be spared from injury.

Maki had been suitably contrite in conversation with Anka, and they had coolly discussed the relative merits of Tenanken integrating with Hinchai in common communion, an act which he now admitted privately had already been done by most Tenanken many tens of thousands of years in the past, for the features of so many Hinchai enemies would pass anywhere as Tenanken. For Maki, the issue was not racial, but cultural and spiritual. It was Tahehto blood which carried the genetic memories binding the Tenanken together, a union intensified by exchanges of the mind-touch in which Hinchai perhaps received, but returned nothing. At the rate they were arriving, Hinchai would be dominant and the Tenanken culture would soon be extinct.

When he entered the main cavern, he saw only two cooking fires were burning, most of the band still sleeping after the feast of the previous evening. He walked around the top of the chamber, stopping and bowing formally as Tel came out of a fumarole, stooping over to avoid cutting her head on a crystal crust.

"Good morning, Mother."

"Ah, you're up early. I presumed you and your father would still be in conversation and memory, so I went outside to watch the sun rise. We will allow the children to play on the bluff today."

"Do you think that's wise? They might be seen by Hinchai who hunt the antlered ones this time of year."

"It's a risk, but they will wear Hinchai clothing, and a guard will be posted. It's necessary they spend some time in sunlight to give their skin a more natural color."

"I suppose, but the color fades quickly. Why not wait until they're to integrate with the Hinchai? Surely that time is soon."

Something flickered in Tel's eyes for an instant. "That decision is up to Anka and Pegre. I have no idea when they will be leaving, but they become anxious. Even now they cook Hinchai foods over our fires; the odors are so delicious from many herbs and spices, and the variety of tastes is marvelous. The cooking skills of the Hinchai have developed far beyond ours, it seems. The caves and our isolation have held us back, yet in several ways I'll miss this place: the coolness, quiet, the sparkle of firelight on the crystal ceilings. But it's not a far distance, as long as my legs are good; I'll return here when I can for my meditations, and your father for reinforcement of The Memories."

Maki's head was pounding. "I don't understand," he said, voice quavering. "You mean you're *leaving* with the others? I thought you were staying here?"

"Oh, no, that's all changed, now. While you were gone, your father put it to a vote of all Tenanken. The children and a few others are the first to leave. But thereafter, within a season or two, all else may join them if they choose to. It was put to a vote, Maki. Only a few have chosen to remain: the very old, near death, those who could not survive the climb to the bluff and down again. If you wish to stay, it's your choice. Didn't your father tell you that?"

"He said nothing about any of this! I assumed only a select few would be leaving." Maki recognized the excitement in his voice, and fought for self-control. "I'm disappointed my father didn't tell me about his own decision to leave; after all, I have returned to be near my parents, and now find I must make a new decision about my own future. It's a surprise, Mother."

"But it *has* upset you; I can see that. Your poor father, so happy to see his son again, and then forgetting to tell him about a major decision in our lives. It could not have been deliberate, and you will have time to consider your own future, with or without us. You control your own destiny, Maki. We might disagree with you, but we respect your right to choose your own way."

She was probing his mind, digging for a response, but he had closed himself tightly, covering what was there with the vision of a waterfall. "I ask only that your choices will not interfere with the lives of others, or put them in danger of harm."

"I'll think about it, Mother. The caves are a dreary place, and I was thinking about that when we were camped outside in coolness, waking up to morning light and the smells of the trees. It's a better life out there, especially for the children, but still I fear the Tenanken ways disappearing with our absorption into the Hinchai culture. That is the issue I must debate, and it will take some time. Father and I talked a lot about this, and in some ways he shares my fears. Surely you know this?"

"We've argued about it since the first days of The Plan. It is only in recent years Anka has become truly convinced integration is the only way to secure a future for the Tenanken. And certain sacrifices will be necessary. I have known that from the beginning, but it has seemed right to me. I have always been the advocate, while your father has been the scholar, relentlessly pursuing justification of The Plan and all the consequences. A great deal of thought, debate and planning has gone into this, Maki. I fail to see how anyone could ask for more."

"As you say, individual decisions have been made. I will take more time to make mine. This conversation has been most helpful, Mother."

"Good, then let us eat something to begin the day properly." Tel put an arm around her son's shoulders, and walked him around the top terrace of the great cavern until they came to a fire burning brightly within a ring of stones, sitting down cross-legged before it. Others had begun emerging from their sleeping quarters, and a heavy odor of wood smoke was in the air. The fire burned quickly into a pile of glowing embers, into which Tel placed yams and powdered sage wrapped in green leaves. Heating stones brought tea to a boil in minutes, and they drank it in silence as life stirred around them.

At a neighboring fire, Baela and her parents cooked their morning meal quickly, the little darting one running to and fro getting sticks and water and various seasonings for her mother, blue eyes ever wide and alert, blonde hair forever falling over her face. Maki watched her with more than casual interest, noting the lengthening, coltish legs, and budding breasts she made no efforts to hide. He caught her eye twice, but she turned away, embarrassed. Her father, Moog, noticed this the second time it happened, fixing an eye on Maki until the younger man returned his gaze to the fire, thinking, *not for you, this little one, not even for a Keeper's son, but for a tall, Hinchai male to make Hinchai babies when her time has come.* He looked again, but now Baela's mother Deda was also watching him. He shrugged his shoulders, and smiled feebly. *No matter. When the time comes, I will be sure both of you are dead, and your daughter will bear the children of Tenanken warriors.*

Tel quizzed him about his friends he knew she disliked so intensely. He explained that Dorald had been smitten by a female in Hidaig's group, and was probably even now in her arms, while Han had decided he would seek a mate among those living near the point where the sun disappeared each evening. He had returned with Maki only to obtain his few personal possessions, and would leave within a day. Maki could see this news pleased his mother, for she had long despised his companions for their unkempt appearances, low intelligence and poor manners, and would now be rid of them forever.

When her meal was finished, Baela raced from the cavern for another day in the sun. Tel smiled as the lithe figure darted past her, shaking her head in mock exasperation at Moog and Deda, who simply smiled back. But Maki was suddenly struck with a disquieting feeling urging him to move. He excused himself, making his way across the cavern and up the exit tunnel to the small grotto which was his sleeping area. Han's traveling roll lay by the exit, neatly tied, but he was not there. Still feeling uneasy, Maki crawled into the grotto and checked his own belongings: skins and furs for a bed, all neatly in place, the pointing weapon rolled up in a skin to one side of the bed, the hand weapon in a bundle beneath it. All seemed undisturbed, and the feeling left him as quickly as it had come. But he had sensed something, a thought or feeling, something dangerous. From whom?

At that instant he heard the crackle of branches as someone pushed their way through the entrance, and he scrambled quickly from his quarters to find Han tying his traveling bundle at his waist. "Ah, it's you. Did you see anyone outside?"

"Only Baela, up that way, climbing on the rocks. Nobody else, but mostly I was getting water in the lower grotto. Why?"

"No reason," said Maki quickly. "Are you ready to go?"

"Yes. I've enough food here for three days."

"I'll deliver more to you. Be sure to stay out of sight, but keep on constant watch for Hidaig. They will travel by night. As soon as they arrive, come to me here in the grotto, but only then. Understand?"

Han nodded vigorously. "I'll come at night, and call you from outside."

Maki grasped him by both shoulders, holding him at arm's length. "We are brothers. Go, now."

102

When Han had left, Maki went back to the grotto, changing the position of his bed so he could lie facing the entrance with ears to hear the slightest sound. He found a few pebbles, and was sprinkling them in a pattern on the floor, a pattern that could be disturbed by an unknown intruder, and then the uneasy feeling was on him again like an invisible hand, speeding his heart so he grunted in surprise, standing up and banging his head against the low ceiling. As pain spread over his scalp, the clutching sensation inside him was gone again, leaving him troubled. He sat down and breathed deeply, willing the pain away, and trying to think. Never before had he experienced such symptoms, yet there was something familiar about them in a subtle way, something close to his everyday life, the power of it misleading him to think—

It was there again, only now there was no disquiet because he had discovered an intention, and with effort he forced into his mind the image of first the tunnel beyond the great cavern, and himself climbing the sloping floor, torchlight showing the way, then the sight of the valley in full daylight as if he were sitting on an outside ledge. Beads of sweat burst forth on his forehead with the effort, but then he felt release, and scrambled from the grotto to a wide fumarole across the tunnel, sloping upwards, from which he could see his sleeping area. He crouched there and waited, ready to spring, ready to kill, holding an image of the valley firmly but easily in his mind.

Waiting seemed eternal. He had hoped for something to happen quickly, but there was not even a sound save distant laughter and shouting from the great cavern. His legs became cramped, and he shifted his weight. Twice he thought he felt something, but both times it was gone quickly, leaving him feeling frustrated and a bit silly curled up in his tiny hideaway. All feeling has ceased to exist in his legs, and he was about to shift his weight again when he heard a twig snap, then branches moving against each other as the entrance opened, and a narrow beam of sunlight fell on his sleeping place. A shadow moved in and out of the light, and then the entrance was again closed.

Maki kept his vision firm, and stifled a cry of surprise.

It was Baela.

She moved towards the grotto hunched over, eyes wide with excitement. Her bare feet made no sound on the rock as she pirouetted on one foot to glance down the tunnel and back again, then she was down on hands and knees, scrambling into his sleeping quarters and somehow avoiding the pattern of pebbles he had placed there. Carefully, and silently, she searched his bedding, finding both weapons and then rewrapping them, leaving nothing apparently disturbed. He waited for her to take something, and felt disappointed when she did not, but the invasion of his privacy and discovery of the weapons was enough to kindle a dangerous anger in him, and so when he moved it was like a mountain cat striking for the kill, and she only had time to turn her head slightly before he was on her, one hand clamping down tightly over her mouth, the other pulling her arm far up behind her back and driving her face-first into his bedding.

"What brings you to my bed, little one?" he growled into her ear. She made a muffled groan, and breath exploded from her nostrils, but otherwise there was no motion beneath his heavy weight, no panicky thrashing about, and so he held her down with a knee while reaching for a small, hide bag ordinarily used for carrying dried meat. When his hand came off her mouth he heard a sharp intake of breath as she prepared to scream, then crammed the hide in as hard as he could and tied it in place with a leather thong crushing her golden hair to the back of her head. With another thong he tied her hands together at the small of her back, then flipped her over and straddled her feather-light body as she looked straight up into his eyes, drowning him in their blueness, and his groin was instantly aching from the hardness of an erection. He spread her legs, pressing against her, but there was no reaction; the blue eyes looked steadily into his without sign of fear or panic.

"Little darting one, they call you, now you don't move so fast. Have you been introduced to adult pleasures yet? No? Perhaps you aren't yet old enough to bleed, but no matter to me. Shall I initiate you, then slit your throat so you won't get into other's possessions anymore? Hmmm?"

He pressed harder, feeling her little mound, and for an instant imagining her rising to meet him, but then she shook her head slightly from side to side, still without fear, and something inside him opened up, releasing the anger, calming him. Sudden realization came that as future Keeper of The Memories, what he was doing was a pardonable but undignified act with a female barely beyond childhood, yet she was of Hanken purity, and weren't they all to die? Perhaps, but not just yet, and besides, some selectivity might be wise. She was intelligent, resourceful and attractive to him, despite her age and heritage, otherwise why would he be straddling her with his organ hard as a spear, and her throat still intact? She would grow up remembering the mercy of her elder, and giver of The Visions. Maki. Her master.

The flint blade jumped into his hand, and Baela's eyes widened in horror as he pressed it against her throat. He felt fear, now, and leaned over so that their faces were only inches apart. "I will make an agreement with you," he whispered. "If you do not scream, I will not hurt you, but otherwise your blood is on my hands, and your parents will die immediately after you. Do you understand this?"

Baela nodded, and made a muffled sound in response.

Maki probed at her mind, and saw nothing. How strange, he thought. Nothing at all.

"No sound, now, as I pull this from your mouth." He pulled the gag down over her chin so it covered her throat. Baela took a deep breath, her eyes never leaving his. His face was still close, organ still hard and erect, but her body was motionless.

"When I look into your mind, I see nothing. Why is that, little one? How is it that you block my entrance so, when I can enter you in other ways?" He pressed against her again, and she looked confused.

"Remember, I said I won't hurt you. But what were you doing in my things? You know I sleep here, you know all my belongings are here. Are you a thief? Must I disgrace your parents over your deed?"

"No, please, don't tell my parents about this! They won't let me leave the caves again if you do. Please!" Baela's voice was a whisper, pleading with him, softening his heart.

"But what you've done is wrong. And how is it you know of my trick with the pebbles? When you entered here you disturbed not one of them. Can it be Baela has abilities we're not aware of, abilities not expected in a Hanken?" Maki thought of the earlier, disquieting feelings, and the pounding of his heart. "Can Baela be some new creature in our midst?"

Baela shook her head back and forth, and a little tear welled up in one eye before trickling down her face. "Please don't tell my parents; I can't stand staying inside all the time. You get to go outside, and make long journeys over days and days. I want to do that, too, but they won't let me. They say I'm too young; well, I'm not! You go out and return with things you've found and, well, I want to see and touch them, but I know you won't like it, so—I look when you're not around. I never hurt anything, and I'm *not* a thief! *Please* don't tell anyone!" Now the tears flowed freely, and she was sobbing and lying there helpless, hands still tied behind her.

Maki felt merciful. And he suddenly felt badly about dominating the diminutive Hanken female beneath him. Despite her miserable heritage, something about her touched him deeply, and not just in a sexual way, although that was also present. She had spirit, and a sense of adventure, most unusual in a female. He sat up straight, hands on hips, looking down at her with great seriousness.

"Do you see your error, then, Baela?"

"Oh yes. Please let me up. I *promise* not to do it again, but maybe sometimes you can show me the things you find outside, and when I get older I can carry, and cook for the warriors like you who dare to explore the Hinchai lands."

"They are not Hinchai lands for long," said Maki softly, then quickly, "I'll let you up, now, but what happened here and what you've seen here is between us. If you tell anyone, I will denounce you as a thief, and your parents will be disgraced. You can imagine what they will do to you after that." He pulled her up into a sitting position, and loosened her hands with two sharp tugs on the thong. She rubbed her wrists, nodding her head in agreement with him.

"I won't say anything at all, but someday—someday—can I travel with you, far away from here?"

What power she had over his heart; he marveled at the compassion he suddenly felt, both the physical and emotional attraction for her, yet when he probed at her mind he felt only a little fear, and perhaps excitement. At being close to him? "We will see," he said, and she smiled sweetly at him.

She scrambled out of his sleeping quarters, and went straight to the cave entrance, turning with a smile. "It is still light, and I've found the nest of a hunting bird with new babies in it. They like me." She pushed aside the branches at the entrance, and disappeared in the blink of an eye.

Maki returned to the main cavern for a day of conversation, eating, and dozing in the company of his father and mother. Later in the day, his light sleep was disturbed by the sudden vision of a giant hunting bird soaring high in the sky, then descending on him with outstretched, bloody talons striking at his eyes.

* * * * * * *

Hidaig's journey to the west consumed eight days for the round trip, and was less than successful. Meandre was even more hostile than expected, giving them an exceptionally brief audience for a Keeper, and asking that all warriors be billeted in the forest surrounding the small cluster of caves occupied by his band.

The old Tenanken still spoke with bitterness about the break between Hidaig and Anka, without sympathy for Hidaig's desire to be a warrior-captain, babbling constantly about Anka's spirituality and compassion until Hidaig feared he would lose his own control and crush skulls. A few warriors were recruited for his efforts, but for the most part they were near-outcasts who had been found undesirable by the females of the band, primitive minds stimulated only by food, bloodletting and sexual pleasures. But they were adequate for his purposes, and they had weapons of their own.

One recruit stood out from the others: quiet intelligence, quick to understand and follow orders, curious about strategy for the coming battle, and constantly alert. Hidaig was immediately suspicious, and watched him constantly. Twice he followed this recruit late at night when the man quietly drifted away from camp to sit by a tree, watching a game trail for no obvious reason, then returning to camp without incident. But on the third night of the march, the recruit made rendezvous with a runner from Meandre, passing on accurate information on force size and attack time, Hidaig himself sitting only a few meters away listening to the entire conversation. When the recruit returned to camp, Hidaig followed the runner towards Anka's caverns for an hour before leaping at him from the darkness, slitting his throat with a flint blade, then disemboweling him in the middle of the trail his band would travel on the following day.

Hidaig prided himself on a sense of the dramatic. The following day he asked Meandre's young spy to join him on point, walking a hundred paces ahead of the others. He enjoyed the sudden gasp as the young one saw the intestines of his runner strung in long loops over the trail ahead, the doomed look when he saw what was in Hidaig's eyes, and the pitiful cry of despair as he fled down the trail, feet splashing in human goo until Hidaig's heavy spear pierced his spine so that he thumped heavily to the ground to shiver a moment before dying. Hidaig ordered the bodies cut into several pieces and buried in shallow graves accessible to the scavengers who would remove all evidence of death within a few days, and then they hurried on to where a few old females waited with eagerness for the attentions of new warrior males.

For two weeks they ate and drank and screwed, and then, forty-strong, they marched to a rendezvous with Han, who awaited them at a rocky prominence within sight of Baela's hiding tree.

She had watched Han set up camp his first day there.

CHAPTER THIRTEEN

SEARCH

It was dawn when the tracking began. Ed's two bloodhounds had gone all over the wagon before dragging him to where the men waited by the rocks. The dogs went frantic when they smelled blood and whatever else was spilled in the grass, and then they took off in a straight line up the hill, pulling Ed behind them in a stumble. Pete had already started up the hill because he had seen the faint gouges of the travois, saying nothing. The dogs raced by him, Ed grinning wildly, but Pete's mind raced in a different way, and he felt despair at what he was certain they would find at the end of the chase. He had seen a skull crushed before, during a fight in the caves, and whether Tenanken or Hinchai the stuff that splattered out from the blows was all the same. Maki was involved. The townspeople would seek revenge, and the time for bringing out the children and young adults would have to be soon.

Jake moved up beside him, bleary-eyed, a rifle slung over one shoulder. Several of the men had gone back for weapons, and the group was now heavily armed. "Don't like it at all, Pete," said Jake. "Normal man can't carry someone the size of Tom up this hill, even two men. It's the critters again, Pete. They've killed Tom, and carried him away to hide. Must not have known his wagon was there."

"That's pretty speculative, Jake."

Jake spat on the ground, and looked straight into Pete's eyes. "No it ain't, and you don't think so either. All the time you spent with old Savas Parkos in that cabin of his, and you never heard or seen nothin'? Come on, Pete, there's some weird folks living in these mountains, and you don't want to admit it."

"Right now, I just want to find Tom."

"Yeah—so do I."

They puffed up the hill, leading the others into the trees, the hounds baying ahead of them. "They're headed back towards town," said Jake. "Stupid—or very smart. All I want is another shot at 'em."

Not likely, thought Pete. With a travois, a Tenanken could run uphill and not be out of breath, and the grass was already straightening where the travois had passed. They were probably a day behind them, and Pete knew where they would likely be now, for above them the trees would soon disappear, giving way to gentle, grassy slopes with outcroppings of granite leading to the canyon which was the home of the Tenanken. What if there was a battle? Could he watch his own band destroyed, especially the children he had worked so closely with? The sense of desperation was there again; he wanted to run ahead and warn them. Run away—run away! The Hinchai are coming to destroy you! Baela, save yourself! Strange, how he thought of the blonde girl at this moment, and then of Bernie, with her long, blonde hair. Would his child be like Baela — or a brute with heavy brow ridges, and no chin. The thought chilled him to the bone.

Up ahead, the hounds were howling long and loud. "Got something," said Jake, and he unslung his rifle. Several others did the same, and there was the sound of a couple of lever actions working.

"All right, sling 'em up!" shouted Ned. "We don't need anyone shootin' themselves in the foot, or blowing away a neighbor. Now sling 'em!"

The men obeyed reluctantly, for the sound of the hounds' baying had filled them all with excitement. They charged ahead through the trees until they reached grass again. Above and ahead of them, Ed was playing the two dogs around a rock outcropping, struggling to hold them when they suddenly became hysterical, howling and snarling, charging into each other.

"Zeke—Mordicai—what the hell's got into you! Stop it. Stop it, now." Ed jerked back hard on the two leashes, trying to separate the animals. "Found somethin', boys. Dogs're goin' nuts!"

Everyone ran up the slope, stumbling over small rocks freshly eroded from the soil, and as they drew near it was only Pete who could smell the fresh stench of death. As the men pressed in close around the frantic dogs, Pete detached himself from them, following a new scent, walking off to the right and further up the hill where there was another rock outcropping. There he could smell new blood—fur—hides—the Tenanken sweat frozen in death. His mind raced. Before him was a pile of rocks most carefully placed to hide a Tenanken secret, oriented with the sun path so a spirit could soar. At dawn. Had it forgotten anything? Would it return? Pete stepped up to the rocks, unzipped his pants, and warm water splattered over the rough granite. Who lay beneath his stream?

Ned called up the hill. "Jesus Christ, Pete, this is no time to take a piss. I think we've found Tom!"

"Coming!" yelled Pete. He zipped up his pants and trudged down the hill to join the others. The dogs were still growling, and snapping at each other, but then Ed lashed out with a boot at both of them until they separated and cowed. He gave one leash to Lyle, and they pulled the dogs away from the pile of rocks, keeping them apart while the rest of the men went to work.

"I don't think I'm gonna like this," said Ned. He removed a rock from the pile, another, then another, Pete joining in, a couple more rocks as the first, putrid odors reached their nostrils. Grim faces looked on as they slowly, carefully uncovered the mutilated body of Tom Henley, sheriff of Crosley, and friend of everyone.

"Aw, Tom," said Ned softly, tears coming to his eyes.

"God damn, what did they do to his head?" asked Jake, turning to look at Pete, but the big man was standing there with his eyes closed tightly, as if what was in front of him might go away if he didn't open them. Tom was there, all right, crammed into a shallow grave on his side, the destroyed half of his head gaping open to the sky, cavity glistening grey and red, and attracting flies buzzing angrily over possession of a morsel here and there. The left front of his shirt was soaked in blood now dried to a black crust, but his badge was untouched, and the wedding band he still wore seven years after Emma's death was in place. His pistol belt was gone.

"He's been shot, too—right up there in the chest," said Jake, pointing.

"Yeah, but I'll bet money it's the head wound that killed him. Jeezus, why am I still looking at this?" Ned turned away, and Pete was there, his eyes downcast, hands stuffed deep into his pockets. Ned took a couple of steps, and put a hand heavily on Pete's shoulder, feeling it tremble. "He was a good man."

"Nobody left," said Pete, his voice far away and quivery. "No wife, no kids, no relatives—dyin' alone—he was a better man than that. He deserved better'n that, Ned."

"Yeah," said Ned, and they leaned on each other for a moment.

"Well, what are we gonna do about it? Sit around and mope, or go out and find the murdering bastards?" Jake's voice was angry, and there were supportive mutterings from the group. "This is it, Ned. We've got to take some action, and I mean clean out these hills once and for all. They've got to be around here close, and that means practically in town. Hell, if you walk up there a few yards you can look right down the canyon and see Pete's place. They may be livin' at your back door, Pete! I say we fan out and scour this whole area clear down to the valley, and on the other side. They've gotta have a shelter, dugout or cave somewhere, otherwise how'd they get through the winter here? Let's do it now, Ned! Now, before they get away for good."

"Hold on, now; first thing we have to do is get Tom out of here, and back to town."

"Only need one man for that," said Ed. "I've gotta get the dogs to home anyway, and I can be back here in a couple of hours with a horse. Dogs need calmin' down before we go on.

"You'll need help loadin' and unloadin'."

"I'll stay here and help," said Lyle. "The rest of you go on."

Ed started to move, but then the dogs were suddenly wild again, baying, and clawing at the ground, pulling him up the hill. "Aw, shit, I've got to get these guys home; they're just too riled up." He jerked back on the leash as the animals dragged him to another pile of rocks, scrabbling frantically against it.

Ned spat on the ground. "Have fun, Ed. Pete just took a giant piss on those rocks."

"I saw, I saw—oh, come *on*!" Ed jerked hard, and one of the dogs yelped in pain. He dragged them both whimpering down the hill. "Sometimes male dogs can get really disgusting," he growled. "Be back in a couple of hours." After a few steps, the dogs seemed to calm down, and trotted obediently ahead of him.

"Okay, we'll split up into two groups, and follow both rims of the canyon down to Pete's place. We can fan out in a line when we get down there. You got any horses, Pete?"

"Sorry, Ned. Stock won't arrive for another week or so."

"So we'll do it on foot. Any objections?"

There weren't any. Rifles were unslung, levers clacking as cartridges were chambered. Lyle offered his rifle to Pete. "Here, I won't need this on the way back."

"No thanks. I meet up with one of those guys I only need my hands, and besides, the law oughta be handling this."

"You got it wrong, Pete. With Tom gone, I'm the law, as mayor of this town," said Ned, "and I'm making this a legal, official search with all of you as deputies. The guys we're after are armed, and they're murderers. Now take the rifle, Pete."

"Yeah, Pete," said someone. "You can use your hands *after* you shoot 'em."

Pete took the rifle, and pulling out the sling to its maximum length, he draped it across his huge back like a kid's toy.

They broke up into two groups, Pete going with Ned and four others along the east side of the canyon, the rest searching thick stands of trees along the west side. As they stepped up to the edge of the canyon headwall, Pete turned inwards, directing his mind like a great bird to shriek warning, and suddenly there came to him a vision of just such a bird soaring into blue sky; he looked up to see it was not a vision, but real. An eagle was circling the canyon far above them, then falling like a released stone to land on a projection on the shear side of a cliff where Pete's experienced eyes caught movement. Baela was there—watching them. Projecting as hard as he could, he warned her to get inside or otherwise hide herself. In response he felt nothing, but then the eagle took off again, flying on a line straight towards them, giant wings pumping air, talons up but head down, turning to watch them warily as it passed close overhead. All the men twisted and turned to follow the flight of the bird, for it was not common to see an eagle so close as this, an awesome sight which to a man was the symbol of the very freedom each sought in the mountains. Even Pete was captivated by the sight for an instant, but he turned his head in time to see what appeared at a distance as a bush moving to join another along the shear rock face of the canyon. She was inside.

"That sure is a purty sight," said Jake. "I remember one time a smart-ass kid from Reno came up here and shot one of those. His mommy gave him a rifle, but never taught him nuthin'. Whatever, he rode home the same day with a busted face and a broken rifle. Can't recall who did that to him, but whoever killed Tom is gonna get a lot worse."

"No shootin' unless I give the order," said Ned. "And that's only in self-defense. Everyone clear on that?"

There were a few assenting grumbles, but for the most part the men were stoically silent, and Pete knew that anything suddenly moving on this day would stand a good chance of dying.

The two groups went off in opposite directions, but soon were on parallel courses along the canyon rims, the men occasionally shouting to each other. So preoccupied was Pete with Baela's safety and the progress of the men who even now approached the thick, stone dome of the Tenanken caverns that he didn't feel the wave of surprise and fear coming from Han.

Just returning from a hunt, Han had nearly walked into the entire Hinchai party before scuttling to his rocky cairn on the hill overlooking the grisly death scene they had just uncovered. He slammed the slab door shut on the apparently random pile of rocks built like a beaver lodge, and sat shivering in the darkness until nightfall.

"See anything?"

"Nothing. Not even a dog turd. This brush is so thick in here you can't see your feet. Hey, do you guys smell wood smoke?"

"No!"

"Keep smellin' it over here. Comes and goes."

"Well, look for an old campfire, or somethin'"

"Look at that mess in the canyon. Goddamned rattlesnake den! Oughta pour kerosene in there, and burn it out."

"There's the wood smoke again! It's getting strong! Way the wind swirls around here, can't tell where it's comin' from."

Pete felt his heart skip a beat. The men on the opposite side of the canyon were moving just below the rotten, granite outcropping providing the lacy network of fine fumaroles from the main cavern ceiling to the outside air. *Someone is still burning a fire in there!* But when he looked down the canyon towards his ranch house, and saw white smoke pouring out of the chimney, the explanation seemed so perfect he smiled naturally. "Oh hell, Ned, they're smellin' wood smoke from my fireplace. Look down there."

Ned looked. "Sure enough. Smoke's blowin' up here from Pete's place! See anything else?"

"Naw!"

"Nothin' over here, either!" They were looking directly at the entrance to the caverns, but all they saw was a thick, scraggly bush growing out of solid rock. Ned kept walking, Pete nearly running into his back in eagerness to keep them all moving. *Is anyone watching us, now?*

And you, Pete-Pegre. Does clothing make you Hinchai? If someone runs from the cave, will you shoot them down like a lesser animal and enhance your status in town, or will you defend those who gave you life, and crush a Hinchai skull?

The thoughts were gone in an instant, leaving his face flushed and sweaty, but nobody noticed because they were now cursing their way through thick underbrush, and black clouds of biting flies swarming about their heads to attack bare necks and earlobes.

They veered away from the canyon to get clear of the brush, and found themselves on a short, steep ridge leading to the valley floor. They looked at Pete's ranch, and thought about cold water or warm beer. A half-hour later that's what they got, plus thick slabs of fresh-baked bread, when they dragged themselves up to the front porch where Bernie was standing, big hands on big hips, a smile on her face as always. Pete was so glad to see her he nearly crushed her in an embrace.

They rested an hour, then crossed the valley and searched the forests for two miles around, finding nothing, returning frustrated, discouraged and angry. The search went on for three more days, and at the time, of course, there was no way any of them could have predicted how, when, or where it would end. Such ignorance allowed the men to sleep well that night, except for Pete, who tossed and turned, subconscious mind struggling to obtain identity. *Hinchai? Or Tenanken? What are you?*

* * * * * * *

From the comfortable saddle in the bough of her hidey-tree she had heard their faint shouts all morning while she watched Han wander through the woods in search of something to supplement his dried-meat diet. She had made herself a yoke of tree branches which fitted to her shoulders so that, when she knelt, Baela became a small bush, or when standing she could turn and blend in totally with a shrub or small tree. The camouflage was imperfect, she knew, but so was Han's vision and mind, and the Hinchai were comically inept at seeing anything in the forest.

She'd been surprised the first morning she saw Han, for the rumor was he'd left the band forever to make a new home far beyond the hills, yet here he was, a few minutes walk from the caverns. So Maki had lied about this also. Once again, she was reminded to distrust the young Tenanken warrior who seemed destined to become the Keeper of The Memories for no good reason she could see except that his father was Anka, by far the wisest Tenanken she'd ever known. But Han was Maki's watchdog, and what was he waiting for? Each morning he appeared at the hilltop across the canyon, still draped in sleeping skins. During the day he scrounged for eating plants, and once took some small animal with his sling. In the evenings he disappeared over the hill again, not to be seen until the following morning.

Today was different. The voices came from the plateau at the end of the canyon, and as Han returned from his hunt Baela watched him stop and cock his head to one side, listening, then stalking. He passed from her view, and suddenly was there again, hurrying this time, backtracking, scrambling up and over the top of the hill, as if being chased. She was still watching the hilltop when other figures appeared in her peripheral vision: clothed Hinchai with pointing weapons, angry faces, shouting to others on her side of the canyon. *Run! Hide anywhere!*

114

The thought rocked her in the tree, and she jumped up like a bird taking flight, scrambling to the ground with the tree between herself and the Hinchai on the far side of the canyon. She bent over double, and a small bush scuttled across the grass to canyon's edge, lodging in a crack by the nest of the great bird of prey who even now circled her young, far above, casting a wary eye on those below. The bird dropped towards her, and she flinched backwards from the nest. *Great danger, but it is there—there, with the Hinchai and their weapons. I'll be seen here.* The bird's talons touched the nest, and pushed off again, the bird shrieking, flying directly towards the Hinchai. *Now! They watch the bird!*

Baela scrambled down the rock face, bare feet searching for tiny ledges and rough flakes, tiny hands jamming into cracks until she felt the wide shelf beneath her, and was nearly running along it, bent double, waiting for a shout or an explosion when they saw her. But once again, the Hinchai could not see; she reached the cave entrance, and pushed herself in among the tangle of branches and brush until a strong hand gripped her arm, pulling her roughly inside, and she found herself staring into Maki's amber eyes at close range.

"Always outside and on the watch, aren't you?"

"I was playing, and they surprised me."

"Who surprised you?"

"Hinchai. Two groups. One's on the other side of the canyon, and another is right above us."

Maki pushed her away from him. "Run and tell the others to put out their fires. There must be no smoke. Hurry!"

Baela leaped like a startled deer, racing down the tunnel to the main cavern and along the spiral of shelves past surprised females preparing to cook a meal, first coals glowing. "Cover your fires! Hinchai are right above us! They have weapons!"

There was a startled cry, and fires were stirred, coals dumped into rock containers and covered, and all looked up at smoke from the making of the fires, still hanging near the ceiling of the great room before diffusing out through the rocks above, and into the Hinchai world.

As Baela completed her circuit of the room in eerie silence, she felt and smelled their fear of the Hinchai, and suddenly it seemed absurd. *Here we are, ready to go out and live with the Hinchai, and we sit here cowering in fear of them, afraid they'll smell our fires and come in here to kill us.* Still, it was an adventure, and Baela loved the drama of it all. She raced from the cavern and back along the tunnel to where Maki still sat on his haunches, peering out through the branches covering the entrance. When he first looked at her, she saw death in his eyes, had a vision of dead and dying Tenanken everywhere in her head, but then he seemed to soften, and beckoned to her. She knelt beside him, and he parted the branches for her to see outside.

"See your so-called friend and teacher," Maki whispered softly.

She looked, and saw Hinchai males, with weapons, and walking with them was Pegre, his own weapon slung across his body.

"He pretends loyalty to us, but out there he is with his own kind. He has become Hinchai, and you would be wise not to listen to anything he says, Baela. He draws us out to live as slaves with the Hinchai, and failing to do that he will kill us all if we oppose him. How can you let this happen to you and your parents?"

Baela looked at him wide-eyed, a child filled with wonder yet somehow not a child, and why was it he could not penetrate her mind at this moment?

Then, *We don't have freedom living in caves. Better to be a slave in sunlight. Why do you hate and fear him so?*

"It will not be this way much longer, Baela, you'll see. We'll make our own place outside, but it will not be under Hinchai domination. My father is old, weak and misled. He'll see, too, but Pegre is another matter, and when the time comes I will have to deal with him personally!"

Maki looked at Baela for approval, forgetting her heritage for the moment, wanting to see a smile or a nod of the head to affirm he was right. Instead he saw large eyes, questioning, but not comprehending. Too young, yet again he was attracted to her there in the gloom at a time when the Hinchai were uncomfortably close.

Maki pondered this, distracted, while Baela sat before him, quietly looking into his eyes, and considering the different methods she might use to permanently disable his pointing weapons.

CHAPTER FOURTEEN

TENANKEN MARCH

Dew turned to sparkling frost in cold morning air, a hint of winter to come, fallen leaves floating in the breeze streaming down mountains into valleys and canyons below. Rustling sounds masked the thumping of bare feet as Hidaig's band, some forty strong, trotted through the forest at a warrior's pace covering six miles in an hour. Once, the early evening before, they had been seen crossing a road, shadow-like figures in a line in front of the wagon driven by Tadeusz Snykowski, returning as best he could to Quincy after a half-evening of serious drinking at the Athens Bar. His entire attention had been focused on the road, until movement ahead redirected his bleary gaze to a scraggly looking bunch of white men with long hair, rags for clothes, carrying spears and axes and falling all over themselves trying to get out of the way as he rattled around a sharp corner only a few miles out of town. He was by them in a flash, hearing a thud in the back of the wagon he would later connect with a huge slash made by something blunt and heavy, and swung with force.

Tadeusz had lived in the area long enough to know there were all kinds of wild folks living in the mountains, and the best way to keep living a simple life was to stay out of their way. He reported nothing to the sheriff in Quincy, went straight to his room in a home only a block from the River Bar and Grill, and collapsed into sleep.

Hidaig kept to the front of the band, setting the pace. His second-in-command, a huge warrior named Kretan, ran at the rear of the column with orders to kill stragglers, or anyone who tried to flee from the coming battle, and since there were no people to kill so far he was frustrated, and ready for war before their journey was even half-finished. The rest followed the back of their leader, lured by the promise of riches and lusty females and an adventure to be recorded forever in The Memories, for they were a poor band with a spiritually dead leader who loved only war, and yearned for the power it could provide.

In the afternoon, Hidaig entertained them with the killing of a Hinchai dog. The animal had followed them as they passed near a cabin, yapping at their heels until Hidaig suddenly turned, fitted a stone in his sling and let fly, hitting the dog in the hind-quarters. As the frightened dog tried to pull itself away with its front legs, whimpering pitifully, Hidaig jerked it up by the hind legs, for it was a small dog, shook it violently until both legs snapped, and his warriors were cheering the animal's screams of agony, then used his flint knife to slowly disembowel it. Death ending the entertainment, Hidaig tossed the body off the trail before the band trotted on.

But the dog's screams had been heard by one Ezra Pike, who lived with his brother Hugh in the nearby cabin. An out-of-work-miner, Ezra was hunting squirrel when he heard the screams, and came running to find the ripped-open carcass of what had once been a sort-of-pet to him. Whatever had killed the dog was pure mean, he decided, and not being a stupid man he carefully climbed a hill and peeked at the trail ahead rather than charging off after his quarry in anger. What he saw trotting along there convinced him that one rifle would not be enough firepower, and so he returned to his cabin and rode into town for help.

It was evening when Hidaig's force arrived at the rim of the canyon, looking down its length to the still sunlit valley where there were several buildings, smoke coming from the chimney of one of them. After a quick look, Hidaig ordered the warriors back from the rim, where it was possible they would be seen from the cavern entrance, not realizing that at that very moment Baela sat in her hidey-tree watching their every movement, and when Han came down the hillside to greet them she was already climbing down from the tree and racing away to tell Pegre what she had seen.

The warriors flopped on their backs in soft grass to rest from the foot-pounding day, while Hidaig took Han aside for a private talk, Kretan trailing behind within hearing distance.

"You're earlier than I expected," said Han. "I should tell Make you're here before it's dark."

"Time for that," said Hidaig, grinning. "Your master can wait for a little while, and there are things I want to discuss with you first. Let's sit."

Han frowned. "Maki is my friend, not my master." He sat down in the grass with Hidaig, while Kretan remained standing near them, leaning on his spear. "What do you want to talk about?"

"I need to find out what we'll be up against. How many able-bodied warriors in Anka's band?"

"Only a few, and all of them will be moving to the Hinchai settlement."

"Not if I can help it," said Hidaig. "You don't really want to see that happen, do you?"

"No, I don't. There will be nothing left but old ones who can barely care for themselves. All the younger Tenanken want to leave. Maki tried hard to talk them out of it, but still they've chosen to live among the Hinchai. It's Pegre who's at fault. He has much influence, and the Tenanken trust him."

"They don't trust Maki?"

"Not completely. His hatred for Pegre is well known, and he has spoken openly about being Keeper someday. Some feel he craves power so much it clouds his good judgment."

"And what about you? Do you think Maki should be Keeper in place of his father."

"Why do you ask? My opinion is not important, Hidaig. You and Maki agreed on a plan to take power, and drive out the Hinchai. My only part is to tell Maki you're here, and I should do that now."

"But I've had second thoughts."

"What?" Han noticed Kretan for the first time. The big warrior had moved closer, was standing near, watchfully.

"I'm not sure Maki is right. After all, Anka is the oldest and wisest elder in recent Memory. He has been both benevolent and democratic, yes? The Tenanken have chosen their way, and he allows it. Who am I, or Maki, to say he's wrong? Maki would even have me kill his father if he resists. Did you know that?"

Han shook his head solemnly. His whole body had grown tense as he sat rigidly at attention. "If you're not going to help Maki, then why are you here?"

"I didn't say I wouldn't help. I just have second thoughts about it. Perhaps it's best if I arbitrate an understanding between Anka and Maki so we can agree on a plan of action that keeps all Tenanken together. Together we are a force, but divided we are nothing. I see no unity in Maki's plan, so I have decided to confront him before his father and force an agreement that brings us all together. It must be a surprise, so I do not want you informing Maki of our presence here until we meet tomorrow. As commander in the field, I'm giving you a direct order. I assure you, Maki will understand."

Han fidgeted uneasily, looking first at Hidaig and then Kretan, who seemed to be watching only him. "Perhaps I can bring Maki here to talk with you."

"No. You stay here for the night, and we will meet him tomorrow." Hidaig's tone of voice was menacing.

Han hesitated, then said, "I don't understand your change of mind, but I will do what you say if you explain to Maki."

"Agreed," said Hidaig, smiling as Kretan picked up his spear and walked away from them. "I certainly don't want to get you into difficulty. Now help yourself to some food, and let's get to sleep." He put a big arm around Han's shoulders, and marched him back to join the others.

It was later that night when Han decided Hidaig intended to take all power for himself. The agreement with Maki had been firm, the plan clear, but Hidaig was the stronger of the two. He would establish a military rule that many in his own band had fled from, particularly the females and young warriors who wanted families. Han sometimes dreamed of a family, though the desirable females ignored him, and Anka's rule was gentle and fair. Hardly a rule at all. Maki must know the change in plans, for they were now against him. He had to warn Maki—now.

He had been lying on his back in the circle of sleeping warriors, looking at the sky lights twinkling above him. He arose silently, taking nothing with him, and crept beyond the circle, looking back several times until he was out of view behind the trees.

Back in the circle, Hidaig lifted himself up on one elbow as a tall shadow moved up to stand beside him. Hidaig looked up into the calm, loyal face of Kretan, spear at his side, awaiting an order.

"Kill him," said Hidaig.

Moments later, an agonized cry broke the stillness of the mountain night.

* * * * * * *

Her bare feet seemed to float above the rock as she raced ahead on the narrow shelf, adrenalin pumping in her veins. At first she had seen a forest of tall spears, and then the warriors. Han had come down from the hill to greet them, and Han was Maki's closest follower. So Maki really intended to take over from Anka. The enforcements were here to back up his claim, and there were few warriors to oppose them. She dared not warn Anka in Maki's presence and so she would flee to Pegre, whom she knew would take action quickly and decisively, as he always had in the past. She hoped he was in the house below her, now, smoke curling lazily from the chimney in twilight. She scrambled down the ridge and into the long grass, heading straight for the house without thought of being seen by anyone but Pegre, so that her heart pounded with fear when the door of the house suddenly burst open and a tall, blonde Hinchai female stepped outside. Baela kept her pace, legs driving as she saw Pegre emerge behind the female, pushing past and trotting towards her with a dark scowl on his face. As they neared each other, Baela shouted to Pegre in the language he had taught her well, "Armed Tenanken are near the cavern, talking to Han. Many warriors are ready to attack us. I came straight down!"

Pegre knelt before her, grabbing her shoulders, face close. "How many?"

She used her fingers to count. "Fifteen at least, maybe twenty. I don't think I saw all of them. They're by the canyon headwall, with spears, axes." Her breath came in gasps. Past Pegre's shoulder, she saw the blonde female rush up to them, and noted the distended stomach of one great with child.

"Peter, what is it? What's wrong?" Her voice was concerned yet soft, her face gentle. Baela felt an immediate liking for her—Pegre's mate. He would choose such a female to share his life.

"We have to get the others out before they attack. It's Hidaig's band, I'm sure of it. He's had ambitions against Anka for years, and now he works with Maki, the young fool." Pegre's teeth were clenched tightly as he spoke."

"Did I do the right thing coming here?"

"Peter," said the Hinchai, "she's speaking Greek! Is this one of your relatives? Are they here already?" Her face stretched into a broad smile, and she leaned over to look closely at Baela. "Oh Pete, she's so pretty, and she's *blonde*. I never knew Greeks could be blonde." She reached out to touch her hair, and Baela smiled shyly.

"This is little Baela," said Pegre suddenly in the other language he had taught her only a little of. "The others are coming from Quincy to Savas's place, and I've got to pick them up. Baela, this is Bernie, my wife."

Her mind whirled at first words to be spoken to a Hinchai. "'Allo," she said haltingly, in a high voice.

"Oh, she's *sweet*," said Bernie, and crushed her in an embrace. "But this is *terrible*. Did she *walk* here all the way from Savas's place? Pete, that's seven miles! She should come right inside and rest."

"Later," said Pegre, standing up and taking Baela by the hand. "I need Baela to help translate. My Greek isn't so good anymore, and their English is *really* poor. I'll take the wagon; a couple of trips oughta do it. God, I wasn't expecting them for another week or two." They were walking quickly through tall grass, Baela almost running to keep up.

"Oh, this is so *exciting*!" Bernie was almost skipping through the grass, grabbing Baela's other free hand, and squeezing it warmly. "But there's so much to *do*! Pete, they can stay in the one cabin we *do* have ready, and the rest can sleep downstairs for a week or so. I'll get the bedding over there right away. But what do I *cook*? They must be *starved*!"

"They've eaten, hon. Don't worry about it tonight. Hot soup, anything simple. Better they get some sleep." Pegre's mind boiled with emotion and dark thoughts.

Baela frowned.

They reached the wagon in front of the house, and Baela climbed in without hesitation. She watched Pegre kiss his mate firmly before climbing in beside her, and in an instant the wagon jerked forward while Baela watched everything with an excited grin. Bernie waved at them as they pulled away, and Baela waved back until her sight was obscured by a cloud of dust.

The wagon bounced and swayed as they climbed the first hill, Baela hanging on tightly. Pegre stared grimly at the road ahead, slapping hard at the two horses. "We'll go in a back way I used many years ago. It comes out near the tree you watch from, so we'll have to climb down in darkness. If Maki is asleep we can get everyone out quietly, and back to the wagon, but again we'll have to climb in the dark."

"There's only one bad spot," said Baela, "but I know a way around it, and the climb is short."

Pegre nodded without looking at her. "So you follow me up, and you lead us back. The older ones will have to stay behind this trip, but I don't think Hidaig will be interested in them. He wants warriors and women, and Tenanken treasure that isn't even there, and when he doesn't find it I'm not sure what he'll do. We'll have to be ready for a fight, even if we get everyone out. If something starts, you stay out of the way."

Baela started to protest, but then something careened around a sharp curve in the road, and they lurched to one side to stop as a spring wagon nearly collided with them. Headed back towards Pegre's dwelling. Baela's head snapped forward as they stopped, and she let out a grunt.

A hawk-faced man glared at them, long neck twisting to get a better look at Baela. "Sorry, Pete, didn't see you till just before the curve."

"Cuttin' it close, Jake. Damn near drove me off the road, and I'm in a big hurry." Pegre's hands gripped the reins so tightly his knuckles were white.

"I was comin' out to get you. The critters have been seen again a little south of town. Ez' Pike came in lookin' for Tom, sayin' they killed his dog. Just shows how often *he* gets to town. Anyway, Ez' says they had spears and axes, and raggedy, old clothes. Ten of 'em at least, and they're headed this direction, but south of town a few miles this mornin'. We're formin' a posse to bring 'em down before they kill someone else. Want to go along?"

"Can't, Jake. My relatives just came in, and I'm on my way to pick 'em up. Especially now, with trouble around. It's nearly dark."

Jake peeked at Baela again. "That one of 'em? Relatives, I mean."

"This is Baela," said Pegre, turning to whisper to her, "Jake is my neighbor."

Baela smiled shyly, cocking her head coyly to one side as Pete looked back at Jake, and thought, *My God, he actually smiled at her.*

"Little blonde," said Jake.

"Right."

"Didn't know there was such a thing as a blonde Greek."

Pete laughed. "We've been sailin' the seas a long time, Jake. Want to know if she has an older sister? She doesn't, but there're some other sisters I think you'll find interesting if you let me go pick them up."

"What about Bernie? She's alone, and those critters are runnin' around loose. If you want, I can watch out for her."

"Thanks, Jake, but she's not helpless. All Bernie needs is her eyes and ears, and that twelve-gauge. She can hear deer tip-toeing around at night, and now I've *really* gotta get out of here. Can't make the curve till you move your wagon. C'mon, Jake. Tell the men I'll try to catch up later, after I get my people settled in."

"Okay," said Jake. "I'll follow you down." He snapped his reins, and the wagon moved past them.

"Hope he doesn't follow us," said Pegre. "Sometimes I wonder how much he really knows." The wagon jerked forward, and they were bouncing and swaying again along the rough road, Jake close behind, gaining speed as they descended the hill. Baela stretched to watch the town coming up at them, a group of Hinchai clustered by one building, waving then yelling as they passed, and Jake stopped there. "Thank God he stopped," said Pegre. "Now we get the others." He slapped with the reins, and Baela squealed as the road rushed by them.

Pegre had changed, or perhaps this was a side of him she had never seen before. In class he was gentle and fun, quick to make a joke or do his little dance that made them fall down with laughter, and at times Baela felt closer to him than to her own father who kept to the silent, dignified, traditional manners of the Tenanken. But now her teacher brooded, heavy brow ridges prominent, mouth pressed into a thin line, eyes black and bottomless. It frightened her a little, this new Pegre, but at the same time she sensed a determination, a power, making her feel safe so that she found herself sitting close enough to lean on him, feeling a startled shudder when they touched.

Pegre gave her a quick glance. "Don't worry yet, Baela. They won't make a move until it's light, and we'll be gone by then. But it's important we get everyone we can *out*, because there won't be a second chance with Hidaig around. We have to destroy his force, Baela, and that means Tenanken can be hurt or killed. I don't want you to be one of them. Do you understand?"

"Yes," she said quietly, snuggling up a little closer, close enough to feel hard muscle and warmth.

"Promise me you'll do what I say, Baela. There won't be time for argument when things start happening."

"I will."

"Good. I'm hoping Maki will be asleep when we get there. You'll have to go in first, because I'll make too much noise. You can push the brush over from the inside to let me in before Maki can make a move. After that, we do what we have to, and get everyone out. Understand?"

Baela nodded, face grim.

Pegre pulled off the main road, and they swerved along two faint ruts in tall grass until they were engulfed by brush and scrub trees, crashing through dried stalks and hard limbs until a graded road appeared, leading up to a freshly painted, dark brown cabin. "This is where *my* teacher lived, when I was young and wanting to learn everything," said Pegre, and there was sadness in his voice. "We'll go on foot from here, but it's a short climb to your tree, and then down to the cave. Ready?"

Baela smiled at him, jumping out quickly when the wagon stopped. Pegre pulled a Hinchai hand weapon from behind the seat and strapped it on, noting the look of disapproval from the little girl. He walked over to the cabin door locked with a new lock, rattled the door, looked sheepishly at Baela and said, "Nothing of value in there, just a lot of old memories. Stay right behind me."

They walked past the privy into thick brush fringing a grove of young fir trees, a rocky base sloping upwards until they were grasping at exposed roots to anchor themselves when loose earth gave way beneath their feet. A few minutes later they reached a wall with a wide crack angling up to the left, forming a rough shelf they ascended easily some twenty meters to the top and a dense stand of trees and thick brush through which a trail had been broken. A few steps later, Baela was looking up in amazement at her own hidey-tree in which she had spent countless hours looking out over the canyon without ever exploring what lay beyond. They crouched by the tree, and Pegre took her elbow in his hand, whispering, "Now, you show me the easiest way to the cave. Remember, everyone will have to follow us back, so it can't be too difficult, even for us older ones."

Baela nodded, and moved out crouched down onto the flat near the cliff, looking for the nest of the great hunting bird, seeing it, and veering to the right towards a wide crack dropping down a meter to a series of descending slabs and the faintly visible shelf along the cliff face. Stepping out on the first slab, she had the usual stomach flutterings, and quickening of breath from the severe exposure to a seventy meter fall straight down to spear-like trees below. Pegre followed close behind, and she heard him grunt when a slab creaked under his heavy step, but in seconds they were on the shelf, watching their feet carefully as they picked their way to the hidden cave entrance in near darkness.

The brush blocking the cave entrance had been woven together to form a wedge-shaped plug most easily moved from inside by pushing. Baela stepped up to the plug, and stood there for a moment, listening, for Maki's bed was only two meters from the entrance, and he was often awake long after darkness. She heard and felt nothing, knelt down and pulled on the brush lightly, wincing when a twig snapped.

The plug gave a little, but moved no further.

It was tied in place from the inside.

Baela looked up at Pegre, shook her head, and he jabbed his fingers angrily in the direction of the cave.

She tried again, the plug snapping and crackling, moving just a little so that a black, rectangular hole opened up on one side. She listened again, for breathing—the scratch of a moving pebble. Nothing. Pegre was kneeling down now at her side. She felt his warm breath on her neck. She crawled forward into blackness, pushing the plug aside with a shoulder, widening the hole to accommodate her tiny frame. A faint gleam of torchlight lay ahead, and she kept her head up, looking for sudden movement or a shadow, or a hand clamping down on her. She swallowed hard and crawled silently through the hole, eyes sweeping the area.

Maki's bed was empty. Baela stopped holding her breath.

She crawled the rest of the way through, then turned and untied the two, braided-hair ropes someone had used to tie the plug in place. Perhaps it was Maki, preventing visitors from sneaking in so close to where he slept. Did he *know* there was a Tenanken force waiting nearby?

Baela pushed on the plug, moving it out an arm's length, and Pegre was on her immediately, crawling past her into Maki's small grotto with the pile of furs and tiny pool of green water. He gestured, and she pulled the plug back in place without tying it, then crawled over to where he was tearing apart Maki's bedding. He found the Hinchai hand weapon, and pushed it under his belt, then picked up the long pointing weapon and thrust it towards her, whispering softly as he pointed to the hole at one end. "Get small pebbles and dirt to make a paste with water, then push it all down this hole until the cavity is filled. Tamp it in hard with a stick, but *don't* touch any other part except this long piece. If you touch *any* other part, the weapon could explode."

Pegre's intensity frightened her, but she sensed a great responsibility connected with this simple task, and so it pleased her to do it. As he crawled out of the grotto to stand up, she was already scraping up a pile of dirt and small pebbles on the floor, and sprinkling water on it with her hands.

"I'll be back quickly, so be ready to leave."

Baela sprinkled harder, mushing the dirt into a thick paste as Pegre disappeared down the dark tunnel leading to the main cavern, leaving behind the nearly burned out torch above the cave entrance. She rolled the paste into little cylinders between her palms, and dropped them one by one into the barrel of the weapon until it was full, then rammed a small stick into the hole as hard as she could and repeated the process. When the stick would no longer penetrate into the hole, she wiped the weapon clean with her hands, and wrapped it in the long fur just as Maki had left it.

Someone was coming up the tunnel.

Baela pressed herself against the grotto wall. If it was Maki, he'd kill her for being here. She wanted to run.

"Where are you, Baela?" Whispered softly.

Pegre.

She peered out of the grotto. He was alone.

"Everyone's asleep, and Maki's with his father. We'll have to wake people quietly, and get them out before Maki awakes. Come on!"

Suddenly she was frightened. Veins at her temples throbbed, and she felt hot all over. She swallowed hard, then followed Pegre's broad back into darkness, reaching ahead of her to touch him until she saw glimmering, yellow light. A few more steps, and they were in the main cavern, weakly lit by a few remaining torches, Tenanken sleeping in clusters around the shelves. Pegre motioned her to stay where she was, then walked out onto the shelves, stopping at each sleeping form, kneeling, poking with one hand, and she felt the Mind Touch again, a vision of herself leading a line of Tenanken along the shelf towards the bird's nest and the trees. People stirred in their sleeping robes, looking first at Pegre and then at Baela, getting up silently and leaving everything behind except the Hinchai clothes they wore in sleep, forming a line to leave their home forever.

Baela turned to lead them from the cavern, and then she stopped, overwhelmed with sudden grief, looking to one side to see Tel standing at a fumarole entrance, looking down on the line of shuffling Tenanken, her eyes dark and sad, but without tears. All felt the wave of love and hurt that came from her, bowing their heads as Pegre rose after awakening one last figure, and looked at his adopted mother with the calm and quiet dignity that reminded Baela he was truly a Tenanken in blood and spirit. No words were exchanged in the tense quiet of the cavern, and then Tel extended both arms towards Pegre, raising them enough so he could see her face. He responded with one arm, and in that instant all felt a surge of energy, an urgency to leave quickly and do what needed to be done. Tel turned stiffly on one heel, and disappeared into the darkness of the fumarole as Baela motioned to the others to follow her out of the cavern.

They left without sound; even two babies strapped securely to their mothers' chests did not cry out. Baela had seen her own parents with Pegre at the end of the line, helping the slower ones. Her grandmother had chosen to remain behind with old friends who could not be moved. She pulled the plug from the entrance, pushing it to one side, then gesturing to everyone to join hands for the precarious walk along the shelf. Most of her flock had been outside only a few times, and she heard the gasps when they first saw the drop off from the narrow shelf ahead. She led them across in a shuffle step, stopping only once when there was a muffled cry and sudden tension in the chain of hands and arms. A young male had stumbled off the trail, dangling in space for one heart-stopping instant before being jerked roughly back onto his feet. But they arrived intact at the slabs angling upwards to the crack, where Baela stood aside to get each one started properly for the short climb upwards. As they came, she counted their number. Including Pegre, three hands and two more fingers. So few? Had so many stayed behind, those who were old or sick? Of course others would join them later, but it was dangerous to stay here now. She whispered to each person to wait by the big tree ahead, and suddenly found herself saying it to her own mother, very adult and serious, while her mother smiled back and patted her on the cheek. Pegre was behind, wrapping an arm around her warmly and pushing her up ahead of him, grunting because the crack was barely wide enough to accommodate his girth.

On top, they found the others huddled under Baela's hidey-tree, looking cold and frightened. It was a clear night, and although the moon had not yet risen, the sky seemed to cast a dim illumination that helped them find the way. The path downhill was easier to see, but they moved closely together in a line, Baela at the end and Pegre in front. As they went over the crest of the hill, Baela glanced back at the bird's nest, wondering if she would ever see the little ones again, imagining herself standing in the tall grass of the valley, watching the mother bird soaring in higher and higher circles until she was a dot in the sky. When Baela came back to her senses, they had reached the bottom of the hill, stopped to rest, and some of the others were looking at her strangely. Pegre came over, and put a hand on her shoulder.

"Ah, the little bird has returned to earth."

Of course, she thought, *he has looked into my mind again, even though he knows I do not like it.* She frowned, and pushed past him to stand next to her mother and father, pouting.

Pegre looked perplexed. "I've offended you with a compliment, but there's no time for anger now. I need your help in translating to the others what they need to do. Please?" He held out a hand.

Baela felt a nudge from her mother, then a harder one from her father, and Pegre had that smile again that made it difficult for anyone to remain angry with him. And so she stepped forward and took his hand, and helped translate his instructions to the older Tenanken who had greatest difficulty with the Hinchai language. But when he was finished, and the line of refugees was again on the move, she pulled on his hand so that he looked down at her, and she said very seriously, "I told you before I don't like it when anyone goes into my head. My visions and thoughts are my own."

"Ah," said Pegre, "now it is clear. But I did not violate your privacy, Baela, nor did anyone else. Here is a question for you to think about while we walk; if you wished your vision of the great bird to be a private one, then why did you share it with us?"

Pegre walked away quickly, leaving her with a puzzled expression on her face. Finally she followed the group at a distance, and hurried until she was at the end of the line. The question made no sense. Share? Never. As a well-disciplined girl-child she had worked hard to remain totally private, as expected of her, keeping all thoughts and dreams and other spiritual things to herself. Sharing was for the true Tahehto who possessed The Mind Touch, not a Hanken like herself, and she felt privileged they would share anything with her. She did not feel inferior, but recognized there were differences between Hanken and Tahehto purities that could not be changed. Her mother and father had taught her this, and she accepted it without resentment or self-pity, though at times, when she was happy about something like a baby animal or a flower or the sweet smells outside she wanted to scream it to the world, but could not find the words. So how could Pegre accuse her of sharing a vision of the hunting bird?

Baela thought about the question until they reached Savas's cabin, coming to a conclusion that could only be impossible— because she was a Hanken child.

Pegre loaded them into the back of the wagon until it was full, everyone crouched tightly together. "I'll have to make two trips. The rest of you will stay inside the cabin until I return. I'll lock you in so everything looks normal. If anyone comes by, stay up against the front wall so they can't see you, and don't make a sound."

Baela translated, although she could see that some had already understood. Pegre unlocked the shiny, new lock on the door of the cabin. He opened the door, and inside was inky blackness, like the cave. For the Tenanken, total darkness was an old experience, and they had no fear of it. Pegre motioned Baela, her parents and two others to enter the cabin. Inside, they sat down on the wooden floor and the door closed behind them, the lock snapping shut an instant later. Baela went to a window and looked outside. Pegre saw her face at the window, smiled, and waved to her, then climbed into the wagon. She laughed at the gasps of surprise inside the cabin, the way the passengers in the wagon suddenly grasped each other in fear, and she wondered if they would enjoy the ride as much as she had the first time.

The wagon pulled away quickly and was soon lost from view, leaving them quiet in the darkness. Baela continued to stand by the mica window, watching the dark shadows and silhouettes outside. A few minutes later, something appeared in her peripheral vision. She jerked her head towards it, and saw nothing, then it was there again, flickering on and off. She watched it steadily as it wound its way down the hill through thick stands of trees, a string of small, dim lights—heading straight for the cabin.

CHAPTER FIFTEEN

NIGHT VISITORS

Pete didn't see the ribbon of lights moving along a hill to the south of Savas's cabin. When he looked back all he saw were frightened faces as the wagon bounced and swerved through high grass on the way back to the main road. Once the ride was smoother his passengers seemed to calm down, relaxing enough to smile at the feel of wind whipping their hair. Quite soon it was an adventure, and there were grins. *How quickly they adapt*, he thought. The intelligence was there; it had always been there. How long since the Tenanken had isolated themselves from their brethren? A thousand years? Ten thousand? Sixty? Even The Memories were vague, distant visions beyond the time of an unnamed Keeper who had enforced the ritual slaying of children favoring their Hanken heritage rather than Tahehto. To purify the race. Followers of these fortunately short-lived horrors had called themselves Tenanken, meaning thick chest, becoming wanderers in exile from the rest of the budding human species that regarded each child as precious in someday populating the entire planet. Then had come the time when there was no place for retreat. The days of the caves began.

Before The Plan.

He was The Plan. Peter, from Crosley. Pegre, from the Tenanken band of Anka, the gentle Keeper of The Memories. It was up to him, now, to bring them outside to sun and trees, back to the race they had rejected and scorned, as if rejecting a part of their own body. The human race: Hinchai, and Tenanken. One people. Coming together. Tonight.

Pete swallowed hard as self-doubt assailed him once again. Surely someone would notice the physical differences. *Look in a mirror at that Tahehto face of yours. Do the Hinchai even notice? Has Bernie ever told you you're ugly?*

He thought about Bernie's beautifully sculptured features.

He wondered about the features of his unborn child.

The road rolled by. Five miles to town, then one. He held his breath as the first buildings appeared ahead, and felt rather than saw heads turn behind him. If somebody stopped him for a conversation....

But the town was empty, both the bar and the hotel dark, not even a dog in sight. What had Jake said? A search party—for critters, he said. More trouble, and at a critical time. He knew the outcome could be deadly. Guns were superior to spears, but only when they had targets to shoot at, and a Tenanken warrior would cut a throat or crush a skull before a sound was heard. The men had gone on a search for Hidaig's band, and he hoped they would stay together in the dark. But where were the women? As he drove through town, every house was dark, no signs of life. His stomach was unsettled; he wanted to belch, but couldn't. He slapped with the reins, and the wagon accelerated out of town, darkness closing in on both sides. He took the short cut up the steep hill, two ruts for a road, horses wheezing. When he paused at the top of the hill there was a collective groan of relief from the back, but then they bounced down another hill and across a meadow to more trees surrounding the ranch.

When he drove into his big front yard, he found it jammed tight with horses and wagons.

Dear God.

Every lamp in the house was lit, and through each window Pete saw a horde of women hurrying around. The back door flew open, and four women emerged with stacks of blankets in their arms, bustling through tall grass towards the two, lighted bunkhouses in the rear of the property, one of them veering towards the barn and disappearing inside.

Pete got out of the wagon after finding a space near his front gate, walked around to the back and held up his arms. Among his passengers, there were no smiling faces. He pointed to his right, up towards the darkened hills, and spoke to them slowly in Greek.

"The canyon, and your old home is up there. You can stand in front of the cave entrance and see where we are now. It is very close. If any of you want to go back, it is your choice, and you can leave anytime. I urge you to stay here at least until Hidaig and his band are gone. It will be safer here, but you are not prisoners. Are there any who wish to leave?"

Nobody moved, though worry was etched on each face.

Pete looked towards the house, the excited faces at the windows, a din of noise coming from inside, and then the front door burst open and Bernie came charging down the porch steps to greet them.

"Remember what you've learned. These people want you to be happy here, so do what they do, and try to smile a little when I go back to get the others. This is the woman who carries my child. Her name is Bernie."

Bernie heard her name as she reached him, and put an arm around his waist, her smile so dazzling it seemed to light up the wagon and the ground around it. "Stew is on, there's plenty of fresh bread to go with it, and the beds are made up. Wouldn't you know every woman in town helped? Came in over an hour ago, after the men left." She wiggled her nose at him. "Well, are you just gonna stand there while the baby gets cold, or do I get introduced?"

Pete helped everyone out of the wagon, introducing them one by one, Bernie putting a hand on each shoulder and hitting them with that smile again. He watched the fear disappear from their eyes, felt it leave their minds. *Oh, my darlin' Hinchai bride, you have your own, special Mind Touch, and they feel it.* His mind raced to keep the new names straight, but when it was over he was certain a couple of them had been incorrect. Everyone mumbled something in return, a few smiling shyly, then clustering around the wagon while Pete tied the horses. When Bernie noticed some of the women looking at her swollen stomach, she patted it happily, and said, "It's gonna be a big one."

Nobody except Pete understood what she'd said, and the remark bothered him. *Not too big, I hope. Not as big as I was when my mother nearly died giving birth to me.*

Pete and Bernie led them in a line to the house, where it seemed the entire town was waiting.

"Where'd the men go?"

"I guess they left about the same time you did. Headed south to Ezra Pike's place armed to the teeth, I hear, and God help those critters if they find them. Shouldn't we have sent for the sheriff in Quincy?"

"Later, maybe. Let's see what they find, first."

"I still think we should have called someone when Tom was killed, Pete."

"Later. We'll talk about it later. Here are the ladies."

They had reached the porch, and the women had spilled out onto it, pulling here and there on themselves, fussing with their hair. Pete was suddenly conscious of how bedraggled the Tenanken looked, like refugees from a distant land, which, in a way, was what they were, looking lost and scared and confused by all the attention.

Nobody heard any names in the babble that followed, Bernie herding them into a warm house filled with mouth-watering odors of stew, fresh bread and a dozen perfumes.

They crowded around a huge, oak table covered with festive cloth in blue and yellow. The table was heaped with bread, rolls, chunks of butter on a plate, cookies and bars, baskets of apples, oranges and pears, and in the center an enormous crock filled with steaming stew. Bernie ladled out stew into bowls for her foreign guests staring open-mouthed at the table, and Pete suppressed a grin. Never in their lives had these people seen so much food in one place, for meat taken by the hunters was usually not displayed before the entire band, and such fruit was virtually unknown to them. They timidly held out their bowls, while Bernie gleefully filled them to the brim and added a wooden spoon.

Everyone ate standing up, chattering noisily, their quiet, dignified new neighbors carefully mimicking every move with spoon and cup. Pete smiled at them one by one, proud as a father, amused by their intense concentration. They gobbled cookies and bars and pears, sampled punch and coffee and tea, and learned the love of buttered bread in seconds. When the eating was over they awaited permission to belch, for it was a Tenanken custom after a feast, and when they realized none was forthcoming Pete thought some of them might burst.

Pete glanced at his watch, then called to Bernie over the din, "I've gotta pick up the others, now! Save some food for them!"

"There's enough here for all the men, too, if they ever get back tonight," she shouted back.

Already the Tenanken seemed at home, fitting right in despite the obvious language problems, looking pretty much like everyone else except for being disheveled. Tenanken and Hinchai—together at last. When Pete neared the door a young Tenanken woman, new name Diana, was answering the question posed by grandmotherly Charlotte Gable, who ran the tiny post office in Crosley. "I come—out—Rhodes," she said painfully. "Is—island." The older woman nodded her head knowingly, for she had heard of the Greek island called Rhodes.

"Is—poor," said Diana.

"Well, you're gonna do just fine here, dear," said the woman.

Pete banged the door behind him, feeling good. He hurried to the wagon—to bring the rest of them home.

* * * * * * *

"Somebody comes," said Baela, and there were startled gasps from the darkness. Peering through the rippled mica windows she counted eight lights, close together, and moving slowly but surely towards them. Still far away; perhaps they would turn, and go another direction, but on they came, descending a small hill, suddenly disappearing from view behind trees and thick brush. She held her breath—hoping, but then the lights flickered much closer, now, one bursting forth from the brush to show tall grass near the cabin, and she saw dark figures moving towards her before she jerked herself away from the window and sat down on the floor beneath it, pressing up against the wall.

There was no sound in the cabin, and she felt everyone's mind go blank, an instinctive Tenanken defense against detection. Her own mind whirled, and then she heard voices, and a dog barked. She crossed her arms over her chest, and squeezed hard.

"Hey Ezra, maybe you'd better feed *that* dog to the critters, too. He didn't even see the Jack till it jumped, and *I* can do better'n that."

"Hell you say, Jake. Ol' Roy sticks to the scent, and we ain't trackin' no Jacks here. They come by this way. You can be sure of it. What's that over there?"

A light gleamed through the window of the cabin. Baela held her breath.

"Shit," said someone, "we've come near three miles. That's Savas's old cabin. Can't be more'n an hour or so to town here. That dog moves."

"Well let's *keep* movin'," said another man. "This whole thing is a waste of time in the dark, and we're out here freezin' our butts off while the wives are partyin' it up at Pete's place. I say we go straight back to town, and start this again in the mornin'."

"Look, we don't know what these guys will do next. For all we know they're killin' someone right now, while we stand here arguing. Or stealin' the town blind, while everyone's over at Pete's."

"Oh hell, Ned, you don't really have any money in that bank, do you?"

"Come on, men, another hour or two, and we're back in town, then we pick up the trail here tomorrow. Hey Ezra, where you goin'?"

"Dog's nervous," said a man so close it seemed he was in the cabin. Baela's heart was thumping hard, and there was whining and a snuffling sound right at her back. "Real strong scent over here."

A clanking and clacking of weapons being readied for action was something Baela had heard before.

"Better get away from there, Ezra. They might be in the cabin."

The dog whimpered at the door, then suddenly started barking. Inside, five Tenanken hearts froze in fear as the animal howled and barked, deep throated.

"Stop it, Roy. Stop it! Naw, they've been here for sure, but not inside. Brand new lock on the door. See?" The door rattled hard in the dark. "Can't even shoot the thing off. How's the windows, Jake?"

There was a face at the window above her, blocking out the faint light of night, and then the bright glow of yellow light suddenly in the cabin, spilling over walls and furniture, a table in the middle of the room. The light flicked off as quickly as it had come. "Looks okay. Nice table. Wouldn't mind havin' it in my place."

"Make Pete an offer, It's his, now."

"Since when?"

"Since Savas left the cabin to him. See anything else in there?"

"Just old furniture and some dishes."

"Let's go. I'm gettin' cold standin' here."

"I gotta piss," said another man.

"So use the privy. Pete won't mind."

The dog was still barking and whining, but had been pulled several paces away from the cabin. A door banged outside.

"Watch out for the snakes in there!" Somebody laughed.

"They come after me, I'll drown 'em," came the muffled reply.

Baela let out her breath in a silent whistle, then the door banged again, and the voices were growing fainter along with snuffling sounds from the dog and the crunch of heavy boots on dry grass.

"Come on, let's go. Damn dog can't smell anything."

"You're just in a hurry to meet those Greek women, Jake. We'll get back in time. They're probably all fat and ugly, anyway. See any of them?"

"Just a little kid."

"Jake likes 'em young," said someone, and everyone laughed just as the dog let out a yelp and a howl.

"Here we go. They went up the hill right here. Come on, Roy!"

"Shit, I do hate climbing."

The noises of crunching grass and breaking brush faded with the whining of the dog and muffled voices of the men, until the only sound was that of air caressing pine needles, and the ever so faint breathing of five Tenanken refugees locked in a darkened cabin.

They sat in silence, afraid to speak, wondering if Pegre would return before morning, but prepared for a long wait. They thought of sunlight, and the cave, tried to imagine standing in long grass in a valley they had seen only from a distance.

Baela shared their visions, quickly becoming bored with them because she had spent much time outside, had actually stood in the places they dreamed about. Her own thoughts returned to the great hunting bird, and this time she tried something new. She imagined she *was* the mother bird, felt herself springing from the nest with powerful legs and a down stroke of whistling wings pushing air beneath her. She arose in lazy circles, higher and higher, imagining the land dropping away until the trees were green dots on yellow rock, and the canyon was a dark gash leading to a valley of rippling green and gold.

She felt wind pulling at the small feathers along her head, the tension as giant feathers in her wings tilted and spread to change speed and altitude, her body wobbling from side to side as updrafts came and went, and she spotted something moving across the valley in a rhythm telling her it was a rabbit. She steadied herself, wings outstretched and motionless, focusing keen eyes on the target, then suddenly folding her wings tightly and dropping like a rock from the sky, the ground rushing up at her before she deployed a wing to brake and maneuver as the rabbit changed direction, then she was dropping again, her victim coming towards her in a blur, and—

"Ohhh!" cried out somebody in the cabin, and was instantly shushed into silence by the others. Baela was startled from her vision, Eagle and rabbit popping out of existence and leaving her shaking in the cold room. Quick breathing in the darkness, some of it her own in frustration and anger at the intrusion of the outcry. Her pleasure had been ruined. Heart pounding, she bit her lip to force back her anger, hugged herself tightly, and pouted—

At that instant, the familiar clattering of Pegre's wagon came to their ears.

They all rushed to the windows, crowding each other for a look. Pegre hurried to the cabin, the door rattled, opened, and they streamed outside, babbling wildly in the Tenanken tongue while Baela sulked in the background. Pegre looked at her for help, but she offered none, and so he understood only a little about what had happened to them. It was enough.

They climbed into the wagon, Baela still pouting, sitting at the back and facing away from the others. She endured her mother's squeals of fear and surprise until they reached the smoother road back to town. Mercifully, she was left alone on the long ride back to the ranch house, but out of the corner of her eye she could see the others watching her silently. Suddenly, she missed her hidey-tree where she could sit and see everything around: waving grass, trees, roiling clouds, and the animals. It was the place where she could dream her dreams. Alone.

By the time they reached town she was feeling better; her stomach growled, and hunger made her forget the anger. Her companions dozed, back-to-back in a huddle, and she watched their heads flop back and forth with each bump. As they finally approached the ranch, a tightness was again in her chest, and her breathing quickened at the sight of all the animals and carriages around the house filled with noisy Hinchai. Was there no need for privacy here?

Pegre parked outside the fence because there was no room left in the yard. The noise in the house came out through an open door, spilling over them in waves. Pegre smiled when they were standing together by the wagon, putting an arm around a young boy newly named Stefen, and taking Baela's hand in his. "This is your new home, and these are your neighbors. See what a good time they're having? Relax, and eat. Everyone wants you to be here."

He led them inside.

People hardly noticed them come in.

Everywhere they looked were Tenanken surrounded by chattering Hinchai women, listening politely with little understanding, answering haltingly and using hands to help make a point, concentrating intensely but without fear. Pegre dragged them to a table filled with food, where a blonde woman, happy-faced and very pregnant with his child was pouring stew from a metal kettle into a giant crock, enveloping herself in steam. Baela's smile was spontaneous, for she saw again the goodness in this woman, and had liked her the first instant of their meeting.

"And here's Baela," said Bernie, ladling out a bowl of stew for her. "Be sure to try one of these, too. Every little girl loves chocolate." She popped something dark into Baela's mouth, laughed when her eyes widened in delighted surprise at the taste, then led her, Pegre and her parents to a relatively quiet corner of the big room. While Baela shoveled food in her mouth, Pegre made the introductions to Bernie. Moog and Deda had become Michael and Dee Astosis, also from Rhodes, and like their daughter they were well rehearsed, falling easily into a halting conversation with the blonde woman. It was an interesting hour for Baela: stomach full of good foods, tastes she had never experienced, animated conversation. Exciting.

Someone shouted, "Hurry up, it's gettin' cold!" The front door had banged open, letting in a burst of cold air and several haggard-looking men wearing heavy boots and jackets. Faces burned red by wind chill, huffing and puffing dramatically, they removed gloves from their hands and stamped their feet on the hardwood floor. Gradually they paired up with women in the room, except for one, the thin, sharp-featured man with sad eyes who stood alone for a time by the stew crock, eating slowly and neatly until he saw Pegre and elbowed his way over to him.

"Hi, Jake. You've met Baela. These are her folks, Mike and Dee Astosis, and this is Jake Price, a close neighbor to us."

Jake nodded politely at everyone. Baela sensed in him a desperate loneliness, a need to be close to someone. It made her sad.

"See anything?"

"Naw. We got as far as Cascade Creek, and the trail disappeared. Pretty sure they followed the creek before coming out again, so we'll have to start all over in the morning. Bad cold out there."

I recognize that voice, thought Baela. *You were very close to me earlier tonight.*

"Sorry I couldn't go with," said Pegre, "but I didn't have much warning about my relatives arriving."

"No problem. We're meetin' at the hotel seven in the morning, if you can come along. Personally, I think it's a waste of time. Whoever we're followin' knows trackin'; for all I know, they was followin' *us* tonight. Spooky out there." Jake looked at Baela with the trace of a smile on his thin lips. "Hi," he said.

"Hi," said Baela, lowering her eyes.

Jake shook his head. "Never heard of a blonde Greek before. Learn somethin' new every day. I'm ready for more coffee, How 'bout you?"

"I'm fine, Jake," said Pegre.

"Well—nice talkin' to y'all. I'm gonna get a cup." He turned suddenly, and shuffled back to the table.

"Nice man," said Bernie, "but a lonely man. Wish I could fix him up with someone, but he's cautious now about getting involved."

But Jake's caution lasted only a few minutes.

They were still talking, Baela's back towards the door, Bernie looking past her. Baela watched the blue eyes moving back and forth across the room, taking everything in, every face, every gesture, reading her guests by sight alone. Her eyes widened, lips curving into an expression of delight. "Oh, did you see that?"

"I saw," said Pegre. "That's Diana, and as far as I know she's unattached."

"He just said hello to her, and she hit him with a smile that would reduce most men to quivering jelly. What a *beautiful* smile."

"I think he's paralyzed," said Pegre, and they both chuckled.

Baela looked slyly over one shoulder. The one they called Diana was leaning against the wall by the door, looking up at Jake Price bending near her, his one hand on the wall, trying very hard to smile. To Baela, the expression on Diana's face was clear; she had looked into the man, and liked what she saw there. Jake was trying to relax without success: face flushed, eyes darting, coffee sloshing in the cup he held in a shaky hand. He mumbled some words, and then Diana touched him without moving. The wrinkles of tension in his face seemed to fade. His hand became steady, and he even laughed at some little thing she said. Baela watched all of this fascinated. *I wish I could touch someone like that, but it may never be—because I was born a Hanken child.*

The evening wore on, and yawns appeared. Gradually the crowd thinned to reveal Pete's relatives sprawled in chairs, some asleep. Bernie hustled the rest of them out, tugging at Jake's arm to finally pull him away from Diana and send him on his way with the promise of another visit soon. The door banged shut, and Bernie flopped into a chair, letting out a deep breath.

"Hoo, I can't take much of this with the load I'm carryin' around."

"I'll clean up," said Pete.

"Pegre—I help," said Baela enthusiastically.

"What did she call you?" Bernie looked curiously at Pete, then Baela.

"Pegre. It's a kind of pet name from the old country. I don't know what it means."

"Oh. Well, it's fine with me if you want to clean up. I've really had enough. Good night, all." She stood up, walking over to Pegre and kissing him full on the mouth. "You too, whatever your name is. I'm glad your people are here."

Bernie shuffled out of the room, looking tired, rubbing the back of her neck, and stretching tall. *Her time is near,* thought Baela. *Very near.*

Pegre had already settled those few Tenanken who were staying in the house. The rest, including Baela and her parents, would sleep in a single bunkhouse fifty yards up a grassy slope leading to rocky cliffs and the high maw of the canyon from which they had come only hours before. Pegre took them there, showed them how to work the lamps, a pump for running water, the indoor privy, all of which they found both fascinating and amusing, and the whole time they were getting settled someone was either pumping water or fiddling with a lamp while the rest murmured approvingly. When at last they had distributed themselves among the beds and figured out how to sleep in them, they sat down wearily and began removing their clothes. Pegre stood at the door, smiling, looking from one to the other, then suddenly surprising them.

"You see," he said in the Tenanken tongue, "we are all together again." And then he closed his eyes, letting out a sigh. The feelings of love, affection and unity washed over all of them. Baela strained mightily to project something wonderful in return, but all that seemed to come was a beautiful smile, and she was satisfied that Pegre saw it, for there was delight in his eyes. He turned down the lamps and closed the door softly behind him. In only minutes the exhausted refugees were sound asleep.

Baela hovered at the edge of consciousness, hearing the deep breathing sounds, the unfamiliar squeak of a bedspring, the rustling of sheets and blankets as someone shifted position. The bird-vision came to her again, and she circled lazily, lazily, gaining altitude, soaring until she could see to all horizons.

A night cry startled her back towards consciousness. An agonized cry. Some animal—wounded. The sound had come down from the canyon, and she wondered why it vaguely disturbed her, but then she was soaring again, spinning dizzily, slipping into a sleep filled with visions of trees and sunlight, as seen through the eyes of a great hunting bird.

CHAPTER SIXTEEN

HIDAIG'S DAY

Occupation of the caverns took place at dawn.

Hidaig moved swiftly and boldly, anticipating little opposition from the female-heavy band of his former Keeper, and though his warriors were not battle hardened, they had developed the hungry look that had to be dealt with if he were to maintain leadership. He sent forth one scout, a slender, rat-faced teenager named Dougal, who reported back that the caverns were quiet with no guards near the entrance, and so at dawn they pulled aside the entrance cover and marched inside without resistance. This was disappointing to the warriors, and particularly to Kretan, whole bloodlust was running hot after the slaying of Han. They turned into the tunnel without bothering to search Maki's sleeping place, and marched straight into the main cavern dimly lit by torchlight.

It was empty.

Cold fire rings were scattered around the shelves, along with small caches of personal belongings, food, a few sleeping robes. Hidaig's first thought was that Anka's followers were hiding in the many fumaroles leading off in several directions, but search revealed only a few old ones who had reached the point in life at which one separates from family, and awaits death. No warriors there. Hidaig's troops dragged them out in a line along the top shelf of the cavern, where their leader marched back and forth, mustering up his fiercest look and snapping his questions.

"Where did the others go, and when did they leave? Tell me, and I'll spare your miserable lives and treat you well until your spirits soar. It is more than you can expect from Anka."

No answer. There was silence in the great cavern, except for the sound of water dripping far back in a fumarole.

"Say something quickly, or you will die many times. Where did they go, and when?"

142

Silence. Not an eye moved. The old ones stared ahead as if blind. Hidaig pointed to one small female, wrinkled and bent, making a random choice. He chose Ba, grandmother of Baela, only to make a point, because he had no time for lengthy inquisitions. He looked at Kretan, and made a chopping motion with his hand. "This one," he said dramatically.

Ba raised her eyes sorrowfully, never to see her grand daughter again, as Kretan stepped behind her, swinging his war axe horizontally against the base of her skull with a loud pop. Fragments of bone and brain splattered on the floor as she pitched forward on her face and lay still. The old ones began keening, tears in their eyes, wringing their hands in grief over the body.

"Once more," said Hidaig, "I want to know where they went, and how long ago. Tell me, or you will all die like this one."

They cried and screamed, going down on their knees, but not one would say a word. Hidaig repeated his question over and over in higher and higher tones, face reddening with anger. Still, they would not speak, and finally he could stand no more and screamed at Kretan, "ALL OF THEM!" The big warrior obliged his master with a grin, swinging his axe in roundhouse arcs as someone began to scream.

"STOP IT! STOP IT! STOP IT!"

The screams continued until the last old one had crashed to the floor. Hidaig jerked around to see Tel glaring at him from the entrance to a fumarole, teeth bared in a snarl, fingers entwined in her thick hair. "Murderer! You come here to kill the sick and helpless because you haven't the courage to face a true warrior! Murderer! MURDERER! Your spirit will wander in torment, and I will spit on it when it passes me in the night! You disgrace all Tenanken left alive; their faces will turn away from you, and you will be Tenanken no more!" Her voice was a shriek, eyes twin beams of fire, face a hideous mask of something half Tenanken, half wolf as she stepped towards them, claws outstretched.

Hidaig stumbled backwards a step as she came at him. Kretan leaped to the line of warriors staring open-mouthed at the spectacle, and snatched up a spear, drawing back his arm to heave it at Tel.

"NO!" cried Hidaig hysterically. "NO! PUT IT DOWN!" Spittle flew from his mouth, his eyes rolling. "SHE IS A KEEPER!"

Kretan hesitated, holding his position, eyes locked on Tel, legs quivering with the tension of coiled muscles as he turned to follow her progress.

"Throw your weapon!" she screamed. "Kill me, too, and spend a spiritless eternity after death as a blind cave lizard licking bugs from the dirt. IT IS MY CURSE ON YOU!"

The huge warrior blanched white, lowering his spear ever so slightly, but holding his position while Hidaig stumbled out of her way as she knelt beside the bodies of the old ones.

"Oh—oh—ohhh," she wailed. "What have we done to bring such evil among us? De? Ba? Show me a vision of my innocence, or invite me to soar with you...."

"What have you done?" The voice was soft from behind him, so that Hidaig twirled, nearly falling.

Anka's moist, amber eyes gazed at him, full of sorrow. Maki came out of the darkness of a fumarole, from where he'd been awakened with his father. A spear was in his hand. While Tel keened her grief and anger, Maki stood by his father's shoulder, eyes darting, suspicious, sensing betrayal.

"If you seek treasure, then take what little there is to find, and go your way. If you were a worthy leader, you would know it is not necessary to kill those too old or weak to oppose. You would know mercy, but it is not within you. It is one reason I was pleased by your leaving. Why have you returned to share your evil with us in such a way, when we have done nothing to you?"

Hidaig put a hand on one hip, posing. "I have been invited to come here—by your son." He looked at Maki, and smiled.

"So, it's *your* ambition that has brought this to us!" shouted Tel. "I was a *fool* to think you had changed, even after all the talk with your father." She gave Maki a baleful stare, gratified when he could not look at her.

"I did not invite Hidaig here to do this thing," said Maki, touching his father on the shoulder. "Father, please believe me. I did not want this to happen."

Anka shrugged his shoulder, so that Maki's hand fell away from him. He looked at Tel with wet eyes, lips pressed tightly together. "You were right all along, but I refused to listen. Forgive me."

Tel sobbed, and bent herself over the bodies of the old ones.

Anka only glanced at his son. "Stand away from me. At this moment, I wish that you had died with your brothers."

Maki winced, as if struck, then turned on Hidaig, who still regarded him with amusement. "I told you to notify me when you arrived. If I'd been with you, this stupidity would never have occurred."

Hidaig made a bowing motion. "Oh, Great Keeper, I do not follow your orders, or those of anyone else."

144

"And where is Han? I sent him to guide you here."

"Ah, Han. He had an unfortunate accident, a fall—on some-one's spear. I must report he is dead."

There was death in Maki's eyes, but he was holding a single weapon and surrounded by Hidaig's warriors, in particular the giant Kretan, who watched his every move. Better to bend with the wind, for if he could reach his sleeping quarters his chances to kill Hidaig would surely improve. Still, he could not suppress a complaint. "I should have known you could not be trusted, should have known you would betray anyone for your own gain," he grumbled.

"Gain?" Hidaig threw back his head, and laughed. "And what do I have to gain here? Riches? Power?" He waved an arm around the cavern. "A few rotten rags, piles of cold ashes, and dead old ones who didn't matter alive. This is my gain? Tell me, Maki, where are the others? Where are the females, and the treasure you said were here? Where are the Hinchai to kill, and the little Hanken brats you protect?"

"They left last night," said Tel, calmer now, "when Pegre came to get them. They are in the valley, with Hinchai protection and powerful weapons. If you go down there you wish a quick death; I hope you will do it, and my son with you."

"Mother!"

"I hear the voice of a stranger. You are not my son. Do what you must, and get out!" Tel lowered her head and Anka came to her, folding his arms around her shoulders as she pressed her face against his chest to muffle her sobs.

Maki looked from face to stony face in the eerie silence sur-rounding them. Even some of the warriors shifted uncomfortably from foot to foot, avoiding his eyes, minds jumbled with dark, pas-sionate and fleeting visions that came from outside of themselves. Hidaig mocked him with a pouting face as Kretan returned the spear to a warrior, picked up his axe and came to stand at the shoulder of his leader.

Hidaig spat on the ground near Maki's feet. "Just look at your face, you, who would be Keeper and warrior king. When you first came to me, I almost believed you could do it, but the more I thought the more I realized you would be raised soft by old ones such as these, vision-heads full of spirits, but no stomach for fight-ing. How could I or my followers serve such a king? Where are your battle scars, Maki? Hmmm?"

Maki's eyes were wide, and streaked with red, breath coming in short gasps as the humiliation was heaped over him like dung. His body tensed, hands opening and closing as Hidaig watched him

145

carefully, but it was Anka who attacked, ancient Anka, Keeper of The Memories, the gentle, spiritual leader who suddenly pushed away his mate with a war cry that thundered from the walls, rushing towards Hidaig with heavy arms outstretched, groping for a throat.

Tel screamed, "Anka, no!"

Hidaig dropped into a crouch, twisting to grab the war axe from Kretan and jabbing it hard into Anka's stomach with one sharp thrust. Anka let out an agonized groan, and collapsed in a heap at Hidaig's feet, grabbing at his own stomach with soft hands never used in anger. He rolled around on the floor, grasping at legs and groin, panting as Tel rushed to him, dropping to her knees at Hidaig's feet.

"He could be dead," said Hidaig, "and remains alive by my choice. I give mercy, Tel, but only because Anka shows courage for one so old, and I have no good reason to kill him. See, his breath returns already; had I used the blade of my axe, his guts would now be spilling out on the floor. Now, get him to his feet."

As Anka rose to one knee, he clutched his stomach and gave out a groan. Something was badly broken inside of him, but he kept this to himself, arising in dignified fashion, making a gesture of dismissal to Maki as the son stepped forward to help him. Maki stepped back, looking stricken.

"I mean you no harm, Anka," said Hidaig, no longer amused. "There is nothing here for me, and what I want is in the valley below us. I will tend to that in a day, and rest here until then. You must not try to leave the cavern, but can wander wherever you wish within it. I need females for my band, and I intend to have them. Gold is decorative, but useless to me."

"There never was any gold," said Tel, but Anka's eyes betrayed the truth.

"I don't believe you, but it's still not important. It's the females I must have, if my band is to survive. There are many males to provide for them, and they will be safer than where they are now, close to the Hinchai devils you insist are our relatives. It is foolish notions like this that have brought pain to you."

Anka hung on to Tel as breath returned; a sharp ache was in the center of his stomach, and he felt nauseous. Hidaig's band was indeed in trouble if these were all his warriors. For the most part they were an emaciated-looking bunch, without spirit, slouching on the butt-ends of stone-tipped spears. He counted twenty of them, but only one, Kretan, stood out as a classic Tenanken warrior, reminding him of Pegre in appearance. Pegre had never been tested in battle.

What use for war these past fifty years? There were no tribes or nearby bands left to make war against.

Except the Hinchai.

His son had betrayed the band, the very thing he had been raised to nurture and protect. How had he become so infected with ambition, and why could he stand there watching while his father was beaten to the ground? Anka felt Maki's sorrow and dangerous anger, but still the young man did nothing. Anka wanted to tell him all was forgiven, but a part of him wouldn't allow it, the part of him that felt betrayed, and despised the betrayer.

Hidaig was still babbling his reasons for attacking the settlement in the valley with a confidence Anka found childlike. His courage came from talk, rather than thought, and Anka ignored him, focusing instead on the steady pain deep inside him. Something was seriously wrong there, but at least the nausea was subsiding. Hidaig was in the middle of a sentence when Anka broke in on him.

"I'm tired. Please, no more talk." He closed his eyes, and leaned against Tel.

"Please let us go—over there—his sleeping chamber," said Tel, holding him and feeling the thump, thump of his heart against her shoulder.

Hidaig was annoyed at the interruption, dismissing them with a wave of his hand. "Take him there, but do *not* try to leave the caves. Kretan! Send two out to find fresh food. I don't care what it is, or how they get it. I'm hungry enough to eat Hanken."

The warriors laughed without humor, for they were all hungry, and now it appeared the booty they had been promised was a lie. To hunt was a chance to get out and see what lay in the valley below. What was there would have to be worth dying for, or Hidaig would find himself fighting a battle alone. Two warriors, carrying spears and slings, stepped forward as volunteers, and Kretan sent them out with orders to return before darkness.

They were never seen again.

Tel remained at Anka's side the entire night, except for two hours near dawn that nearly took her life.

* * * * * * *

Their private grotto ended a twenty-meter fumarole leading from the rear of the great cavern. Extending from the grotto, with its tiny pool and piles of sleeping furs were several smaller fumaroles, all of which dead-ended after only a few meters. But one curved sharply in a helical way to a passageway, more a subterranean crack than a tunnel, leading to the upward slanting corridor to their favorite ledge from which they often watched the outside night. It was the place at which three of their now dead children had been conceived.

Over the years the passageway had become their special secret, giving them a way to escape the cavern for a private moment. Tel thought of this as she watched the labored breathing of her mate-of-two lifetimes, hearing the faint wheeze at the end of each exhalation. In the great cavern nearby, warriors slept, sprawled out on ledges, spears at hand while Hidaig talked, pacing back and forth, anxiously waiting for his hunters to return. Tel could think of only one way to send a distress signal. Fire. Any light coming from the cave area would be a sure sign of danger, if seen by Pegre, giving him time to prepare for fight, or to flee.

Finally, her inner clock told her it was night, but barely so. Perhaps he would be outside, at least for a moment. At this distance the mind touch was a whisper in the wind, not to be relied on. It must be now, though she knew the risk was considerable. If Hidaig caught her, even his superstition would not prevent her death.

She searched the grotto for what she needed, feeling with her hands because of the dim light of her tiny lamp of tar-saturated fur. Anka's meditation crystal, a thumb-sized piece of clear quartz, twinkled at her from a shallow niche in one wall. She fumbled in and around the sleeping furs, pulling out small, hide bags, checking their contents, putting them back again: herbs and seeds, crushed and dried flowers, a dark crystal with which it was said she cast spells, but was really just a pretty thing she couldn't throw away, and finally her flints. One thing worked in her favor; this time of year the ledges were covered with dried leaves, twigs and small branches blown there by the wind. She would have a plentiful supply of burning material.

Anka moaned as Tel crawled out of the grotto. *Dear one*, she thought, *I fear your pain, but I must leave you for a little while.* She crawled on, the little bag with her supplies dangling from a long thong draped around her neck. It was an effort to move upwards; the walls were smooth, and her knees protested the pressure as she pressed feet hard against rock to gain friction for pushing ahead. Dim light from the grotto disappeared, and she was advancing by feel and memory in total, inky darkness. In the crack the climb was easier, the channel an inverted triangle with solid bottom and rough walls where hands could be placed flat for balance. She moved quickly along the channel without a stumble, until she saw the glimmer of light coming up from the floor. A hole was there, dropping into a snarl of short fumaroles, one leading to the torch-lit tunnel thrusting upwards to outside ledges.

Tel crouched at the edge of the hole for several minutes, listening, probing for a thought or vision. Nothing. She slipped through the opening, and with a short slide was in the tunnel. She could hear faint voices coming from the main cavern. Watching her feet to avoid loose stones, she hurried upwards, a sense of mission coming to her along with a sharp pain in her chest. She slowed to the point that the pain was a dull ache, and the exit to night appeared ahead, wind hitting her face as she crawled out onto the narrow ledge. She crawled along it on hands and knees, picking up twigs and dried leaves caught in cracks and crevices in the rock, disappointed at how little she found to burn. One larger limb was lodged in a crack above head. When she stretched high to reach it, something gave beneath her foot, and for one horrible instant she felt herself toppling backwards over the edge and into the trees below. She jackknifed her body back onto the ledge, heart thumping so wildly she saw flashes of light before her eyes. She stretched again, grabbing the limb and angrily jerking it free before breaking it into pieces with her hands. It would be a small fire, visible for only a short time. She arranged the sticks in crisscross pattern over the tinder she took from her bag, added some leaves and twigs, then went to work with her flints.

She hunched over her work, batting the pieces of hard stone together until the first wisp of smoke arose from the tinder. Cupping her hands about the glowing fluff, she blew on it gently, adding twigs until a tiny flame burst forth. She added more twigs as the flame grew, a small breeze encouraging it. Only when she added the few large pieces of wood could she feel heat, a transient thing of only a moment. There was no more wood on the ledge. She watched the little fire burning brightly within sight of the valley for only a few heart beats, then crawled back along the ledge and into the tunnel.

Her hand brushed a hairy ankle, and strong hands seized her, pulling her roughly to her feet and shaking her furiously.

Hidaig.

"So I'm not imagining strange sounds in the tunnel. Perhaps you will tell me how you got here without being seen, eh? And what have you been up to? Let's see."

He released her, got down on his hands and knees, and crawled out onto the ledge, dragging a spear with him and looking to his right.

"This is a bad thing you've done, Tel."

Her mind whirled. If she pushed hard, he might go off the ledge—or grab her—or run her through with the spear.

Tel fled. Hair streaming behind her, she stumbled down the tunnel as fast as old legs would take her.

Hidaig hesitated, then crawled outside, reached out with his spear and swept the now weakly flaming signal fire off the ledge and down into the canyon below. When he crawled back inside, he could still hear her feet pounding the floor of the tunnel. He leveled his spear and charged after her, having made the decision that even though she was a Keeper, he, Hidaig, was now chasing only a doomed, old woman.

But Tel had a good head start, heard him now, and knew he could quickly catch her if she remained in the tunnel. On her left were countless fumaroles leading to nowhere, except in one tangled cluster. It was already in sight, and she darted into it, twisting painfully around two corners, legs burning from the short run. She took a deep breath, palms pressing down on smooth rock, and pulled her self up into the ceiling with a grunt, the sounds of Hidaig's feet right behind her. Her feet were last up in the darkness, and she rolled away from the opening as her pursuer thundered past in the tunnel, never breaking stride. A few seconds later she heard him screaming at someone in the main cavern.

She'd been seen. Hidaig would realize she had somehow reached the tunnel from the grotto. Any minute they would search for her, but their time was running short. Hidaig planned to attack the valley settlement in the morning; she's overheard him talking about it. Only hours to dawn, and he'd have to be in position by then, so if she could find a good place to hide....

Pitch darkness, and she moved back towards the grotto by feel, despairing that her signal fire had not been seen. It was so tiny, and surely Hidaig had quickly destroyed it. Her efforts had only endangered her life, and what about Anka? But he knew nothing; he hadn't even seen her leave. Surely they wouldn't....

Suddenly she was filled with a terrible fear.

She scrambled forward in the crack, calling up visions of what she had seen under torchlight, checking against what she felt with feet and hands until she found what she wanted, and stopped abruptly to feel the rock on her left. A wide crack above a quartzite nubbin, a jagged cut up the shallow wall to the ceiling, or so it seemed at first sight. In fact, the wall ended in a shelf just below the ceiling, invisible until she was right there. Now where was the crack?

She clawed frantically with her hands, and found it.

The climb upwards was harder than she remembered. How long had it been? And she'd had a torch then. Now, in blackness, she moved by feel as the floor dropped further and further behind her. Not a vertical climb, but steep enough so that a slide back to the floor could break her old bones. Her hands hurt from gripping rock, growing weaker by the second, but then as she reached forward for a new hold there was nothing but air. She explored over her head, and found the ceiling. Inch by inch, feeling ahead, she pulled herself onto the shelf, a rocky womb at the top of the wall.

Exhausted, and feeling secure in her hiding place, she slept—

And was instantly awake.

To light—and voices.

Yellow light flickered on the ceiling near her face, though her hiding place was in darkness. Below her a scraping sound came from the direction of the grotto, followed by a mumbled curse.

"Here it is. Above their sleeping chamber."

There was a short pause of silence.

"Can you hear me?" There was a scraping sound, perhaps a spear against rock. "Can't even turn around in here. I'm in a kind of tunnel."

There was no answer. The light was moving below her, now, and she heard the crunch of footsteps. "Where are you?"

Suddenly she heard a reply, quite faint. The footsteps quickened, the nearby ceiling again fading to darkness. "I see a light! Can you hear me?"

Another muffled reply. Whoever it was must now be near the exit. There was another scrape of spear against rock. "Here! Over here. I see your shadow."

She heard Hidaig's voice. "A tunnel. So she came through here."

"Empty, now," said the other Tenanken.

"She must have come out again when I passed here the first time. There's too many of these things to hide in, and she can't help them now. Check the tunnel again, then join us in the big cavern. We have to leave soon. Tel can rot here by herself, and bury her dead. Hurry!"

Tel's heart froze. Bury her dead?

The footsteps were below her again, light moving across the ceiling. She held her breath as the light stopped, moving around in a circle, then forward again towards the grotto. A moment later it flickered out, plunging her into blackness. She kept her mind blank for several minutes, dozed again, but the thought of climbing down the wall in darkness jolted her awake. She felt around a long time until she found the crack, listening for voices, hearing them loud, quickly fading to nothing. Silence lasted an eternity. They could be waiting quietly for her to come out. But it must now be morning, and Hidaig would surely spare no warriors as cave guards during the attack. Her risk was calculated.

Slowly, steadily, she climbed down the crack to the tunnel floor, and picked up a fist-sized pebble for a hand weapon. Soon she was at the grotto, looking down at it from the ceiling.

Anka was not there. His sleeping furs were in disarray. She listened carefully, heart pounding, then dropped feet first into the grotto, and peered along the short tunnel to the great cavern.

Someone was lying on the cavern floor.

Haltingly, she crawled out of the grotto, and looked around. The cavern was empty, warriors and bodies of the old ones gone. But in front of her lay the broken and bloodied form of her life-mate. She hurried to him, leaning over to touch his mutilated face, blood trickling from his mouth. His eyelids fluttered, opened, amber eyes showing recognition. He opened his mouth to speak, but all that came out was a horrible gurgle.

"Oh, dear heart, what have they done to you?"

Anka managed a weak smile, then gurgled again.

"I think they have killed me," he said.

CHAPTER SEVENTEEN

WATCHERS

It was daylight when Baela was startled awake by her mother's moans. She looked over at the thrashing form on the bed next to hers, certain that moments before she had heard her grandmother's name shouted in the room. Baela herself felt vaguely uneasy, an uncomfortable frightening feeling of emptiness, then sorrow, then nothing, as if a piece of her mind had been suddenly cut away. She sat up abruptly, looking around at the sleeping forms, then at her mother, whose eyes were now open, face glistening.

"Mother, what's wrong?" whispered Baela.

Da stared at her a moment, still returning from sleep, blinking her eyes twice and licking her lips. "I had a terrible dream about Mother. She called to me, and it was like she was in shadow, reaching out at me. I tried to touch her, but something pulled her back into darkness, and then I felt—no, I *feel* like I've lost her. I feel like I'll never see her again."

"She's in the cave, Mother."

"I know. It was a dream, Baela—only a dream. Go back to sleep, now." Da closed her eyes.

Baela sat quietly for a moment, listening to her mother's breathing slow and deepen. All the others were asleep, and here she was, wide-awake, instantly bored. She sat on the edge of the bed, swinging her legs and waiting for the dull feeling to come and tell her to sleep some more, but it didn't come, and then she heard a door slam at the big house a hundred paces away. Someone else was awake! She'd slept in her clothes: jeans and a thin, white blouse with tiny, yellow flowers on it. Shoes and socks she had taken off, already deciding not to like shoes because they strangled her feet. She tip-toed bare-footed to the door, and let herself out into the vastness of her new world, the big house and grass before her tinted orange as the orb of the sun peered over the edge of a nearby hill. She marveled at

153

the sudden warmth as the fiery ball lifted into full view, and she was immediately thirsty.

Baela watched Bernie carry a box from the house, put it in the back of Pegre's wagon, then go back inside. In a moment she reappeared with a cloth satchel, and Pegre was behind her, a long pointing weapon in one hand. These items also went into the wagon, while Baela watched silently, bothered by the sight of a weapon in her teacher's hand.

They saw her as they turned to go back into the house. Pegre waved, and Bernie gestured at her to come inside with them. "Breakfast is on the table!" she shouted, while behind her Pegre smiled, pointed first to his mouth and then to the house. Baela understood, and trotted happily through tall grass to reach them, arriving smiling and a little out of breath.

"Mornin', Darlin'," said Bernie, and then to Pegre, "You think we might have one who looks like that? Bounces through the grass like a young deer." She put an arm around Baela's shoulders. "Hot cakes and sausage this morning. We need to fatten you up a bit."

They went inside to another table filled with food. Pegre and his mate had already been eating. Bernie bustled around the kitchen, and plunked a full plate in front of the girl, delighted by the hungry look on her face. Coyly, Baela mimicked everything Pegre did with knife and fork, buttering her hotcakes, pouring syrup, carefully cutting a piece and putting it slowly into her mouth. Pegre laughed at her expression when she tasted the sweetness. He laughed again when she tasted the sausage, delicious, but stinging the inside of her mouth.

"Everything's new," said Pegre.

"Do you like it, Baela?" asked Bernie.

Baela nodded vigorously, mouth filled with food.

"Good. There's plenty more, now; you just ask." But then Bernie's smile faded, and she looked at Pegre, who Baela had learned was called Peter or Pete by the Hinchai. "When're they coming over?"

"Any minute. The plan is to get back by dark, but it didn't work out that way last time. I really don't expect to find anything."

"All those men, and all those guns. I don't like it, Peter. I've got an uneasy feeling in the pit of my stomach about the whole day."

"Baby's kickin' again." Pegre smiled.

"Baby's fine, and not long in comin'. I want him to meet his father, so don't you go gettin' yourself shot out there. If these are hill people you're after, they'll go to ground in daylight, and you'll never see 'em."

"Don't have to. We'll have four dogs with us. They followed a track clear to the creek, but we've got to pick it up again. It's only a mile from here, Bernie."

"Everybody goin'? Jake, too?"

"Yeah, everybody."

"Great. Every woman in town is left alone today."

"I'm sure the people we're after skipped our area yesterday." Pegre looked at Baela, knowing she sensed his lie even though her understanding of English was still poor. She was leaning over her plate, chewing thoughtfully.

"You're not back by dark, I get the women together, and we come lookin' for you. I can handle a shotgun as well as any man, Peter."

Pegre reached over, and touched his mate's chin. "Okay, okay. We'll be back by dark. Anything happens here, you lock yourself in the house, and use the shotgun. Don't forget our guests in the bunkhouse, and upstairs. Several of them can give any man a good fight."

Bernie was silent for a moment, but Baela could feel and smell her fear, now, detecting a sudden unease of her own, a sort of apprehension that remained after she left the table. She helped Bernie wash the dishes and utensils at the sink, drying each piece as she had regularly done with simpler things for her parents in the cavern. Pegre went outside to wait, and in a short while they heard the rattling and clop-clop of wagons and horses pulling into the yard while Pegre directed traffic to parking places. Bernie sped up the washing, then wiped her hands and left the house while Baela finished her drying chore.

One wagon was parked close to the house, and in the back were four huge dogs, sleek, black coats and lolling tongues. The men were heavily armed and grim-looking, different from the scene of the welcome the night before. Some of them waved to Baela when they saw her standing by the window, and so she went out on the porch for a closer look. When she got there, the dogs took one look at her and started barking furiously, deep-throated sounds that turned into moans and then howls until one of the men stepped up to the wagon and screamed right into their faces. The howls became whimpers as Baela nervously stood her ground, knowing the animals sensed she didn't belong there, that she was one of those they searched for. Likely it was the basic Tenanken diet that produced a unique flesh odor the dogs could smell even at a distance. With time, it would disappear, and for now she was safe. She wondered what Hidaig and his band would feel like when the dogs were on their heels. From two nights before, she knew what it was like to be the hunted.

The men piled back into the wagons, Pegre getting in with the hawk-faced man she knew as Jake. Baela saw kindness and sadness in the slender man's eyes, noticed the way he looked all around after seeing her on the porch. It occurred to her that he was searching for the Tenanken female called Diana, the one he had hovered around during the welcome just hours before. She was surprised at how quickly a bond was forming, for Tenanken males were traditionally aloof around females, carefully choosing their mates on the basis of hearth skills rather than feelings or emotions. These often came later, as with her own parents, who had become quite close only after her birth, and now often coupled for the pure pleasure of it.

Bernie went to the wagon, and kissed Pegre as reins snapped and drivers yelled, the vehicles pulling out of the yard and moving slowly in a line up the dirt tracks towards the hill. Soon they had disappeared beyond the trees, and there was silence. Bernie came back on the porch, eyes welling up with tears, and putting an arm around Baela's shoulders. "Wish he wouldn't have gone with 'em today. Don't know why, but I've still got a bad feelin' about this whole day."

They stood and watched the trees for a moment, then went back inside as the first Tenanken adults emerged sleepy-eyed from the bunkhouse to feel the sunlight on their faces.

* * * * * * *

Maki waited anxiously on the ledge, surrounded by warriors who had brought him quickly outside when Tel's attempted signal fire had been discovered. He was afraid for his mother, though he knew her cleverness was underestimated because she was female. He knew also that she was an experienced wanderer of the cavern mazes. She could blank her mind well, and if determined not to be found she would not be found. But her foolishness had only incurred Hidaig's anger, accomplishing nothing and again putting her own son in an awkward, dangerous position. Obviously, Hidaig had decided to take power for himself, but he lacked both the intellect and spiritual presence to be Keeper. Maki still hoped that Hidaig would accept his usefulness in coaxing support of the conquered band for their new leader if the son of their old one were made spiritual advisor and Keeper of The Memories. From this base he could be patient, for the day would come when a devoted follower would slit Hidaig's throat, and all power would be his. For the moment, he would bide his time and survive. But he feared for his mother—and his father, feeling nothing coming from them.

Kretan emerged from the cavern, Hidaig close behind. Both glared at Maki.

"Have you found her?" Maki probed with his mind, scratching at the barrier Hidaig had raised. Its presence worried him. What was he hiding?

"We don't have time to search every tunnel and hole, but eventually she'll have to come out There are more important things to do. My question to you is, do you stand with us this day, or must we throw you into the canyon? I have no desire to constantly watch my back."

"I join with you, Hidaig, but Pegre is mine, and I ask you to leave him to me. I will need my weapons."

Hidaig thought for a moment, Maki feeling the weak probe, and letting him see hatred there, all seemingly directed at Pegre, and so there was reason for trust. Hidaig ordered Kretan to retrieve Maki's weapons from the cave, and shortly after the huge warrior reappeared with a fur bundle under one arm.

The bundle contained the rifle, but the pistol was gone. *Pegre*, thought Maki. As the others watched him suspiciously, he levered the rifle just enough to see that a projectile was in place. Probing lightly, he could feel the tension and fear all around him as he fingered the weapon.

"You know how to use this?" asked Hidaig.

"I have killed Hinchai with it before. Today, I will use it to kill Pegre." He closed the breech of the rifle with a snap, and looped the weapon across his chest. "I will do it at close range, so I can watch his face when his body explodes."

"Such strong feelings for an enemy," said Hidaig. "I will keep you in front of me today, and if you point that weapon in my direction Kretan will run you through. Those are his orders."

The big warrior smiled, and fingered the sharp, stone tip of his spear.

"I understand," said Maki, "that I must prove my loyalty to you. You will feel differently at the end of the day." He hoped that Hidaig would sense only his hatred for Pegre, and not the other feelings he now kept shielded from the probe: his hatred of Hidaig for betrayal, the mixed love and resentment he felt for his parents, and overwhelming guilt for having stood by passively while his father was struck down. But all these things would not have happened without Pegre's plan to take the Tenanken from the caves, and so he focused the blame on the one who would be his victim this day.

They moved out in a line, Maki, Kretan and Hidaig bringing up the rear, climbing to the end of the canyon past Baela's hidey-tree, and close to where both Tenanken and Hinchai had been buried under stone, one remaining there still. Far below them, on the canyon floor, beneath thick pines, beetles and worms began work on the corpses of several old ones and a loyal friend named Han, whom Maki had already forgotten.

They rounded the end of the canyon, and came back along the other side, past the open entrance of the cave they no longer attempted to hide, because soon there would be nobody left alive to hide it from. They picked their way along the edge until the canyon veered sharply towards the valley, and there they went back into the trees, following them out to a sharp ridge descending to a grassy floor dotted with buildings. Pegre was in one of those buildings. Pegre, and his Hinchai mate. Maki focused on a vision of killing them both.

Hidaig called them to a halt at the edge of the trees, and there they sat down to watch and wait as the sun rose, turning the valley golden. The buildings were near; it would be a charge of three hundred paces down the ridge and across a field to reach them. There was activity at one building, a door banging and a Hinchai female rushed out with something in her hands, which she deposited into a vehicle before going back inside. When she appeared again there was a big male with her, and they loaded more things into the vehicle.

"There, you see Pegre," said Maki. "The other is his Hinchai mate, and she carries his child." The disgust in his voice was impossible to conceal.

Hidaig squinted, and looked closely. "So it is. He is not exactly as I remember him, but we were younger then. I see fat from the easy Hinchai life." He chuckled.

"Don't be deceived by sight," said Maki. "He's strong, and his spirit is not diminished. Remember, he's mine."

"Yes, yes," said Hidaig, smiling. "Ah, what have we here?" He pointed to another building, from which a figure had emerged into the sunlight. "They have another child?"

A young girl with long, blonde hair stretched lazily, bringing slender arms up over her head, then running towards the other building. Maki recognized her immediately. "No, that is one of the Hanken from our band. The rest of them must be in the building she came out of. If we attack now, we might catch most of them asleep."

Hidaig shook his head. "Not so fast. I don't know how many are inside, or the number of males who can fight. Pegre must have at least one pointing weapon, so surprise will have to be the main element of our strategy, and the strike must be swift. If pointing weapons are used against us, our numbers will mean nothing. We will wait until we see who is down there, and exactly where they are. Now, we watch."

Hidaig leaned back against a tree, and Kretan squatted on the ground beside him. Maki remained in front of them, sprawled out on his stomach, chin on hands to watch the valley. For a while, there was nothing to see. Baela had gone inside the house, and it was quiet outside. Sunlight warmed his face, eyelids fluttered, closed. He even dozed.

The clattering and shouting jolted him wide-awake. He watched the vehicles pull up to the house, bristling with weapons and full of Hinchai males. He turned and looked at Hidaig, who smiled back smugly.

"If we had attacked a few minutes ago, you see what a nice welcome we would have had? It is a good thing to be patient, and if my guess is right we will soon have no opposition to worry about."

In seconds Pegre came out of the house with a weapon, and all the Hinchai males got back into their vehicles. They drove away quickly, and Pegre's mate went back into the house, closing the door behind her, but in the next few minutes the Tenanken of Maki's band came one-by-one out of the longer building and walked over to the house, disappearing inside. Maki looked at Hidaig expectantly.

"Not yet. We want the vehicles far away before we do anything; all those weapons could destroy us in minutes. We can wait. I count five males who can give us any kind of fight, and they might even decide to join us. It's the females we want, anyway. Patience, Maki. I'm sure that's a hunting party we saw; they won't be back before dark, and we'll be far from here by then."

They waited.

The day grew warmer. Tenanken went back and forth between the house and long building. A few wandered around the fields and visited a wider, higher building some two hundred paces from the house. The structure was unfinished in places, connected to a fenced-in area used to keep animals, though there were none there, now, and the wood was not painted in colors like the other buildings. By early afternoon most of the Tenanken had retired to the long building to sleep, for the heat had become intense, and was a new experience for them. Pegre's mate appeared a couple of times, hanging clothes and bedding on a line behind the house, but otherwise it was quiet.

"It is time," said Hidaig, and Kretan and Maki were immediately on their feet, the rest following more slowly. "Form two lines, equal in numbers," Hidaig ordered, and the warriors scrambled to obey. "I will lead this group, and attack the house. Kretan, you take the others and occupy the long building. All Tenanken males can choose to join us, or die. Take the females alive if you can, but kill any Hanken in the group. I will not tolerate them in my band. Maki, you go with Kretan and show us you can conduct yourself like a warrior. Your ambition may yet be fulfilled. Are there any questions?"

There were none.

"Move quickly and boldly, and none of us should be hurt. Now move!"

They moved out in a line down the ridge, descending quickly until they reached grass, and the line became two, snaking towards the house and long building.

* * * * * * *

During the morning the canyon breathed in, sucking streams of air from the valley to the headwall to fan the glowing embers until a root smoldered. Only a stick or two remained from Tel's scattered signal fire, but new life was added with dried pine needles, twigs and cones, and now the root. For hours it had smoldered, growing hotter with each tiny gust of wind, tendrils of smoke appearing and disappearing, and then there was a tiny flame igniting more pine needles and a cone. The flame grew hungrily, dancing in the wind and reaching out for food, a joyful light in the gloom beneath the trees. A squirrel came by and stood on its tail in surprise at the sight of the flame, staring at it with black eyes. The flame frolicked before the squirrel with a surge of new life, whipping close so that the animal blinked its eyes at the wave of sudden heat and darted away through the trees, heading instinctively towards the open valley below. The squirrel had seen fire before, and knew what it could do. To stay in the canyon was to die, and so it fled.

The single flame grew to a vortex of fire, heating the air around it. The velvet mat of pine needles began to smoke, and beetles burrowed frantically to escape the heat. Around the vortex a firestorm grew, swirling and leaping until suddenly the canyon floor exploded in flame reaching upwards for closely packed trees, and in seconds the canyon was a living hell of fire sweeping towards the headwall.

For two hours the flames consumed everything in the canyon, even the wretched bodies of dead Tenanken and two hapless deer that had been late to rise that morning. Flames reached far above the canyon rim, sending a column of smoke two miles into the sky, hot air rising so quickly that a miniature cumulonimbus cloud formed right over the area and gave birth to light rain which cooled the canyon when there was nothing left to burn.

By that time, many people had died in the valley below.

CHAPTER EIGHTEEN

FIRE

"You sure are grim this mornin'," said Jake. "You mad at me for somethin'?"

The concern in his friend's voice shook Pete from his reverie, chin in hand, staring out at passing trees. "Daydreaming, Jake," he said, reaching over to put at hand on the man's shoulder. "You drive, and I daydream. I'm not in favor of this search party, you know. I've got a nasty feeling about it."

Jake smiled. "I've got a feeling about it too, Pete, but it ain't bad. I think this is the day we're gonna find those suckers, and I'm gonna get another shot at the son-of-a-bitch who tried to kill me. Remember when y'all thought I was nuts talkin' about the critters? Now here we are chasin' them. I think it's great."

Pete patted the bony shoulder affectionately. "You were right, Jake. You knew before any of us, but when you haven't seen those guys it's a little hard to believe."

"Yeah, and I was drinkin' a lot then. Thought they was some kind of monsters 'cause I never saw wild white people before. What do I know?"

The men ahead of them had turned off onto a side road, and Jake slowed to make the turn. "Didn't see Diana this mornin'," he said.

"Wasn't up, yet. Only one of the kids got up early. They were all tired last night."

"Pretty girl. What's her last name?"

Pete thought fast. "Galleos, I think. She's distant family; hard to keep up on all the names. Yeah, I saw you talkin' to her."

"Only speaks a few words of English, but we seemed to get along okay, and that smile of hers can just about knock a man down. You mind if I call on her sometime?"

"That's between you and Diana, Jake. Good luck."

162

It was the first time Pete had seen Jake really grin since before Ester had left him.

The road ended at the little creek meandering through the valley, a rushing torrent in spring now barely a trickle. The men piled out, weapons clacking as they were checked and loaded. Pete figured there were fifty guns among the group, and every man a good shot. No matter, because by now Hidaig had surely moved in on the cave to find only a few old ones with Tel and Anka, taking what little there was to take and leaving. He would not be so foolish to risk a confrontation with the firepower of the entire town. He would leave the area right away, and likely head south. But somehow it seemed he was near, a kind of malevolent spirit hovering over Pete and his friends, threatening them. The feeling had nagged at Pete since early morning, and now the nagging was urgent, forming a little cramp in his stomach, a fluttering pain that would not go away.

Jake pulled his knapsack out of the back of the wagon, opened it, tipped it so Pete could look inside. Nestled beside a canteen and food bag were several half-sticks of fused dynamite. "Heavy artillery," said Jake. "Those critters get near me I blow them to kingdom come." He closed up the sack and slung it over his back while Pete held his rifle. They followed the ragged line of men to the creek where Zeke and his big dogs were already working the opposite embankment, and it was only a few minutes later when the animals huffed and whooped, dragging their master off through the trees, the rest of the group charging through cold water after them.

To Pete, the trail was clear, a line of heel marks on pine needle-covered ground. There were some with him who also saw the signs, experienced hunters with prey instincts approaching that of The Mind Touch, and at times Pete wondered if in fact it was also a Hinchai gift, neglected and unused over the long centuries. Did they feel his own apprehension at this moment; did they feel a strange warning of immediate danger that squeezed their intestines and made their throats tighten?

They charged up the hill, all men excited by the baying of the dogs, slipping and sliding on soft earth and grasping at roots to pull themselves upwards near the summit, where they stood panting and sweating.

They were at the headwall of the canyon.

Pete looked over to the side, and gulped. The brush covering the entrance to Anka's caverns was pushed aside, the black maw of the opening now clearly visible. For the moment, they were moving away from it. The dogs had found something beyond the canyon rim, and were howling excitedly. The men stumbled after them to a clearing by large granite boulders, where they found scraps of corn-cob and what looked like jerky, which the dogs greedily snapped up.

"Okay," said Zeke, "it looks like they bedded down here. Grass is bent, garbage all over the place. You know, it's just a little ways over to where we found Tom. Shit, they was probably here watchin' us, 'cause we followed the canyon back just below this spot."

Another man yelled from nearby, and they drifted over to look at the big splash of blood he'd found on the ground. A line of red trailed from one puddle to a second, smaller one at a spot where the pine needles were scraped away to show dirt. All of them shuddered. Someone or something had died in agony here, tearing up the ground. Ned hunkered down, and touched the blood. "Pretty old, I'd guess. Probably a dog or a deer."

"Yeah? Is that what Tom was?" asked Jake.

"Let's get on with it," said Ned.

"But where to?" asked Zeke. "Scent's so strong here the dogs don't want to leave. Besides, it's noon, and I'm tired from draggin' two hundred pounds of dog. Let's eat."

No opposition. They sat down in the clearing, and ate the lunches they'd brought along, and for a while Pete thought they might go back the way they had come, leaving the caverns undis-covered. But it was Ned, munching bread and strolling along the canyon rim, who first saw the man-sized hole in the wall and let out a whoop that scared them silly.

Pete thought fast, and moved faster. While the others went to Ned, he angled off in the other direction, crossing the canyon at the edge of the headwall and climbing around the rock where the nest of the great hunting bird now lay empty. They hadn't seen him yet when he found the crack leading down to the long shelf by the cav-ern entrance; he raised a foot to step into it, but stopped when there was a sound behind him.

He turned, and found Jake grinning at him from a meter away.

"Right behind you, buddy. Didn't think you were goin' in there alone, did ya?"

The best answer was no answer. Pete slung his rifle across his back and descended the crack looking forward, swallowing hard again at the sight of the canyon floor over forty meters below. Jake scrambled happily behind him like a skinny lizard until they stood on the shelf, breathing hard, and not from the effort. "Aren't you gettin' a bit old for this?" asked Pete

"Speak for yourself," said Jake, pleased with himself. The oth-ers saw them, then, and hollered.

"Hey, what're *you* doin over there!" shouted Ned.

"Sneakin' up on 'em," said Jake sarcastically.

Everyone got the meaning, and shut up while they edged their way along the shelf, Jake right at Pete's back.

"You think anyone's in there now?" asked Jake.

"I doubt it. You have a light?"

"Nope."

"Never mind. I got a candle here," said Pete, and Jake looked at him curiously.

They stepped up to the entrance, and listened. There was a faint moaning sound coming from the blackness. "Big cave," said Jake. "I can hear it breathin'."

From their left came the sounds of rifle actions working. "Jee-zus, don't anyone get trigger-happy and shoot the first thing that moves over here," yelled Pete. He unslung his rifle, pointed it at the blackness, handed the candle to Jake. "Light it for me. Here's a match."

Jake lit the candle, handed it to him. They stepped inside, a soft glow spreading ahead of them, the moaning suddenly loud in their ears. Pete moved the flickering candle to the right, then quickly back again in surprise. Maki's sleeping furs were still there.

"You see that? Someone's been sleepin' here, all right." Jake pressed so close one shoulder was digging into Pete's back. "Sound's comin' from the left. The real cave must be down that tunnel." He pushed Pete in that direction, sniffing the air. "You smell the wood smoke?"

"Yes," said Pete, and he snicked back the hammer of his rifle. The tunnel seemed forever until they finally reached the main cavern in darkness except for the faint glow of light that Pete played around on the walls, past burned out fire-rings and torches, scattered pieces of garbage left carelessly on the floor. Pete lit a torch, handed the candle to Jake.

"This is it," said Jake. "This is where they lived; I remember the stink of their hair, and it's here. God, Pete, this is close to your place. All the time they was right at your back door. We'd better get goin'."

Pete didn't answer, didn't seem to hear. The light continued to move around the immense cavern, darting in and out of fumaroles and tunnels, pausing at a fire ring, moving on, stopping for a long pause at what looked like a streak of blood on a rock, then flickering out.

"Hey!" shouted Jake, grabbing onto Pete's belt.

Pete shushed him. "Listen for a minute," he said.

Jake hung on, listening, but all he heard was Pete's breathing growing slower and shallower, until it seemed he wasn't breathing at all. His own heart was pounding, the darkness closing in, suffocating him. His fingers twisted Pete's belt, and then suddenly a match scratched and the light was on again, a blessed glow of relief.

"Okay, they're not here now, but they were here. I want to get back to my place, Jake, and right now."

"Yep, especially with the women down there. Right behind you, Pete." Something had changed in the big man's voice, thought Jake. It was deep, soft, without emotion.

They retraced their steps, Jake taking a deep breath when they stepped out into sunlight again.

"What'd you see?" shouted Ned, the others lowering their rifles.

"It's a big cave, and people been livin' in it, all right. Empty, now," said Jake. Pete moved along the shelf again, following the canyon towards the valley, Jake right behind him. The big man said nothing. Didn't even look back.

"Hey, where you goin'?" shouted Ned.

"Back to Pete's place. It's awful close, Ned, and he's worried about his people."

"I'm beginnin' to think those guys have left the area by now, but we're gonna backtrack and see if we can pick up another trail. Four hours or so, and we'll meet you down there."

"Okay," said Jake. "See you then." Ned and the others were already moving up towards the canyon headwall while Pete was charging off in the other direction without a word, big feet picking along the narrow shelf like the hooves of a mountain goat. He stopped once to sniff the air, looked back briefly, then charged on.

"I'm comin'," shouted Jake. He put one reassuring hand on the rock wall and shuffled cautiously along the foot-wide path hanging above certain death by seventy meters.

Quite suddenly, there was an odor of wood smoke. Strong. Blowing up the canyon. Jake looked down at the valley, and Pete's house. No smoke coming from the chimney. An instant later, he felt a warm breeze on his face, surprising him because all morning there had been a chill in the air. The odor of smoke was continuous, now, and below him at the edge of his vision he thought he saw light and movement, but his path was so precarious he didn't dare lose concentration on the placement of his feet. Even when wisps of smoke curled over his boots, he watched only the shelf and moved carefully ahead, beginning to sweat, and below him there seemed to be a rushing wind. *Never mind. Watch your feet, and stay alive.*

And his world exploded in a hell of flame.

A low whooshing sound filled his ears as the blast of heat seared one side of his face, and instantly he was pressed to the wall by towering flames reaching up for him from the canyon floor. Wind generated by the fire buffeted him on his narrow perch so that he turned to get both hands on the rock with his pack-covered back towards the flames. He heard Pete yelling something he didn't understand, and shouting from somewhere up the canyon was nearly drowned out by the roar of the fire as he crab-walked the shelf one agonizing step at a time, feeling the heat now in his boots and legs and butt. Hotter and hotter. He smelled singed hair, and something sharper, and knew he had begun to smolder. Any instant now he would burst into flame like a match, eyes burning and pain making him reach for his face, letting go of the rock and losing his balance to topple into the inferno below him. Exit Jake Price.

No. He crabbed faster, grunting, seeing only his feet, sweat pouring into his eyes to blur his vision. Pete yelled again, and this time the voice seemed near.

"It's movin' up the canyon, Jake! A little further, and you've got it. Come on, a few more steps!"

Now his chest hurt, and he was coughing, and for one heart-stopping instant his right hand slipped off the wall, twirling him backwards to a new blast of heat that nearly blew him from the shelf before his left hand, wedged in a crack, snapped him back again like a recoiling spring.

"Come on, Jake. A couple more. Here, grab my hand!"

Jake saw a blur that was his feet, and crabbed again. Strong arms grabbed him, and there was the odor of garlic.

"Christ, you're eyes are watering hard. Here, sit down, and we'll clean 'em out."

"You guys all right over there?"

"Yeah, but it was close. Fire started right below us when we were comin' down. Jake was in the middle of it."

A cloth was pressed into Jake's hand, and he wiped his eyes clean. The smell of singed hair was strong, now. His hair.

"Look at that thing go!" yelled Ned. "It's gonna clean out the whole canyon!"

"I've got to get Jake to my place! Nothing serious, but we should take care of some burns."

"We'll go down from this side, and meet you there," said Ned.

Jake opened his eyes. Vision was clear, and Pete's square face was right in front of him. Across the canyon Ned and the others were disappearing into the trees, headed down towards the valley. When he turned, the skin on the back of his neck hurt like hell, and he saw a wall of flame near the headwall of the canyon, moving away from them like a wave surging against a shore. "Am I burned bad?" he asked.

"Don't see any blisters coming, but the hair's gone back there, and the skin's red. Pretty lucky, Jake. If we'd been comin' *towards* the fire when it started, we'd both be cinders now. It started right below you; must have been smoldering for a long time to blow like that."

"You don't think it was set?"

"Don't see how, unless they were right there when it went up. Anyone down there now is dead, I can tell you. Come on, let's get at those burns."

The shelf had blessedly ended at a ridge, and the walking was suddenly easy. Pete's house was directly below them, bunkhouse and barn even closer, and Pete looked back at him with a grin, but an instant later the grin was gone. The big man stopped so fast Jake ran into him. Jake followed his gaze, and saw a line of men running down from a knoll by the mouth of the canyon, crouched over, wearing tattered rags for clothing and carrying spears and axes. They moved in organized fashion, splitting into two groups heading separately towards the bunkhouse and the main house.

It was not Ned and the other men he saw.

It was the critters.

"Pete—," he started to say, but then his friend let out a scream that sent a shiver throughout his body. It started deep in Pete's chest, as a growl, and came out as a shriek, primal and terrifying. Pete charged away from him and down the ridge, massive arms flailing the air while Jake twisted painfully to unsling his rifle and stumble along after him.

In the rush of adrenalin that followed, pain was quickly forgotten.

CHAPTER NINETEEN

WAR

Bernie saw the fire from the kitchen window, and went out the back door for a better look. At first it was a bright glow in the canyon, without smoke, and then quite suddenly there were flames leaping above the trees. Her houseguests had gone back to the bunkhouse, but now a few of them came outside to watch, pointing and chattering animatedly among themselves. She saw Baela race towards the barn, blonde hair streaming behind her. A moment later she appeared in the hayloft doorway, pointing towards the canyon and shouting to the others, but Bernie couldn't understand anything. At first she didn't understand when Baela suddenly pointed again in a different direction, screaming shrilly, driving the others into a panic. Some raced towards the house, while others ran inside the bunkhouse, slamming the door shut. Diana and two other women pounded towards Bernie, pointing towards their left and shouting at her. Her head turned, in slow motion it seemed, and suddenly she understood.

Trotting towards her across the fields from the direction of the burning canyon was the filthiest group of men she had ever seen in her life.

Instantly she recognized the danger, but never before had she felt so vulnerable. Never before had she felt so slow—so pregnant, and the baby was kicking madly. The other women stormed past her and scrambled into the house. She watched the attacking men, stooped over, splitting into two groups, one heading straight for her, and finally she seemed able to move. She rushed inside and locked the back door, then shut a window and locked it too. While the other women cowered in the kitchen by the windowless back door Bernie walked briskly to the front door and bolted it, then glanced at the line of white men coming towards the porch: filthy, clothes hanging in rags, primitive spears and clubs in their hands, long hair hanging

169

in brutish faces and over shoulders. *Jake's critters*, she thought. *These are Jake's critters. But they're men. White men.*

The big window was the soft spot of the house; they would come through there. Bernie opened a closet by the front door, pulled out a twelve-gauge shotgun, stretched to reach a box of shells on a shelf. She crossed the front room when the first of the attackers was already on the front porch, face pressed against the window, grinning evilly. She stood in the kitchen doorway, loaded two shells into the weapon and snapped it shut. Four men were on the porch, now. The front door rattled.

Bernie stepped backwards into the kitchen, yanked open a drawer by the sink and took out all the carving knives she could find. She put them on the counter, looking sternly at the frightened women, and pointing. No translation necessary, the women grabbed knives with both hands and retreated again to a corner. Bernie stood in the doorway, leveling the shotgun as the men outside began pounding on the window with their hands, pressing their faces close to look inside. They seemed hesitant, unsure. Out of a corner of her eye she saw someone move past the kitchen window, and then there was a pounding on the thick back door, bolted shut. A heartbeat later the window of the kitchen burst inwards, followed by a massive, hairy arm groping around the corner, reaching past the sink and towards the door. Diana growled, raised a butcher knife in both hands and struck four times in rapid succession.

Blood sprayed over the sink. The man outside howled, and the arm retreated. The women were not whimpering, now, but angry. Their eyes flashed, and they screamed at the men outside in a language unlike anything Bernie had heard before. Guttural, fast. Now they stood their ground, but they were only four women with knives—and a shotgun.

A crowd was on the porch, at least seven men still hesitating, feeling the glass with their hands. Perhaps they would decide it was too dangerous, and go away. Bernie's finger curled around one trigger of the shotgun as a new face appeared at the window. A tall man with chiseled features, less brutish than the others.

"Hidaig," said Diana, and Bernie wondered fleetingly what that meant, but there was no time to dwell on it for the new man had stepped back and was swinging an axe towards the big window. His knees were bent, and he swung horizontally, head down. The glass tried to bend, but was not given time; it shattered into several large pieces falling onto the living room floor, a spray of smaller slivers sticking in furniture along the opposite wall.

Bernie took two steps into the room, and aimed the shotgun.

Two men scrambled over the windowsill.

Bernie fired at point-blank range.

The explosions were deafening, and the women screamed. The first shot blew away the face of one attacker, the second nearly cutting a man in half at the waist as Bernie reloaded. Blood sprayed over the attackers and the porch, but on they came, another three men, and Bernie cut them down like grass blades, slamming their bodies back over the windowsill.

She backed towards the kitchen, grasping for the box of shells on a counter. Three more men came across the sill, eyes wide with fear, but the taller one on the porch, the one who had broken the window, was screaming at them, driving them on. For an instant she realized they didn't understand the gun, didn't understand it wasn't loaded yet, and could do no harm. She reached behind her, and found the box, scrabbling with her fingers for a shell and loading it as the attackers edged forward, but then there was no more time to even aim. One man sprang at Bernie, she thrust the shotgun into his mouth and jerked the trigger.

A human head bounced into one corner of the room.

They had their filthy hands on her, now, grappling for the weapon. She threw her weight into them, and at first they seemed surprised by her strength, but then reinforcements came and suddenly she was struggling with four men. As they pushed her into the kitchen, the back door burst open, flooding the room with light as the other women fled from the house to whatever fate awaited them outside.

A fist struck her face once—twice, and then in her stomach. *Oh God, the pain!* The baby's feet pounded inside her. *They're killing my baby*, she thought. *They're going to kill both of us.* She struck back with the shotgun butt and felt bone break, but them a fist hammered into her ribs and she cried out, loosening her grip. The weapon was ripped from her hands as they pushed her against the sink and again there was a hard blow to her stomach. Tears streaming, she clawed at their faces as they struck her repeatedly in the face and ribs as she covered up to protect her child, dropping to her knees under the rain of blows.

Her head snapped back. A hand was snarled in her long hair, and she was being dragged across the floor, arms crossed over her stomach. Pieces of glass drove into her back and buttocks and she screamed in pain, vaguely aware of the front door slamming open and then the porch was beneath her, rough splinters tearing at her clothes.

Shouting. The ground was now beneath her, for they had dragged her off the porch. Her hair was released, and her head hit a rock. Barely conscious, she looked up to see a blurred figure standing over her. More shouting, and then a gunshot! The figure above her turned, and then from far away came an animal scream that sent a chill through her broken body. She closed her eyes, and waited for death to come.

* * * * * * *

From her perch in the hayloft, Baela screamed at the others to lock themselves inside. Hidaig and his gang were attacking; they would kill all but the females, but for Baela this was not reassuring. She knew what the outcast gang leader thought of Hanken, and she would surely die if they captured her. The attackers came in two lines, one veering towards the main house, and she thought of Bernie: alone, pregnant, and Hinchai. They would slit her open and leave her to die slowly, or crush her skull with an axe if she was lucky. She screamed Bernie's name, but there was no movement in the house. Below her, Tenanken ran to the bunkhouse, some females to the main house, and one male towards her in the barn. Moug. Her father had seen her.

No, she thought, *don't come here. Stay with mother.*

Moug raced silently towards her, motioning her with a sweep of his arm to get out of sight, but it was already too late. The first line of attackers had reached the bunkhouse, were pounding on walls and the door, and Baela could hear the screams of those trapped inside. But three attackers had split from the group, and were chasing her father. One she recognized as Maki, and she flushed with anger. The traitor was now in the open with his conspirators, and she wished that somehow he would not live to see darkness.

As the warriors gained ground on Moug, Baela searched the loft for a weapon and found one, a long, metal fork with needle-sharp tines that could run through the muscle of even a Tenanken warrior. She hefted it, gratified by the light weight, stepped up to the edge of the loft and kicked at the wooden ladder leading up to it from the barn floor. It was nailed solidly to the loft, would not come loose even when she kicked with all her strength. She was still kicking when Moug appeared in the entrance to the barn. Stepping to one side of the doorway in half-gloom, he looked around desperately for something to fight with, eyes wide like those of a cornered, frightened animal. Baela tensed, starting to throw the fork down to her father, but it was too late to react at any speed for the attackers had nearly caught up to him when he reached the barn.

A warrior she had never seen before appeared in the entrance, spear in hand, looking up and seeing her, moving forward, and then Moug stepped from the shadows and kicked him hard in the crotch.

The warrior dropped his spear and fell to both knees, clutching at himself. Moug pounced, grabbing for the throat and rolling his intended victim over, squeezing hard. The warrior's feet beat a crazy rhythm on the floor, hands clawing at Moug's face, but then a shadow fell over both of them. A huge warrior appeared in the doorway, war club in hand, and the biggest spear Baela had ever seen in the other. He swung the club in a high arc over his head as Baela screamed. Moug saw motion out of the corner of an eye, shrinking from the blow, but there was a loud snap and crunch as the heavy stone club struck first shoulder and then head.

Moug rolled over on his side, and lay still.

Baela screamed again, tears streaming down her face as Maki entered the barn, looking from her to the figures on the ground: one still as death, the other writhing angrily now, scrambling to his feet in terrible fury.

The one who had struck down Baela's father now moved towards the ladder to the loft, but Maki screamed at him, "Leave her! She's mine!"

The huge one fixed amber eyes on Baela, amused, then turned to his companion who had just risen, still holding his crotch. ""So we will take her," he said in a deep voice, "and throw her scrawny body down to the point of my spear." He slammed the spear shaft into the ground near the ladder, grinned as his comrade pushed past him unarmed and began to climb up to the loft.

Baela stepped back two paces from the ladder, and leveled the big, metal fork, gripping with tiny hands.

The warrior's head appeared above the loft floor. He grinned, showing rotten teeth.

His shoulders and thick body appeared; he grasped the top of the ladder and started to step up onto the loft floor.

Baela lowered her head, and charged.

The fork struck in the hard chest of the warrior, burying itself deeply.

The attacker let out a gasp, blood spurting with air. His hands groped at the wooden shaft sticking out of him and he toppled over backwards, ripping the weapon out of Baela's hands and slamming hard to the floor below.

Baela's heart pounded, her weapon gone. Nothing but straw remained in the loft, not even a stone. The giant below her looked up and chuckled, then pushed the shaft of his spear even deeper into the ground. He smiled at Baela, and began to climb the ladder.

"Why kill her, Kretan?" asked Maki calmly from the doorway.

"I will take her to Hidaig on my spear. He will be pleased." Slowly, patiently, Kretan slithered up the ladder.

"Very well," said Maki, and he bent over to pick up the spear of the warrior killed by Baela.

Her only chance now was quickness and speed and light, flexible bones like those of a bird. Once she had briefly experienced flight by leaping from her hidey tree, executing a forward roll when her feet touched the ground, and taking up much of the shock in her back and one shoulder. The height had been what she now faced, perhaps three times her own length. If she landed wrong it would all be over. Even done properly she must come up on her feet in a sprint to get past Maki and out of the barn. And what then?

Baela thought of the great hunting bird, and stretched out her arms like wings as she backed along the edge of the loft away from the ladder. Kretan's head appeared above the edge of the loft, grinning in anticipation of touching her, saliva glistening on his chin. Her foot slipped on the edge of the loft, and she teetered a little, gasping in surprise at what she saw below: Maki, arm drawn far back with the spear, running forward to gain momentum, eyes fixed not on her but on the back of the huge warrior named Kretan, releasing the spear with a grunt, and then the strangled cry.

Kretan's eyes bulged as he screamed in pain and fury, four inches of the stone spearhead protruding out from his chest, blood spurting. Pump, pump, pump, the life drained from him in an instant. He collapsed over the top of the ladder in a red pool, and was still.

Baela looked down as Maki kicked over the big spear that had been waiting to receive her, and he saw the question in her face.

"It was a private vengeance," he said, "but I did it for you, too. Jump down, now, and I will catch you. I promise, Hidaig will not harm you, because it is my will that you go unharmed. He needs my support to consolidate the band, and you can help, Baela. You can make life better for your parents and friends if you stand by my side in this, because they all have affection for you."

"You try to trick me," said Baela sharply. "You hate all Hanken; I've heard you say it. You think we all should have died at birth."

Maki shook his head and looked up at her pleadingly. "No, I don't feel that way about you, Baela. You have intelligence and spirit, and when I'm Keeper I want you at my side. Just you, Baela. Nobody else."

Suddenly the girl with long legs and budding breasts understood the power she had over the ambitious young man. She put her hands on her hips, and looked down at him seriously. "When you say by your side, you expect that I will lie down with you."

Maki nodded.

"You expect I will have your children."

"Yes," said Maki softly. "Now jump down quickly, and I will catch you. There's no more time for talk."

Baela thought—considering her options.

She leapt into the air, and fell into Maki's outstretched arms.

He caught her with a grunt, holding her for an instant close against his chest, feeling the slender arm around his neck and smelling her sweet breath. He put her down on her feet, but grabbed an arm when she tried to twirl away from him.

"My father's badly hurt; I have to help him. Let me go!"

"He's dead, Baela. There's nothing we can do, now."

"No! Please!"

"He's gone, and we have no time to argue. I'll bring you back when the fighting is over, but now you come with me!"

"Father—" she said, tears running down her face as Maki pulled her away from the huddled form and out of the barn. She stumbled after him, squinting in the sunlight and again hearing the screams of the battle.

They had run only a few steps when the first shots rang out.

Popping sounds. Maki flinched, ducking his head and unslinging his pointing weapon while maintaining a firm grip on Baela's arm.

"What is it?" she asked.

"Stay close to me, and move quickly." Maki pulled her close, put an arm around her waist and they trotted towards the bunkhouse which the attackers had still not penetrated, the scene chaotic as warriors stumbled around and fell, one breaking away and running towards them, the popping sounds continuing. When he was a few feet away, a red hole appeared in his forehead, and then his head exploded, showering them with blood and pieces of bone. Baela screamed, and Maki crushed her to him as they ran for their lives.

* * * * * * *

Pete charged down the ridge, a crazy bull looking for something to crush, eyes fixed on the house with attackers already on the porch. He hit the grass and vaulted a fence like an eighteen-year-old, without breaking stride, Jake calling out in vain for him to wait, but again all that existed were the figures on the porch, *his* porch and *his* house, pounding at the window, and then he saw Hidaig swing the big club, heard the window shatter and the first explosion from inside the house. Bernie's shotgun. She was fighting them—alone. Pete growled in rage, baring his teeth as the shotgun went off again, two, three times, slamming bodies back onto the porch. *They will kill her; they will kill her, then slit her open and kill our child. Because I wasn't there.*

Hidaig was barking orders on the porch, oblivious to the crazy animal charging at him. Another explosion, and then the back door to the house flew open, spilling out women.

"Diana!" called Jake from behind him. "Over here!"

The women ran towards Pete and Jake. One warrior saw them from the porch, starting a chase but freezing in his tracks when he saw Pete coming. Another came around the house, swinging a club and striking one woman to her knees, retreating to the porch as she bounced up flailing at him with a knife in her hand.

Pete saw the mob drag a kicking and screaming woman from the house. *Bernie. Dear God, they've got Bernie. My wife—my baby.* She lay in a heap on the ground, surrounded by warriors, and Hidaig was stepping up to her with his club.

Pete screamed a primal sound that came from the pit of his soul. He leveled his rifle waist high and fired, a warrior spinning away from the crowd, holding his side before collapsing on the porch. As he chambered another round a warrior ran towards him, spear raised for a throw, body shuddering and them crumpling to the ground when Jake opened fire. Jake fired again, knocking down another warrior as the group turned and saw them coming. Where was Hidaig now? It was Hidaig he wanted. *I will crush skull, then feed your brains to our child.* But there were no children—yet. His unborn child lay with its mother in the dirt before their home, threatened by beings from another world, who showed no pity.

He would show no pity.

Pete screamed again, firing as he charged, warriors scattering and falling before him. By the time he reached Bernie the rifle was empty; he threw it to the ground and snatched up a war club. So many years since he'd had such a weapon in his hands, but it felt comfortable and natural, and when the first warrior came at him with a spear he parried delicately, then swung by spinning his entire body, shattering the Tenanken head in an explosion of gore. The three remaining warriors fled around the side of the house as he reached Bernie and knelt beside her, vaguely aware of Jake's puffing arrival to stand guard behind him.

"I'm here," he said, panting. "It's all right, now."

Her face was bloody and swollen. She rolled over on her back, and held out her arms for him, tears gushing over her face. "Oh, Pete, they've hurt the baby. I have a terrible pain inside me, and the baby isn't kicking. Oh, Pete—our child—"

"It's all right," he said. "We'll take care of you. Relax." As he spoke, his head swiveled, searching for Hidaig. Jake seemed to read his mind, and knelt beside him.

"The fight's moved to the bunkhouse, but they can't get in. You want to find someone, I'll stay with Bernie, Pete. I'll take care of her for you."

I've brought them to this. I led them out of the caverns and down here to die. I am responsible for this. Pete grabbed up the war club, and put a hand on his friend's shoulder. Jake reached out to hand him something.

Two sticks of dynamite, and a small box of matches.

"Something for the cause," said Jake.

Bernie groaned, and clutched at her belly. Jake looked down at her. "If I have to, I'll die for her, Pete. Go on, now."

Pete grabbed Jake awkwardly in a hug, then turned and headed towards the bunkhouse, where warriors still pounded at the heavy door. He ran within twenty meters of the milling crowd, then knelt in the tall grass and struck a match. The fuses on the dynamite were incredibly short, and he had no experience with explosives.

The warriors had built a small fire by the bunkhouse, feeding it with loose scraps of wood, carrying flaming pieces over to the building to start a much bigger fire. A warrior tending the fire looked up and saw Pete kneeling in the grass. When he saw the match his eyes widened, he stood up, spear in hand, and walked deliberately towards Pete. He had walked only a few steps when he stopped with a sudden shudder. A small hole appeared in his chest, oozing blood. The warrior stood there, looking confused, and then his eyes rolled upwards; he sank to his knees, and toppled over on his side.

Now Pete heard it, the crackle of gunfire, off to his right, the whine of bullets coming in like bees. Screams. Two more warriors staggered and fell by the bunkhouse. Pete lit the fuse of the dynamite, watched the fuse burn all the way down, then flipped it towards the bunkhouse and dropped to the ground. The dynamite exploded in the air, knocking everyone hard to the ground within a radius of twenty meters. For a moment Pete could hear no sound except a high-pitched ringing; he stood up groggily, gripping the war club, stumbling forward.

The warriors panicked, darting away from him around the bunkhouse and across the grassy field towards the blackened and smoldering canyon beyond. Gunfire was continuous; Pete looked to his right, saw Ned and the others kneeling in a line by his fence, aiming and firing with careful deliberation. One by one, the warriors fell under rifle fire and lay still. Pete trotted after them, looking for Hidaig, finding Baela instead, firmly in the grip of Maki. The traitorous son of Anka was dragging her with him towards the canyon, a rifle in his hand. Pete changed direction and went after them, trotting faster until he was running. They hadn't seen him, hurrying to escape the hail of bullets which somehow avoided them, not looking back but ahead to where the steep ridge came down to meet the grass. And there, waiting for them on the ridge, a spear in his hand, stood Hidaig. Grinning.

Pete gained ground with each step. By the time they reached the ridge he was only a few meters behind them. They scrambled up to the flat rock slab where Hidaig stood, spear leveled.

"Kill the Hanken slime!" screamed Hidaig.

"She comes with me!" yelled Maki. "I promised her—"

"I said kill her! Now!" Hidaig drew back his arm with the spear.

Maki twirled, getting himself between Hidaig and Baela, and pushing the girl to the ground.

Hidaig's arm thrust forward, his spear piercing Maki in the throat. Maki let out a gurgling cry, releasing Baela and his rifle, grabbing the shaft of Hidaig's spear with both hands and yanking it from him. As life pumped out of him, shock came; he teetered on the sharp edge of the ridge, then fell off it and spun lazily to the ground meters below.

Hidaig grabbed Baela's hair in one hand, the rifle in the other, stepped forward and put one foot firmly on the girl's stomach to hold her down. Pete roared, and charged up the ridge, swinging the club up in a high arc over his head.

Hidaig calmly leveled the rifle at Pete, a horrible grin on his face—and pulled the trigger.

The explosion was loud enough to drown Baela's scream, the breech of the weapon blowing apart and sending splinters of steel and brass upwards into Hidaig's eyes and face. As he staggered backwards, reaching for his face, Pete's club came down with terrible force to destroy his head from crown to brain stem with a sickening plop. He toppled off the ridge to join Maki in the dirt below as Pete pulled Baela to her feet.

"Okay?" asked Pete.

"Okay," she said, but her eyes were filled with tears. Below them, Ned and the others were advancing across the grass, and there was one more rifle shot.

No prisoners were taken that day.

"Bernie's hurt; I've got to get back to her. Come with me." Pete gave Baela's hand a squeeze, then rushed towards the house. Baela hesitated, then started after him, but halfway to the house she changed direction, heading towards the barn.

Bodies were scattered in the grass, and Pete smelled death. Tenanken were piling out of the bunkhouse, a few following him as he rushed past. Ahead, a small crowd had gathered around Bernie, still on the ground by the porch, and an awful thought crept into Pete's mind. *What if I lose her? What's the sense of all I'm doing if I lose my wife and child?* But he was relieved to find her alive and conscious, managing a weak smile from her battered, swollen face when he bent over her, and then she burst into tears. He knelt down, and took her hands in his.

"I hurt so bad inside, Peter. I hurt so bad."

"It's all right now, hon. Lots of people here to take care of you."

Jake put a hand on Pete's shoulder. "Hope you don't mind, but she complained a lot about pain on her left side so I pulled up her blouse and checked. No bleeding or swelling, but a pretty good bruise comin'. She might have a cracked rib, Pete. They really pounded her, but Jeezus, Pete, she killed *six* of 'em."

"It's not just my side, Peter," said Bernie, squeezing his hands hard. "What scares me is the baby not moving, and I feel pain there too. Oh—there it goes again!" Bernie closed her eyes for a moment, then opened them wide. "Oh, God," she said, "it's starting!"

"What?" Pete was surprised by her sudden alertness.

"I think it's coming *now*! Get me to a bed. I'm *not* going to have my child born in the dirt."

Pete gulped, then looked at the faces around them. "Three on a side, and keep her back straight. We'll lift together, and take her to the bedroom by the kitchen."

Six men lifted her gently from the ground, and she groaned. They carried her inside the house, broken glass crunching under their boots, and put her on the brass bed she shared with Pete.

"Now what?" asked Jake. "Is she really gonna have a baby now? Hell, we need a doctor here."

"Nearest one's in Quincy, and Bernie's in no shape for a ride," said Ned. "Besides, our horses 'n' wagons are all back at the creek. Any volunteers for a run back to town?"

A couple of hands went up. "Okay, Ed and Zeke, it'll take you an hour if you really hump it. Stop by as many houses as you can, and tell the women to get right over here. I know Audrey's done some midwifin', and some of the others, maybe. Zeke, bring some shovels back. We've got maybe thirty bodies to bury somewhere."

"We gonna talk about this, Ned?" asked Jake.

"Later," said Ned. "Right now we need action, not words, unless you want to smell the stink."

"The mouth of the canyon is a good spot," said Pete, "and it's safe on my property. Whoever these people were, I doubt they have relatives to come lookin' for them."

"Maybe," said Jake thoughtfully, "but what we're doin' ain't legal."

"Later, Jake," said Ned, but the end of the conversation came when Bernie moaned again.

"Can you get some women here? Things are really startin' to happen!" she yelled.

The men crowded out of the room in confusion, Pete remaining at her side. Only a minute later Jake returned with Diana and two other women in tow. Pete looked at them, and without hesitation spoke in classical Tenanken.

"Please help her. Our child is ready to be born."

Diana squealed with delight, clapping her hands together but then becoming stern, pushing both Peter and Jake out of the room and slamming the door behind them.

Pete looked at Jake, and managed a wry grin. "I've just been thrown out of my own bedroom by a woman who isn't even my wife," he said.

They occupied themselves with the other men for two hours, shoveling broken glass out of the front room and boarding up the big window. Everyone crowded into the house, wanting to help, and in an hour a steady stream of women was marching back and forth between the bedroom and the kitchen. Near dusk, Diana emerged from the bedroom with a smile, took Pete by the arm and led him to Bernie. The women had cleaned and bandaged her wounds, and she had on her favorite nightgown, a white thing that made her hair seem even more golden. Her face was swollen and purple on the left side, one eye nearly shut so she had to turn her head to look at him. "See, I'm pretty again," she said weakly.

Pete felt out of place. Awkwardly, he said, "Do you still hurt?"

Bernie took his hand in hers. "The contractions are regular, now, but my side doesn't hurt so much when I lie still. And Pete, the most wonderful thing, a little while ago Diana was examining me, putting her hands over my stomach to see how the baby was positioned, pushing back and forth a little and Peter, the baby moved! I felt it move! Then as soon as Diana took her hands off me it was quiet again. She says the head is placed right; everything's ready to go. Our first child will be born right in this bed. Oh, it feels tight down there!"

She was babbling, euphoric. Pete sat down on the edge of the bed. "Can I touch?" he asked, and she nodded. He put both palms gently on her abdomen and immediately felt movement as if the child had been startled. He closed his eyes and let the love feeling well up in him, imagining it flowing through his hands to child and mother. A tiny heel moved slowly past his hand once, twice, then pushing outwards sleepily. He opened his eyes, and found Bernie crying.

"He knows his daddy's there," she said.

He sat with her until after darkness as the contractions grew stronger, coming at shorter and shorter intervals. People came and went, including Baela, who wanted to feel the baby and laughed when it moved for her. Diana and two other Tenanken women were a constant presence, waiting patiently for the moment. Pete looked at their calm expressions. *The memories of tens of thousands of birthing years are with you. Please use them to help the ones I love.*

Well after dark, Bernie yelled, then grunted and arched her back with terrible force. Diana pushed Pete out of the room, explaining, "room too small. No space enough." Steaming water was brought in, along with all the linens in the house. The door slammed shut.

Pete was jittery, standing in a front room filled with nervous men. When Diana came out briefly he followed her to the kitchen. "I should be in there to help," he pleaded.

Diana looked at him sharply. "Woman know what to do. No time to talk—work!" She bustled past him with a boiled knife in her hand, and slammed the door behind her.

"Aren't you supposed to start pacing, now?" asked Jake, and some of the men laughed uneasily.

"I'm gonna take a walk," said Pete. "It's getting too close for me in here." Nobody followed him when he left the house to sit on the edge of the porch and look out at the silhouettes of trees. Darkness hid the bodies piled to his left where they had been dragged. One of them was Maki, Anka's last son, unceremoniously dumped with a pile of Tenanken outcasts, perhaps the last of their kind.

The change was not coming; it was here—now. Tenanken and Hinchai as one people. It was right; again, he felt it, and now, very soon, the first child of their joining. What kind of child? The question chilled him. His own features were heavy, but not Tahehto like those of his father. Would the child be brutish? Would Bernie scream at the sight of her newborn, wondering how such a thing could come from her, what monster had entered her to conceive it? Sweat beaded on his forehead as he thought about it, but then his reverie was interrupted by the arrival of Zeke in his wagon, carrying shovels and a passenger. Audrey Miflin, red-faced and heavy-busted, waddled past him into the house.

"Calm down, poppa. We'll have that baby of yours born in no time."

But in a few minutes she peeked out the front door. "Hell, they don't need me in there; everything's goin' fine. Old country medicine. Better stick close, though. It's gonna be pretty soon." Audrey grinned happily, and ducked back inside.

Pete directed Zeke to a spot at the mouth of the canyon and walked back to sit on the porch while ten men went to work with the shovels. Ned came out of the house, and sat with him for a while.

"We've been talkin'," said Ned, "and I hope you'll go along with this, even though it's against the law. It's just that we've got ourselves a nice, quiet town up here, and what would it accomplish if what happened today ever got out?"

"All those dead. How can we not talk about it?"

"Well, we're sure as hell gonna try not to. All of us came up here for the peace and quiet, and we're gonna keep it that way. The vote was unanimous, Pete. We're not sayin' anything to anybody about today. It never happened, just like Tom bein' killed. Tom had nobody but us, and we got the guys who killed him. That's fair enough, and nobody will mourn the critters we're buryin' out there."

I can think of a couple, thought Pete, remembering the feelings he'd had in the cave that day. *If they are still alive.*

"We got them all, Pete, every one. A couple of our own got banged up pretty good: Bernie, one of the other women, and then the guy we found in the barn, the little girl's father."

"Baela?"

"Yeah, that's the one. Her daddy, she said. Bad bang on the head, shoulder busted, a couple of dead critters by him, one pierced clean through with a stone-headed spear. Hell of a fight that must have been. Bad concussion, and we've got him upstairs. He's been babbling all evenin' in a weird language, sort of speakin' in tongues. Touch and go for now, but we'll ride it out with him."

182

"Where's Baela?"

"She's with him, now, and her mother."

There was a shout from inside the house.

"What do you say, Pete. We keep quiet about all this? Bury the dead, and get on with it?"

Pete thought for a minute, but it was hard to concentrate. What was all the yelling about? A new beginning for the Tenanken, safe in a quiet place, and time to learn the Hinchai ways. Their own settlement, and friends. Future lovers. Children. Quiet time was needed— not invasion by outsiders.

Now men were talking by the open door of the house, and from somewhere deep inside came an agonized cry.

"Yeah, that's fine, Ned. We keep quiet about all of it."

"Good," said Ned, slapping him on the back.

Jake stuck his head out of the doorway. "Better get in here, Pete. Things is happenin' fast, now; women runnin' all over the place."

Pete and Ned both scrambled to their feet, Pete beating him to the door by a step. Inside was chaos, men packed together, pushing up towards the bedroom door, falling back when Audrey rolled out of the kitchen with a pot of something steaming and threatened them with it before the door slammed behind her. Over the din in the front room Pete could hear women's voices beyond the door, and then Bernie grunting, crying out, grunting again. Suddenly there was another cry, but this one higher pitched and coming in bursts.

A baby's cry.

It got very quiet in the front room, everyone listening. Finally, Jake sidled up to Pete and put an arm around his shoulders. "From what I hear, you have just become a poppa," he said. "Congratulations."

The door opened, and Audrey bustled out.

"Can I?—" Pete began.

"Not now. Mister Pelegeropoulis is not yet presentable to his public." She held up something long and bloody. "I'll wrap up the cord for you to keep." She busied herself in the kitchen, then pushed past Pete and into the bedroom, but women were in the way so he couldn't see Bernie.

A boy. He had a son. The firstborn was a son, and in the Tenanken traditions it was a most favorable sign.

At last the door opened to him, the women stepping aside from the bed and he saw Bernie lying there, battered looking but smiling serenely, and cuddled tightly next to her a tiny human being wrapped in a blanket. For Pete, there was no sound or sight other than those two before him in the bed; he stepped forward, sat down next to them, touched Bernie's face, then pulled aside the blanket to look at the face of his son.

He was beautiful.

A well-shaped head was covered with blond fuzz. Tiny mouth, but generous nose in a square face with well-defined cheekbones, and when Pete's face drew near, the baby opened coal-black eyes, squinted at him, then turned his head and made sucking sounds.

"He's a big baby," said Bernie softly. "Maybe twelve pounds."

Pete leaned over and kissed her, first the cheek, then the mouth. Control failed him for the first time in his life; tears welled up in his eyes, and streamed down his cheeks. "Are you okay?" he asked, voice quavering.

"I am now," she said, then pulled his head down and kissed him firmly while the baby squirmed against her, mouth searching for a breast and finding it.

They watched the baby suckle for a moment while the other women left the room, closing the door behind them. "Do you have a name for the baby?" asked Bernie, then quickly added, "I think he should be named for his father."

Pete thought. The baby suckled, and hiccupped.

"How about Peter Savas? The father and his father."

Bernie smiled. "That's nice, and very Greek." She looked down at their son, his mouth clamped on a nipple, a tiny hand massaging the breast. "That's your name, little guy. Peter Savas Pelegeropoulis. Quite a mouthful." She jiggled the nipple in the baby's mouth, and laughed.

They sat alone with their son for several minutes, and then Pete opened the door so the neighbors and Tenanken relatives could see the new addition to planet earth. One by one they smiled, made funny sounds and strange faces at the child. Jake seemed wistful when the baby clamped onto his index finger and held fast; he looked up, caught Diana smiling sweetly at him, and blushed a deep red. For those moments, the room was filled with both friendship and love, between two peoples.

Outside, under the cover of darkness, ten men worked on— burying the past.

CHAPTER TWENTY

A SPIRIT SOARS

They rested calmly in the inky darkness of the cavern, waiting for death to come. Anka's head rested in Tel's lap and he moaned in a deepening sleep that frightened her more with each passing moment, yet she did not try to wake him.

They had hidden in the tunnel above their sleeping quarters before Pegre and the Hinchai had come into the cavern, getting out of sight just in time because Anka's movement was slowed by pain so severe he had fainted twice while trying to stand. In the end he had crawled to their grotto, where Tel had nearly burst her heart pushing him up into the tunnel. Now they sat an arm's length from the exit hole, a pile of large, sharp-edged stones within reach so that any attacker would be assured of a rude, even fatal welcome. Tel had felt Pegre's Touch, closing her mind in fear the other would sense her, and then they had gone away. There had been the odor of wood smoke, and still later the popping sounds she knew were made by Hinchai pointing weapons. She had expected Hidaig and his gang to return and search for her again, so hot had been his anger, but when he didn't return she assumed he had gotten what he wanted or the battle had gone badly for him. Now she waited, feeling the life ebb from her mate, wondering about the fate of her last son. A traitor. But her son. The feeling that he was no longer alive tortured her in the darkness.

A sound.

Voices. Faint at first, and the crunch of a pebble grinding rock.

Tel closed her mind, and picked up an axe-shaped stone. Her heart thumped rapidly.

The voices were quickly louder, and she could hear words; suddenly The Touch was there, familiar and loving, and something even stronger, a vision that made her heart soar. Pegre was here again, and Baela with him.

"Pegre!" she shouted. "We're here, above the grotto!"

"Tel?" The voice was male, and deep.

"Over here! I cannot move!" Anka's head shifted in her lap, and he groaned. Now she could hear Baela chattering nearby, light flickering up from the exit hole. Tel tapped the floor with the rock in her hand until a bright glow flashed in her face.

"They're up here!" cried Baela, scrambling up through the hole. Pegre was right behind her, grunting as he squeezed his bulk into the tunnel, and then the two of them were pressing warmly against Tel, looking down at Anka's battered form.

"It's bad," said Tel. "Hidaig beat him, and left him to die. When he coughs, blood comes."

"It's cold here. We should make a fire and get him to a comfortable place. Baela, take these and light the torches in the cavern. I think there's a fresh one by the grotto." Pegre handed Baela a small box of wooden matches; the girl nodded, and dropped out of sight down the hole.

Pegre moved Anka out of the tunnel and into the cavern, carrying him like an infant. Anka's head tilted back, mouth open. *He's dying*, thought Tel. *I will lose him soon, now.* She followed them into the cavern, where Baela had lit a few torches that flickered dimly. "Most of the torches were burned out," complained the girl.

Pegre made a hot fire that warmed them all, and Anka stirred, eyes opening to look at the faces above him. He smiled when he saw Pegre, and grasped a big hand in his. "How is it in the valley?" he asked.

Pegre was solemn. "There was a battle yesterday. It was bad, but Hidaig and his band are no more. Two of our band were injured, one seriously, but he will live." Pegre put an arm around Baela, and pulled her close. "This little one killed a warrior."

"And what of Maki?" asked Tel softly. "What has happened to our son?"

Pegre hesitated, and shook his head sadly. "He's gone, killed by Hidaig after the battle was lost. In the end he saved Baela's life. He was not evil, Tel, and died for what he believed in." It was perhaps a lie, but Pegre hoped it would lessen the pain.

Tears welled up in Tel's eyes, but she did not cry. There was only numbness at the verification of what she had felt earlier.

Anka closed his eyes, keeping his own grief private.

"In this bad time, there is happier news," said Pegre. "My mate has given me a son; he is strong and beautiful, both Tenanken and Hinchai, the best of both. You must see him, and I want both of you to come and live with us."

186

"Ba, too," said Baela. "Where is she?"

"The old ones are resting," said Tel.

Anka opened his eyes and gurgled a reply. "Perhaps Tel; it will not be for me. It is over for me, but I thank you." He patted Pegre's hand affectionately, and closed his eyes again.

Tel nudged her mate, fearful he would die any moment, now. "Anka, there is something you must yet see. Baela has a gift for you, if you can stay awake."

Baela looked puzzled, but Pegre gave her shoulder a squeeze and said, "It's a special gift, Anka."

"From a special child," added Tel, knowing Pegre's mind.

"Eh," said Anka, and opened his eyes curiously.

Tel leaned close to Baela, speaking to her in a whisper. "Do you remember the great hunting bird with the nest at the top of the cliff?"

"Yes."

"Good. I want you to imagine you are that very bird, soaring high up in the sky, and totally free. There are no limits to how high you can go, or what you can see. Let your imagination soar with you."

"I do that," said Baela, still puzzled, "when it's quiet, but how—"

"Just do it now, and we will try to imagine what you are seeing. It is a little game we play for Anka."

Baela shrugged her shoulders. "All right."

Tel turned to Anka. "Baela will imagine something, and we will try to guess what it is. Are you awake?"

Anka nodded sleepily.

"Go on, Baela," said Tel.

So Baela closed her eyes. For a moment she was still in the cavern, warm by the fire, smelling torch fumes and wood smoke. But then she relaxed, looking out over the tops of trees on the opposite side of the canyon, her heart beating rapidly with the excitement of life. The chicks burrowed beneath her, hungry as always, demanding food. It was time to hunt again, and so she leapt from the nest with a thrust of talons and spread her giant wings to sail out over the canyon. Two wing beats later she caught an updraft, and began to climb.

"Ho," said Anka, but his voice was faint.

Wind whipped her feathered face, and she felt the delicate tensions of wing tips spreading, bending to trim her flight; she thrust downward and rode the thermal in a slowly ascending spiral, the earth slowly spinning below her. She did not hunt yet, but flew for pure joy—for life. The sun was bright above her, below, the trees were green dots, but something compelled her to go on, to explore. Never before had she risen so high, so alone. Mountains appeared on one horizon, and on another a blue sea. Now the horizon was curved, the world below a giant, blue ball, the sky turning dark, and the sun a well-defined glowing disk. She was attracted to it, found herself tempted to fly towards its warmth, but holding back. It was not a place for her to go—not yet. Perhaps someday, when her spirit soared in death. In the meantime her hungry chicks were waiting, and she had responsibilities. Reluctantly, she made a final turn in a black sky, folded both wings half-closed and dropped like a stone towards the giant globe beneath her.

"Ahhhh," said someone in another world, or did she imagine it?

Baela plummeted into blueness, then haze, trees and ground re-appearing and then flying below her a huge, fat bird with a long neck, moving at great speed. A slight spread of wings to break her own velocity, a twisting turn, then dropping again, talons opening to hit the bird with terrible force, breaking its neck, and grabbing firmly, wings beating hard to hold up the new weight. She floated down in a glide, the family meal hanging beneath her like a rock, the chicks seeing her coming from afar, shrieking, flapping their stubby wings. When she landed they were tightly squeezed together in the nest. Lovingly, she tore off chunks of flesh from the long-necked bird and fed them individually to her impatient children. *Mother is home, and now we eat. Can there be any finer life than this?*

She awoke, startled by Anka grasping her arm. Firelight flick-ered in the gloomy cavern, and The Keeper was looking up at her with great intensity. "You have the First Mother's gift, Baela, and the golden hair. The Hanken Mother of us all has somehow returned in this terrible time. Such power! Can it be that our world is a round ball floating in blackness? I think you show me the beginning of my journey, to a place of new life better than the one I have endured for too long. I am old, far too old. My visions are old, and no longer im-portant. I have worried about you and the other Hanken children; I have feared you were not Tenanken, that the Mind Touch was lost to you. But such power! Such things I could not imagine!"

Anka paused, exhausted by his outburst. Something gurgled deep inside him. He patted Baela's arm, and again closed his eyes. "You haven't shared your gift with us before."

"But she has," said Tel, "many times, without knowing it. Many of us have flown with the great bird, but to Baela it was a private thought she guarded as her own. She has resented the intrusion of

The Mind Touch, but now I hope she sees it for what it can be: an intimate sharing of souls."

Baela listened to their words, but did not understand their meaning, did not comprehend what was truly happening to her. For with the budding of breasts and flaring of hips had come the power of the first Hanken mother.

To a golden-haired Hanken child.

Once every hundred generations.

Anka fumbled at his throat with one hand, and gave instructions in a dying voice. "Tel will use the Mind Touch to help you recall those memories important in your new world. Pegre has also recorded them. Baela, never forget those who have come before, for their blood is in yours; your physical and spiritual strengths are from them. The Mind Touch is from your Hanken purity; encourage the other children to cultivate and use it. When they are saddened, give them a happy vision; when they are alone, let them soar with your spirit-bird. Take care of them. Tel will instruct you, and show you the ways."

"Yes, my heart," said Tel, her voice cracking.

Anka pulled a thong loop over his head, and held it up to Baela. Hanging on the loop was the clear, doubly terminated quartz crystal of meditation he had worn since youth. The crystal had become a symbol of his spiritual leadership. "Put down your head," he said. "This is yours to wear until you are ancient like me, and choose to give it new life with someone else."

He raised himself slightly, slipped the loop over Baela's head, and fell back exhausted into Tel's soft lap. "It is done," he gasped. "Tel, will you come with me to the ledge where we watch the night lights?"

"You should rest, my heart, and it will be cold on the ledge."

"Is it dark?"

"It is near dawn," said Pegre solemnly. "If you wish, I will carry you to the place."

"Please," said Anka.

Pegre gently lifted him, Tel and Baela following with two torches as they climbed the spiral of shelves in the main cavern, and then up the long tunnel to the place where Tel had tried to build her signal fire.

"Wait for us here," said Anka. "It will not be long." And then he crawled painfully out onto the ledge, Tel right behind, finding the smoothed place where they had sat, and loved, so often.

They cuddled on the shelf, and watched the stars disappear as the sky turned orange. He took her hand, their heads touched. Tel closed her eyes as The Mind Touch wafted slowly, lovingly over her, and she knew it was for the last time.

She was running down a steep hill, afraid she would fall, but Anka, running beside her, held tightly to her hand, pulling her along and grinning in the bright sunlight. Several children cavorted ahead of them, heading for tall fir trees lining a creek cascading over polished rocks down the hill to meet a larger stream stretching out across the valley floor. When she reached the stream, out of breath, the children were splashing in it, trying to catch small fish with their bare hands, plunging their heads in to grab at the darting, silvery shapes and sputtering icy water when they came up for air. Their prey were too elusive, and so they tired of the sport, racing on to the trees and climbing into them, calling for Anka and Tel to follow.

It was somehow a familiar place; she had been here before. Anka pulled her to a large cottonwood forking into two trunks three meters above the ground. He released her hand, and began to climb. *Silly thing*, she thought, *you're too old to climb*, but he ascended easily to the fork as the children yelled encouragement, then peered over the edge and beckoned for her to join him.

Tel scrambled upwards as the children squealed with delight, watching her progress from the branches of neighboring trees. She knew it was crazy, but not real, and pulled herself upwards in the vision, feeling the rough bark on her hands and feet until she reached the fork and a depression, and rolled into it on top of Anka, cuddling with him there. And then she remembered this special place, the place where her first-born had been conceived—before the Hinchai came.

For a moment the noise of the children ceased as Tel nestled in Anka's arms, her head against his chest. *Is this goodbye? Is this goodbye, my heart?* Anka did not answer, but held her tightly, and then the vision changed.

From the ground below came sounds of the new language. Tel peered down and saw two adults with four children strolling up the hill among the trees. Hinchai. She felt fear, and then her precious children, the future of the Tenanken, were calling to the strangers. She wanted to scream a warning, but Anka put a hand on her shoulder, and she was silent. When she dared to look again her children were clambering down the trees, shouting to those on the ground. A moment before they had been naked, but now they were clothed, showing only bare arms and legs; they ran to the Hinchai, frolicking with their children while the adults looked on with amusement.

The happy group began moving down the hill, back towards the Hinchai village in the valley. Tel's throat tightened, and she felt a horrible ache in her heart. The Hinchai were taking her little ones from her, while she hid fearfully in a tree, tears flooding her eyes. She looked again, vision a blur; the group had stopped, the Hinchai male turning towards her and suddenly she realized it was Pegre. Pegre! Like her own son, like Maki. Where was Maki? Oh yes, he was gone away—far away. But Pegre! Where was he taking the children? She must go with them wherever it was, otherwise who would teach them to remember all that had gone on before them? And now he was beckoning to her to come down and join them, the children jumping up and down excitedly. She turned to Anka, her face a pleading mask.

Anka shook his head wearily. "You go. It is not meant for me. I'm tired, and I want to rest here for a long time. I want to rest here forever." He closed his eyes.

"No!" shouted Tel. "I cannot leave you!" She grasped his hand tightly in hers.

"Then I must leave you," said Anka, and gave her hand a gentle squeeze.

The vision dissolved to blackness, and she heard Baela's gasp from nearby. Tel opened her eyes to the light of a morning sun, Anka slumped heavily against her, head on her shoulder. One look at his face, and she knew he had left her forever.

She cuddled his body until it cooled, until the agony was too much for her to hold, and then she screamed her grief to the universe: streams, trees, hills, animals in early morning sleep, the Hinchai who now gave her children shelter. She screamed until Pegre came out to tenderly lift the lifeless form and take it back down the tunnel, giving her what comfort he could, and then she stayed on the ledge, moaning and keening her sorrow until the sun was high overhead, and she was dizzy from the unaccustomed heat. When she crawled into the tunnel, Baela was waiting for her, eyes swollen and red from a burning of tears. The girl took her hand, and looked straight into her eyes. "I felt him leave—like the bird," she said, and exploded into tears.

Tel took the little face in both hands. "Oh, Baela," she said, "you are so very special, and soon I must tell you of another who has soared."

They clung to each other as they walked down the tunnel, the shadows of Pegre and his burden flickering ahead of them. And by the time they reached the cavern, Tel understood the meaning of Anka's last vision.

CHAPTER TWENTY-ONE

HOMECOMING

Bernie stood at the kitchen window and looked out at the season's first dusting of snow reflecting orange in the twilight. A line of happy Greeks was coming towards her from the bunkhouse, holding hands and pulling each other playfully down the hill. It was a carnival atmosphere, crackling with excitement, and she expected any moment to hear music and see dancing in the house.

A blast of cold air hit her as the back door opened and Jake came in with an armful of wood, smiling at Diana standing at the sink, peeling potatoes. He kicked the door closed, and stomped snow from his boots.

"Not here yet?"

"Nope, but pretty soon, I hope. Roast is nearly done," said Bernie. "Get that fire stoked up good, Jake, so we can leave it alone tonight."

"Yes, ma'am," said Jake, grinning again.

Bernie turned back to the sink, noticed Diana's eyes follow Jake. She whacked at a potato with a knife a couple of times, and nudged Diana mischievously with an elbow. "Do you like him?"

"Oh yes," said Diana. "Jake a gentle man. I make good wife for him."

Bernie laughed. "Does he know that yet?"

"He will," said Diana, and then they laughed together.

Outside, the Tenanken gathered in a cluster to share warmth, facing an orange sky left by the departing sun. There was among them a sense of completion, the end of a journey that had taken thousands of years and would continue with a new beginning when the sun rose again. Tonight, with the return of The Memories, they would be spiritually whole in the new world they had hidden from for so long. They waited impatiently, stamping their feet and milling around, smelling the food cooking in the house but refusing to go inside for fear they would miss first sight of Pete's wagon. The wait was not long before they saw it.

There was murmuring, and someone went into the house to tell Bernie her guest was arriving. Diana came out of the house, walked over to Jake to stand beside him, and there was more murmuring when he put an arm around her shoulders. Bernie came out a moment later with the baby in her arms. Peter Savas, the beginning of a new race and recently fed, peered contentedly from the folds of his blanket, then yawned mightily as the wagon bounced towards them.

The wagon rolled into the yard and clattered to a halt. Pete got out first, smiling and waving, walking to the other side. When Baela got down there was excited chattering among the group about the huge, quartz crystal hanging from her neck, and then it got quiet again. Very quiet. Pete leaned over a sideboard, and slowly lifted an old woman down to the ground.

To say she was old was somehow not enough, for this woman was truly ancient: a thousand wrinkles covering her face, shoulders hunched, amber eyes reflecting an eternity of hardship and sorrow. Here was the family matriarch, uprooted and far from home after losing her husband of a long lifetime, yet despite her bent body she held her head erect, and her eyes were alert. Pete steadied her on one side, Baela the other as the old woman shuffled on a line towards Bernie and the baby. People called out to her. Tel? Her name was Tel? The rest was gibberish. Bernie doubted she would ever understand the Greek they spoke.

They came together as the happy throng closed in around them. Bernie towered over the old woman, and slouched a little to show her the baby.

"Bernie," said Pete, "this is Telesa Samos. For many years she was mother to me, and in many ways has been a mother to all of us refugees. Now we will take care of *her*."

"Welcome to our home," said Bernie graciously.

Amber eyes scanned the child and its mother. A gnarled finger touched a fuzzy cheek. Peter Savas cooed, and kicked his feet. The old woman stared intently at the child, probing his stomach, checking each tiny finger and toe, then looked up at Bernie. Tears were running down her face when she took a step forward to hug Bernie and Peter Savas to her with surprising strength. "Good baby," she said in a deep, guttural voice. "Good woman—my Pegre."

Baela let out a squeal of laughter, but the rest were somber.

"Let's go in to eat," said Pete, "to celebrate Tel's first night in her new home—and all of us being together again."

Old country ties, family ties, thought Bernie, happy for all who would sit at her table. And then the most incredible thing happened as they walked towards the house. It was as if Bernie were suddenly swept up from the ground to soar far into the sky, so high she could see the sun already below the nearby hills. Higher and higher she went, gasping with surprise, then plummeting back to earth.

"Ahhhh," said a collective voice around her.

Pete opened the door, and they went inside for the welcoming feast.

ABOUT THE AUTHOR

JAMES C. GLASS is a retired physics and astronomy professor and dean who now spends his time writing, painting, and traveling. He made his first story sale in 1988 and was the Grand Prize Winner of Writers of the Future in 1990. Since then he has sold six novels and a short story collection, and over forty short stories to magazines such as *Aboriginal S.F.*, *Analog*, and *Talebones*. Jim writes science fiction, fantasy, and dark fantasy. He now divides his time between Spokane, Washington and Desert Hot Springs, California with wife Gail, who is a costumer and healing dancer. There are five grown children and eleven grandchildren scattered around the country. Jim also paints mountain, desert, and red rock scenics in oils and pastels, and is often heard playing didgeridoo and Native American flute. For more details, please see his web site at:

www.sff.net/people/jglass/